I0583870

MURDER AT CLASSY KITCHENS

A Marcie Rayner Mystery

J.C. Eaton

CAMEL PRESS
Kenmore, WA

CAMEL PRESS

Epicenter Press
6524 NE 181st St.
Suite 2
Kenmore, WA 98028
www.epicenterpress.com
www.camelpress.com
www.coffeetownpress.com
For more information go to: jceatonmysteries.com

All rights reserved. No part of this book may be reproduced or transmitted in any form or by any means, electronic or mechanical, including photocopying, recording, or any information storage and retrieval system, without permission in writing from the publisher.
This is a work of fiction. Names, characters, places, brands, incidents, media, and incidents are either the product of the author's imagination or are used fictitiously. Any resemblance to actual persons living or dead, businesses, events or locales is entirely coincidental.

Cover design by Rudy Ramos
Author photo by Florine Duffield

Murder at Classy Kitchens
Copyright © 2021 by J.C. Eaton

ISBN: 9781603817264 (Trade Paper)
ISBN: 9781603817295 (eBook)

Printed in the United States of America

For Marilyn and Joy,
who make this world a kinder, gentler place

Acknowledgments

High-wire acrobats would never attempt to pull off their feats without a sturdy net underneath them. As writers, we are fortunate to have such a net in the form of family and friends who support and encourage us.

Thank you to our readers Susan Morrow and Susan Schwartz (all the way in Australia) for catching scene inconsistencies, typos, and grammar faux pas. And thanks to our techies, Larry Finkelstein and Gale Leach, who never turn away our frantic calls. You folks are amazing.

Without our extraordinary agent, Dawn Dowdle, from Blue Ridge Literary Agency, none of this would be possible. Dawn has been the cornerstone of our writing endeavor and we could not do this without her.

And to our editor, Jennifer McCord, at Camel/Epicenter Center Press, we are indeed in your debt. You always take our manuscripts and move them to the highest level. Thanks for stretching us as writers and storytellers.

Most of all, we thank you, our readers, for giving us a reason to turn on the computer every day and start writing.

CHAPTER 1

NEW ULM, MINNESOTA, MARCIE RAYNER'S APARTMENT

I wasn't sure which sound woke me up first but it didn't matter. My arm reached across the nightstand to shut the alarm and grab the cell phone. All with my eyes closed. I could barely pry them open to slide the arrow on the phone but somehow I managed.

"Huh, hullo."

"Marcie! I thought you'd be up by now. I keep forgetting we're an hour ahead of you in Florida. It doesn't matter. You should be awake by now. Don't you have to be at work?"

"My alarm just went off and yes, Mother, I have to be at work. What's up?"

"Has your office been hired to work on that Brazilian tourmaline theft? You know the one I'm talking about. It happened years ago and they never caught the thieves. This morning on Good Morning America, they said the case was re-opened with a new lead in the Minneapolis area. So naturally I thought—"

"You thought wrong, Mom. Max and I aren't handling any jewel thefts, especially one of that magnitude. It's an international jewel theft ring as far as I know. That means global agencies like the International Criminal Police Organization – Interpol. And they'll be working with federal and state agencies, not a local detective one like Blake Investigations."

"Well that's good news as far as I'm concerned. According to what they said on the news, those thieves are extremely dangerous and will do whatever it takes to ensure no one encroaches on their operation."

"Nice to know."

"Want to know something else?" My mother babbled a mile a minute. "They think they have a new lead because more of those priceless tourmalines have leached out of the country."

"Leached? They used the word leached?"

"Yes. Leached."

"Well, you don't have to worry. All we've got on our docket are run-of-the-mill cases. Nothing to raise an eyebrow."

"Tourmalines. Can you imagine? I always thought diamonds were the most sought-after gems. I especially like the chocolate variety they advertise every Christmas. But apparently these tourmaline gems are rare – a blue green kind with pink hues in the center of the crystal."

"Listen, as much as I'd like to chat with you about gemstones, I really have to get going. I'll call you later this week. Okay?"

"Okay honey, and thank your lucky stars you're not dealing with that case."

I thanked my lucky stars the conversation was short and I was able to take a quick shower, feed the cat and select a decent outfit. I grabbed coffee on my way into the office and made it to work with time to spare.

"Finally! Classy espadrilles instead of suede ankle boots. Just right for summer," I announced as I opened the door to Blake Investigations and gave Angie, our office secretary, a wave. "We never have any weather in between winter and summer, huh?"

I darted across the outer office and headed to the door to my own private one. I'd been with Max Blake, an amazing private investigator and family friend, for over a year. He literally saved me from what would have turned out to be a rather boring and mundane existence running crime statistics for a small community college in St. Paul, Minnesota. Convinced that I was detective material, he never let up. Besides, I needed a fresh start after divorcing my charming, yet philandering husband.

Now, with an official Minnesota investigator's license and a few heavy-duty murder cases behind me, I was beginning to feel like the real deal.

I reached for the doorknob when Angie shouted, "Hold on, Speedy Gonzales. There's someone in your office who wanted to see you. The guy refused to sit out here."

"Hogan? That doesn't sound like him. He's so chatty. Besides, he left late yesterday afternoon for Biscay. Damn, Sundays go by too fast. He should be at that brewery of his. They get started shortly after dawn."

Angie gave her frosted curls a quick fluff with a hand and adjusted the collar of her pale blue silk shirt. If I had to describe her in one word, it would be stylish. She shook her head. "Not Hogan. I would've told you if it was your boyfriend. This guy wouldn't give me his name but said you knew him."

I crinkled my nose and turned the knob. "Okay, Angie, I'll see for myself," but the last few words faded as I stepped into my office.

"Jordan? What are you doing here?"

I hadn't seen Jordan Rayner since our divorce papers were finalized over two years ago. I'd heard from former co-workers of mine in the St. Paul Community College Safety Department, that he had taken another teaching position in Minnesota, this time at the University of Minnesota-Twin Cities. I didn't need to know more. We didn't have kids. I got the cat, kept the last name because it was much cooler than Krum, my maiden name, and we went our separate ways.

"How's Byron?" he asked, getting up from one of the chairs near my desk. It looked as if he hadn't slept in days. Soft stubble on his face and dark circles under dark brown eyes that gave his face a haunting look. No matter. It didn't detract from his overall appearance – the classic tall, fit, boy-next-door. At least he was dressed with the same flair he always had. Whatever was going on, Jordan wouldn't think of leaving the house without a tailored shirt and traditional style chino trousers.

"You didn't drive all this way to ask about the cat. And by the way, he's doing fine." I tilted my head giving him the once over. "Why didn't you call? You obviously knew where to find me."

"Because I wasn't so sure you'd see me and I really needed to see you. Listen, can we please sit down and talk? It's important."

I nodded. "Unless you're sporting a new look, I'm wagering you didn't get a heck of a lot of sleep last night. Want some coffee?"

"Yeah. I could use a cup."

I turned back to the door and asked Angie to bring in a cup of coffee for him. "One cream, no sugar."

"You still remember," he said.

You'd be surprised at what I still remember.

"Okay, suppose you tell me what's going on." I plunked myself in a chair adjacent to my desk and motioned for him to take the other seat. "I really hope you didn't drive all this way because you realized what a screw-up you were and wanted another chance. We *are* over, you know."

"Oh holy hell, Marcie, I was a screw-up and I'm damn sorry about it but I moved on, too. Moved on, got re-married, and Oh, for the life of God! They think I murdered my wife!"

At that instant, Angie walked in and put Jordan's coffee on the desk. "Do you need anything else?" she asked.

My mouth was wide open but no words came out. Instead, I shook my head and she closed the door behind her. Jordan took a slow sip of the coffee and leaned toward me. "Tawn. That was her name. Tawn Hamlin. We'd been married for a little over eight months. I need your help, Marcie. I didn't kill her. I'd never do a thing like that. I adored her."

Tawn Hamlin. The name sounded familiar but I couldn't quite place it. It was one of those cutesy names like Bambi that evoke images of Las Vegas showgirls. Jordan held the cup of coffee and his hands shook. The guy was a seasoned liar when it came to cheating but as far as killing went, Jordan would be one of the last people I'd ever expect. Heck, this was a guy who nursed a praying mantis when one of its legs got injured. I doubted "killing" was even in his vocabulary.

He looked down at his coffee and kept shaking his head. I was so stunned by his revelation that I sat there in silence for what seemed like ages. Twice I opened my mouth but I quickly caught myself before any callous or sarcastic words came out.

"I need to hire an investigator, Marcie, in order to find out who really murdered my wife."

"You're in Minneapolis, right? There are tons of topnotch private investigators there. Why me?"

"Because you never quit. Because you're relentless when it comes to analyzing and figuring things out. Like my affairs."

"That wasn't so hard to do."

"For crying out loud, I need someone who knows me in a way no one else does. You're that person. And you know I would never be capable of committing murder. Face it, I'd be a case and a number in any other investigation firm. With you, I'm a human being. So, will you do it?"

I didn't answer his question. Not right away. "You said 'They think I did it.' Who's 'they?' The police? What did they tell you?"

"Not what they told me, more like how they kept questioning me over and over again. I could tell they were anxious to make an arrest but they didn't have any evidence."

I looked him right in those dark eyes of his. "Why you?"

"No surprise, there. The husband is always a person of interest in these kinds of things. And I don't exactly have a strong alibi for the time of death. I was home, alone."

"Jordan, if I do agree to help you, to take on this case, you need to be absolutely and totally honest with me." I threw my hands in the air and stood up. "Geez, look who I'm asking."

"Marcie, please! I've gone three days without sleep. Ever since two police officers showed up at the house to tell me my wife was found dead in the Classy Kitchens showroom."

Classy Kitchens. Of course. That's where I'd heard her name. It was a while back but I was positive I'd seen her on one of those family news segments. She was a designer for million- dollar kitchen renovations out of Minneapolis. And if I wasn't mistaken, she'd even done a stint or two on HGTV. I must have missed the news coverage about her murder.

"You'll need to start at the beginning," I said. "Everything."

"So you'll do it? Take the case?" Jordan's eyes were wide and he looked hopeful.

"So I'll decide. And don't leave anything out."

Jordan put his coffee cup on the desk, lowered his head and swallowed. "Tawn came back about a week ago from Atlanta where she was doing a guest feature for one of those "flip or flop" shows. Everything went off without a hitch and she was back at Classy Kitchens with a full plate. She was juggling three reno jobs and all of them were bears, according to her. But that's what she liked best – the challenge."

I grabbed a pen off my desk and a small pad. "Where exactly is Classy Kitchens located?"

"The showroom is actually in Edina, near the Galleria Shops of Distinction. Impossible to miss. It's like a landmark or something. But Tawn spent most of her time on site. You know, at the various residences where the work was being done. We're not talking simple gut jobs and replacements with the usual granite countertops and stainless steel appliances. Classy Kitchens creates designer dreams, everything from customized brick ovens to elaborate carousel features."

"You've lost me. As you know, I'm fine with a microwave and a dishwasher. What on earth's a carousel feature?"

"Parts of the kitchen are literally built on carousels that move so that the kitchen can face different outdoor areas for entertainment. Beaucoup bucks."

I rubbed the back of my neck. "Oh brother. Okay, pick up from Tawn's arrival back from Atlanta. Did she have any problems with anyone? Any issues?"

"Like I said, everything was fine. For the next four days she went to work and other than her usual grumbling about impossible clients, nothing was out of the ordinary."

"Did she work a normal day? Nine to five?"

"Usually, but not always. Sometimes she stayed late in the showroom, working with clients to design their fantasy kitchens."

"Alone? Just her and the clients? No other employees?"

"Uh-huh. The business has a security company but the guard doesn't get there until nine. She was usually out of the place by then. Except for…" He stopped for a minute and took a breath. I could see his hands were clenched together. "The night she was found. Three days ago. The main entrance doors were still open when the guard arrived a few minutes before nine. He found her on the floor behind a kitchen island in the Tuscany section."

"Section?"

"Yeah. Classy Kitchens has entire sections that feature a particular motif."

I didn't say a word but mentally rolled my eyes. What kind of monies do these clients have? Then I remembered the homes on Lake of the Isles Parkway outside of Minneapolis when I was on another case. I answered my own question – too much money.

Jordan continued with his explanation. "According to what the police told me when they came to my house that night, she was found face down and it appeared as if she'd been hit on the head with a blunt object. They found a heavy-duty aluminum meat mallet under a barstool a few feet away with blood on it. Didn't take a rocket scientist to surmise it was the weapon."

"What about fingerprints? Could they lift the prints from the handle?"

"No. Whoever used it had to be wearing gloves."

I tapped my teeth for a split second. "Isn't it a little odd that the killer would use a meat tenderizer? Not the kind of thing most people carry around with them."

Jordan furrowed his brow and reached for his coffee cup again. "I probably should have mentioned this. Classy Kitchens is fully stocked. Everything. Pots, pans, utensils, the whole shooting match. Clients apparently like to see how the designs can accommodate the cookware."

"Whoever murdered your wife either knew where to find that heavy-duty mallet or they just got lucky."

"You think it was spur of the moment and not pre-meditated?"

"I'd have to take a good look at the forensic report but if she was found face down with no sign of a struggle, I'd say someone knew exactly what they were doing. What did the police list as the official cause of death?"

"Blunt force trauma to the head with a heavy serrated object.

The toxicology report isn't back yet from the lab but I don't think that will change anything. So, will you take the case? You know me, Marcie. I'd never do anything like that."

"Just answer one more question for me. Were you cheating on her?"

"Hell. We were only married eight months."

"That's not an answer. Were you or weren't you? And don't you dare lie to me."

Jordan looked down and spoke softly. "Only once. Tawn was in Orlando doing a show. I don't know what the heck got into me. I wasn't thinking. I'd had a few drinks at a sports bar and hooked up with a student from Northwestern. It was a one night stand. Never saw her again."

"You don't change, do you?"

"Don't let this be a deal breaker, Marcie. Maybe I can't keep it in my pants. I'll give you that much, but I'd never lift a finger to hurt anyone."

No. You hurt them in other ways.

"You'll need to sign a contract with Blake Investigations and there's a retainer to pay. We accept cash, checks and all major credit cards."

"Marcie, I—"

"One more thing. You should hire a lawyer. Even though you haven't been officially charged with anything, you need to be prepared. You need legal counsel. Don't talk with the police unless you've seen an attorney first."

"I don't know what to say except thanks. I mean it. Every word."

"Thank me when we find whoever wielded that cooking utensil."

CHAPTER 2

Angie was more than happy to assist Jordan with the paperwork and give him a receipt for the retainer. I told him I'd get started on the investigation later in the day once I finished with my scheduled appointments.

"Remember," I said, sounding more like a schoolteacher than an ex-wife and newly hired private detective, "hire a lawyer and don't talk to anyone alone."

It was awkward seeing him out the door and I imagined he felt the same way. A few minutes later, Max breezed in. He'd been working surveillance for an electronics company that suspected some of its employees of theft.

He spun his head around and glanced outside. Then he looked at me. "Was that who I thought it was? Hard to tell, the guy was halfway down the block but I caught a glimpse of him when he opened his car door."

"Yep. It was. Jordan Rayner in the flesh."

"Don't tell me he wants to rekindle old flames?"

"No. He wants me to put out a fire. He re-married and his wife was found murdered. Three days ago in Edina. He thinks he's a person of interest. Guess I wasn't paying too much attention to the news."

"Whoa. Let me grab a cup of coffee and I'll meet you in my office. You didn't take on the case, did you?"

Angie waved the contract in the air from behind my head and Max let out a sigh.

"The retainer's on his Visa card," she said. "I think he'll be good for the money."

Max took a step toward Angie's desk. "His money's not what I'm worried about. It's the emotional involvement." Then he stared directly at me.

"There is no emotional involvement," I said. "That part's over. But I don't believe for a minute he killed his wife."

Max didn't say anything. He poured himself a cup of coffee and walked directly to his office. I gave Angie a shrug and followed him. I plopped myself down in one of his comfortable faux leather chairs and waited for him to sit down next to me.

"You're not defending him, you know. That'll be up to his attorney if he gets charged. You've been hired to find out the truth and you damn well better be prepared for what you uncover." He finally sat. "Well, let's hear all the details."

I told Max everything Jordan had told me, including his hanky-panky with the student from Northwestern. He didn't seem shocked. Not about the girl or the fact Jordan didn't have a solid alibi for the timeframe of Tawn's death.

"A meat mallet, huh?" Max gave his chin a quick rub. "Fully stocked kitchens in that showroom? Unbelievable. And here I thought Doris and I had hit pay-dirt when we got a convection oven."

I chuckled. "Guess I'll begin with the police report and a visit to Classy Kitchens. I need to find out who in their employ might've had a motive for murdering their designer. Jordan also told me Tawn was doing a balancing act with three demanding clients. I'll need to interview them as well."

"Edina, you said?"

I nodded.

"You can thank me later, but I've got a friend who works for their police department. Each year he keeps putting off retirement. Good thing, too. I'll give him a call and see if I can save you some time with the police report. If we're in luck, he'll either email it to us or fax us a copy by the end of the day."

"Us? Will you be working the case as well?"

"Oops. Wrong word choice. Not us – you. You're getting pretty seasoned by now and if you can approach it without any past history of Jordan's getting in the way, you'll be fine. Of course you can always run things by me like usual. I'd be put off if you didn't."

"Thanks Max. I really appreciate it."

"Hey, it's not because I don't want to double team this one with you, but I'm overloaded as is."

Just then, Angie knocked on Max's door. "Marcie, your first scheduled appointment is here. I told her to go right into your office."

"Great. I'm on my way."

I thanked Max again and spent the remainder of the morning with clients and paperwork. Angie grabbed us sandwiches from the deli at Max's insistence since none of us felt like going out to eat. Besides, Max had "accidently" tossed his kale and radish salad into the trash muttering something about twigs and rabbit food. It wasn't as if he was particularly overweight, but his wife kept a tight eye on his paunch for fear it might expand. Meanwhile, Max kept a tight eye on his light brown hair for fear it would turn gray.

At a little past three, Angie put a four page fax on my desk. "It was addressed to Max but he said it was meant for you."

"The police report? He got it already?" I was ecstatic.

"I don't know how he does it, but I swear that man knows everyone in this state."

"Everyone of consequence," I said. "Tell him thanks."

I glanced at the time on my computer screen. I had an appointment at four but that gave me plenty of time to see what the police investigators in Edina had uncovered about Tawn's death.

The report included a detailed description of the scene including the position of the body and the possible murder weapon. Also included was a copy of the autopsy report. I gravitated immediately to its findings - subdural hematoma as the consequence of blunt force trauma with sharp force injuries. In layman's terms, someone hit her upside the head with one heavy mallet.

At least one question was answered—the fact that there was no sign of a struggle. She never saw it coming. According to the report, Tawn was at a computer work desk in one of the Tuscany kitchens and she had headphones on. Someone obviously snuck up from behind. The computer was still running a design program.

The description of that particular Tuscany kitchen, complete with island, matched everything Jordan had told me. The only thing I was missing was the forensic report - lab work, trace evidence, DNA, and toxicology. Given Max's connection in Edina, I was certain I'd be privy to that information as soon as it became available. Meantime, I had to resort to old fashioned sleuthing and since I didn't have anything on my docket for the next day, I planned to spend it in Edina, scoping out kitchens that I'd never be able to afford if I lived to be two thousand and ten.

That night, I wolfed down some leftover lasagna and called Hogan. Usually he phones me around nine but I didn't want to wait that long to tell him about Jordan for fear of losing my nerve. Even though our relationship had moved along steadily,

I didn't want anything to jinx it. We met when the co-owner of his brewery in Biscay was found murdered on the premises and Hogan joined a growing list of suspects. Thankfully, he didn't remain there.

I caught a quick breath and spoke. "Jordan Rayner came into the office today. You know, my ex. His second wife, Tawn Hamlin, was found dead in Edina. They'd only been married eight months. He believes he's a person of interest. Swore to hell and back he didn't do it."

"Whoa! That's one heck of a way to begin a phone conversation. Guess it beats, 'How was your day?'"

"Um, that's not all. He begged me to take on the case. To find out who killed her."

"You didn't agree to that, did you?"

"I, er…"

"I'm not objecting, I'd be surprised, that's all."

"Well, I did. Please don't get upset but—"

"It's okay. I'm not upset. Shocked maybe, but not upset."

"Good, because it's strictly business. I've told you what a jerk he was, still is, as a matter of fact, but that's a story for another day. Anyway, I don't believe he killed her."

"It doesn't matter what you believe, that's up to his lawyer."

"Yikes! You sound like Max. But I didn't tell him the real reason I took on the case."

"Which was?"

"I wouldn't want to live the rest of my life with people thinking I'd once been married to a killer. I mean, even if he wasn't the killer but was found guilty due to circumstantial evidence or something. Pretty callous on my part, huh?"

"No, not really. No one wants to walk around with a stigma. Still, it has nothing to do with you. But working this case…are you sure you're up for the emotional residue that's going to come along with it?"

"Did Max call you and share notes?"

Hogan laughed. "Seriously, there's always past history. That sort of thing."

"I'm way detached by now. Besides, I'd be tackling it like any other case. Talk to the people who worked with her, talk to her clients, find out what they knew. Study the timeline, review the evidence—."

"Look for clues. I know. I know. I haven't forgotten that jaunt in the Mystery Castle. You mentioned clients. Consider me your unofficial and unlicensed sleuthing partner if you wind up having to meet any of them in their homes or out-of-the-way places. You never know."

"Forgot talking with Max! Does my mother have you on speed dial?"

"I mean it, Marcie. If Jordan didn't kill his wife, one of those clients of hers might very well have done the deed. What do you know about where she worked?"

"She was the head designer for Classy Kitchens in Edina. Have you heard of it?"

"Classy Kitchens? Who hasn't? They were featured recently on Good Morning America. Not that I was watching, mind you. I got the lowdown from Trisha at the diner."

Trisha was one of waitresses at the Triangle Diner in Biscay where Hogan's brewery, The Crooked Eye, is located. I got to know her during another murder investigation.

"So you know it's pretty high-end. Jordan said it's located by the Galleria Shops of Distinction, between France and York Avenues in Edina. That should tell you something."

"Yeah, re-mortgage the house if you plan to shop there."

"Funny. Anyway, I plan to drive over first thing in the morning. I wasn't planning on giving any advance notice. Thought I'd mill around first and see what I observe. Then, I'll ask for the owner or manager and go from there."

"This Tawn Hamlin, what about her past history?"

"That's where my internet searching begins tonight. Jordan was in pretty rough shape when he came into the office today so I didn't delve too much. Tawn was only found dead three days ago in one of the Tuscany kitchen showrooms at Classy Kitchens."

"*One* of the Tuscany kitchen showrooms?"

"Yeah. One of them. I think I'm going to be in for the surprise of my life when I scope out that place tomorrow. Too bad you have to work."

"How long before you can get your hands on the police report?"

"My hands and eyes have been all over it. Max has a friend on the police force in Edina. He was happy to call the guy and pull in a favor for me but he can't work the case with me. He's already inundated. Anyway, Tawn died of blunt force trauma to the head with a serrated sharp object. Specifically a heavy-duty meat mallet. I may never tenderizer a steak again. Anyway, the police found the weapon not too far from the body."

"Like I said, let me go along for the ride if you find yourself having to meet alone with a client at their place. Especially if you think he or she could be a suspect."

"You've got a bear of work schedule at the brewery. The ride alone from Biscay to Edina is grueling with all that city traffic once you leave the boondocks. Don't worry. I'll be fine. Max insisted I carry a concealed weapon. I like to think of it as my other jewelry."

Hogan laughed and we said our goodnights. I spent the next two hours trying to dig up anything and everything I could on

Tawn Hamlin from all sorts of internet sites, beginning with the most obvious – Classy Kitchens.

By quarter to ten I was bleary-eyed but better informed about Jordan's interior designer wife. Tawn Hamlin wasn't her real name. Big surprise there. Nope, I put a few clues together and found one Mary Ann Locaste from my own neck of the woods – Mankato. Maybe I could use Hogan's help after all.

CHAPTER 3

I spent more time than usual selecting something to wear for my visit to Classy Kitchens. And while I consider my professional attire to be stylish, I wanted to convey a sense of affluence even though I wasn't rolling in dough like their usual clients. I wanted to mosey through the showrooms and chat with the personnel before I whipped out my license and introduced myself. With that in mind, I opted for one of the few designer outfits I owned – an off-white AMII V-necked blouse with light gray straight leg pants. My pair of leather wedge heel sandals completed the package. Perfect for the start of summer.

I'd let my blond hair grow so that that bob cut I previously sported was now more of a shoulder-length style. Much easier for tossing into a ponytail or an upsweep. It only took me a minute or so to get it into a loose chignon and apply a light gray shade of liner to accent my hazel green eyes.

By quarter to seven I was heading north on Route 15. From there, east on the 212 at Glencoe. Then, the snarling city traffic from the major freeways that surrounded Minneapolis and its suburbs. I arrived at Classy Kitchens an hour and forty five minutes later. Not bad for morning traffic and a ninety mile trek. The last cup of coffee I drank had worn off somewhere between Chaska and Edina. I stopped at a Starbucks for a quick refill before locating the Galleria Shops of Distinction and the nearby Classy Kitchens.

Jordan was right. The place didn't need an introduction. It took up an entire city block and had its own parking lot, thank goodness. A few European high-end cars snubbed their noses at me when I locked my car door and walked to the front entrance. I imagined the employees parked around back because no one on a salary or commission, for that matter, could afford those vehicles.

Classy Kitchens screamed ostentatiousness before I even set foot in the door. Two perfectly manicured topiaries in giant urns graced the front entrance and a marble walkway in front of glass doors completed the package. A far cry from The Home Depot or Lowe's. I stepped inside as if million-dollar kitchen renovations were as common as changing place settings for me.

What I didn't expect, no thanks to Jordan, was a greeter at the door who handed me a map of the showrooms and ushered me into a lavish foyer.

"Welcome to Classy Kitchens," he said. The guy appeared to be in his twenties. Tall, thin, clean shaven. Maybe a college student juggling his schedule for extra income. I nodded and he continued to speak.

"If you already have an appointment, please proceed directly to the customer lounge on your left. Someone will be right with you. If you're perusing our showrooms, the map will indicate the section. Please be assured, we cannot possibly showcase all of the architectural styles we create, so don't be discouraged if you fail to see what you envisioned for your remodel. Our staff will most certainly be able to accommodate you. Should you require assistance, our concierge desk is located adjacent to the Asian fusion kitchen off of the main hall."

Following that spiel, I was certain the guy was either a theater major or he had elocution training before Classy

Kitchens left him at the door to give customers their first impression of the place.

"Thank you." I glanced at the map and then at him. "I understand you've lost your designer, Tawn Hamlin. Please accept my condolences. Tell me, were there…I mean, are there other designers who are conversant with kitchen transformations?"

The greeter took a breath and responded automatically. "We are saddened by our loss. And while no one can replace Tawn, she worked with two extremely capable assistants, both with degrees in interior design. In addition, Classy Kitchens is in the process of securing another lead designer. Is there anything else I can help you with?"

"Maybe. Is the kitchen where Tawn was found open to the public or are the police still securing evidence? I wouldn't want to inadvertently walk into a place where I don't belong."

He clasped his hands making a sharp sound. "The entire Tuscany wing is open. Our showrooms were closed the day following the incident but the police removed their crime tape and we opened a day later."

Not wanting to press him further, I thanked him and headed straight through an enormous glass door that opened into the first showroom – French country style. From there, I moved to early American revival and nearly choked. Our founding fathers never would have imagined weathered gray shaker cabinets, soapstone countertops, and farm sinks with faucets that cost more than my car. The 1950s retro kitchen astonished me. I remembered my grandmother telling me how happy she was when they replaced linoleum and got rid of "those God awful rounded refrigerators."

Apparently she wasn't the only one. I overheard a woman telling a man, whom I presumed to be her husband, that if they were going to spend a near fortune on their kitchen, she most certainly wanted it to look that way. Muttering something about

French provincial, the woman and her companion left the revival kitchen and made a left-hand turn to another section.

I glanced at the map and decided it was time to scope out the Tuscany section. While the greeter didn't tell me exactly which kitchen was the one where Tawn was killed, I figured I might be able to do that on my own. Providing of course, the island and the work desk were adjacent to each other.

Tuscan styled kitchens must be in high demand because there were four showrooms, each sporting different décor and appliances. Two of them had islands. The others had peninsulas that graced either side of the oven and sink. All of them had computer workstations and all of them had tables and chairs for the clients. I immediately ruled out the island kitchen with the arched ceiling and terra cotta floor. Or was it brick? The workstation was in an alcove that served as a butler's pantry. That left only one option and I immediately made my way over there.

Unfortunately, I wasn't alone. Two gentleman were arguing, albeit quietly, about whether or not to "go full Tuscan or embrace the more flexible Mediterranean style." I don't know what came over me but I blurted out, "Mediterranean has a cleaner, bolder look and won't be passé." I didn't have any idea what the heck I was talking about but I hoped it would move them into another space. It did. One of men muttered, "I told you," and they took off.

I stood in the last place where Tawn Hamlin had been and I studied the area carefully. Not only the kitchen, but the access to the room from other areas. It was a nightmare. Her assailant could have snuck up on her from anywhere. Any kitchen, any section, any wing. I made it a point to locate emergency exits and there were three of them, all of them with signs that said an alarm would go off. Clearly, the front entrance was the only option for egress and the killer had to be lurking around the place before the business closed for the day. Given the alcoves, pantries, and butler prep areas, it wouldn't have been too hard. And, if it was an employee, he or she could have stayed behind in the office area by the front door or even a restroom.

By now, I was certain all trace evidence had been removed but that didn't prevent me from opening drawers and cabinets as well as peering behind the vases and bowls on the counters. Nothing. It was time to check out the Asian fusion kitchen and the concierge desk.

A svelte, middle-aged woman with light ginger hair that framed her face, looked up from some paperwork and smiled. "May I help you? I'm Renata Florio and I can get you started if you'd like."

"Nice to meet you, Renata." I opened my bag and showed her my Minnesota Private Investigator License. "I'm Marcie Rayner with Blake Investigations and we've been hired to look into Tawn Hamlin's death." I avoided the word *murder* so as to avoid any hint of an accusatory tone. "I'd like a moment or two of your time."

Without waiting to be asked, I took a seat at the oval oak concierge table and pulled out my iPad.

"The police took our statements days ago. I don't think there's much more I can tell you," she said, quickly folding a piece of paper that was on her desk. I was able to catch a glimpse – Beaumont Collections. I figured it was some high priced company that sold jewelry or ridiculously priced objets d'art. Renata shoved the paper into the middle drawer and pulled a post-it note from a pad. "Can't you speak with them?"

"Our agency has been in contact with the police but not everyone asks the same questions to move an investigation along. No right or wrong, but sometimes we look for different things."

Renata stretched her arms in front and I immediately took note of the large gold clasp bracelet on her wrist. It had to be costume jewelry. She tapped her finger on the desk and shrugged.

"Not much to tell you. I left work with Brom and Alexis, Tawn's assistants. It was a little past five. We close at five every day except Mondays and Fridays when we stay open until six. I didn't hear about what happened to Tawn until the following day."

"No one called you?"

"No, I came to work as usual but there were police all over the place and that yellow crime scene tape was everywhere. Neil came to work, too. He's the weekday greeter."

"Yes, I met him a few minutes ago. What about Brom and Alexis?"

"Brom was off that next day and Alexis was on site with a client. She found out about the murder when she arrived at her client's place and the woman turned on the morning news."

"Didn't you find it surprising that no one called you prior to let you know? Surely the police must have notified the owner once the body was discovered."

"They might have, but Mr. D'Angelo, the owner, never called me or any of us for that matter. Maybe he was in shock or something."

Or maybe he had to cover his tracks.

"Do you remember who else was here that morning?"

"Of course. Roger, the security guard from Top View Security, Neil, like I said, and Mr. D'Angelo. Silvano D'Angelo but he goes by John. John D'Angelo. He always joked that his first name sounded more like an Italian restaurant owner than a man who established a construction and design company."

I chuckled and made a note in my iPad. "What about a cleaning service? Do you have night cleaners? Where were they?"

Renata folded the post-it paper back and forth. I was positive the end was going to break off. "Two cleaning ladies arrive at five in the morning and work until nine when we open. The police were already on scene when they got here and Mr. D'Angelo sent them home. Once a month, the showroom undergoes a deep cleaning but that isn't scheduled for another week."

"Renata, is Mr. D'Angelo the only owner of Classy Kitchens?"

"He owns the company, if that's what you're asking, and my direct deposit indicates Classy Kitchens, no other name."

"Other than the owner, the designers, Neil, and you, does anyone else work here at the showroom?"

Renata shook her head. "Mr. D'Angelo uses an accounting company for payroll and that sort of thing but they're located in St. Paul. As far as the building renovations go, he has his own contractor who works off-site in conjunction with our designer and the assistants."

"Do you have a name?"

"Leo McCellan. McCellan Contracting out of Minneapolis."

"I've heard of them but I thought they only built new houses."

"New *and* expensive," Renata replied. "If you were to check out the builders for most of those fortresses and castles on Lake of the Isles Parkway or in Mendota Heights, I'd wager McCellan was the builder. Classy Kitchens doesn't just do renovations. Often times, we're contracted with clients to design and construct their interior kitchens even if it's new construction with a different builder."

"Doesn't that get a tad awkward?"

"It can, but Tawn had a way of gracing over things when it came to working with two separate parties, not to mention the clients."

"I know this sounds cliché, but can you think of anyone at Classy Kitchens who might have had an issue with her?"

The words flew out of Renata's mouth before I could finish. "Absolutely not."

"What about her clients? Do you know who she was working with?"

"You'd have to speak directly with Mr. D'Angelo for that. I do the initial intake for new customers but the negotiations are left to Mr. D'Angelo. I do know Tawn was handling multiple assignments."

"What about her assistants? You mentioned Alexis being on site with a client the morning following the murder. Do they have different clients? How does that work?"

Renata appeared to be more relaxed with that question. She stopped fidgeting at her desk and looked directly at me. "Brom and Alexis work under Tawn's supervision but they have special projects of their own. For example, Brom might be working on the acquisition of hand-painted Talavera tiles in a specific color pattern while Alexis might be working with a client to design a specialized window treatment. We're not your run-of-the-mill contractors. The assistants handle vital components of the entire project. Oh my gosh. I'm speaking as if Tawn's still here…"

"It's okay. I understand. Listen, I know you're busy and I don't want to take up your entire morning." Off to my left, I could see a young couple waiting to approach the concierge desk. "I'll leave you my card should you think of anything at all that might assist us. Oh, and one more thing – Would it be possible for me to have a word with Mr. D'Angelo?"

"I'm afraid that's not possible. Not today, anyway. He called earlier and said he wouldn't be in. After days of dealing with the police and the press, I think the man's ready for a breakdown. Maybe you can stop back later this week?"

"I'll call first, to be sure. What about Brom and Alexis? Are they available?"

Renata turned her head to yet another glassed door. *What is it with this place and glassed doorways?* "Alexis should be coming back any minute from a work site but Brom's not with anyone. I'll buzz him and tell him you're on the way."

"Thanks, Renata. I really appreciate it."

She picked up the phone on her desk and tapped a button. "Brom, a private investigator needs to speak with you. I'm sending her in." Then, she leaned forward and whispered, "You don't think…I mean, if you've been talking with the police, that any of us could have done it…if you were going to look anywhere, I'd start with her husband."

I could feel my throat tighten and I let out a dry cough. "What makes you say that?"

"He and Tawn had been arguing ever since she got back weeks ago from Orlando. Maybe it's nothing but I'd look close to home if I were you."

CHAPTER 4

I wondered if Tawn had found out about Jordan's fast-lived fling and that was the cause of the dissention. Expressionless, I looked at Renata. "Um, thanks. I'll keep that in mind."

She pointed to the doors that led to the designers' offices. I thanked her again and walked straight inside.

While I wouldn't describe their workspace as lavish, it was certainly accommodating for the clients as well as the designers. Four separate offices opened up into a living space that featured comfortable couches, a large coffee table and a credenza that housed a Keurig coffee maker and a glass carafe with what appeared to be iced water with lemons.

No sooner did I step into the room when a lanky man in his late twenties or early thirties rose from his chair in one of the offices and walked toward me. Short-sleeved button-down shirt sans tie, light beige chinos, and Nikes. Office casual to say the least. His short curly hair matched the dark color of the frames on his glasses.

"Hi! I'm Brom Wilton, please have a seat." He motioned to the couches. "We're the only ones in here at the moment. Alexis, the other design assistant, is still in the field and Tawn…well, I suppose that's why you're here."

"Marcie Rayner. I'm with Blake Investigations out of New Ulm and we've been hired to look into her murder. I was hopeful you might be able to answer a few questions even though you've already given a statement to the police."

Brom positioned himself on the couch across from mine and spent the next few seconds shifting in his seat. "Are you consulting with the police?"

"We've been hired by a separate party. I'm not at liberty to disclose the details but I can tell you that the police are fully informed and have been more than willing to share their information with us. And while we possess a copy of the initial crime scene report and autopsy findings, it's the one-to-one conversations that help us in our investigation."

"I'm not sure what I can tell you. The last time I saw Tawn was the day she got killed. She was working on one of her projects when we all left for the day."

"We all?"

"Alexis, Renata and me. It was a little past five."

"Other than Tawn, was anyone else still in the building? The owner, perhaps?"

"I really didn't give it much thought but I don't think so. It's not as if Mr. D'Angelo tells us his comings and goings. And, his office is across the hall, cattycorner from the concierge desk. Not as if he was in here. As far as I know, it was only Tawn working."

"What about the greeter? Neil?"

"Oh geez. Neil hightails out of here as soon as the clock hits five. Or six, if it's a Monday or Friday. What I don't get is how someone could be murdered in a building that's locked and armed. The only people who knew the code, other than Mr. D'Angelo and Tawn, were Renata, Alexis, and me."

"Not Neil?"

"No, Definitely not Neil. Only the office staff. If you ask me, Tawn would've had to let her assailant into Classy Kitchens but that doesn't add up either. According to what the police said, Tawn was taken by surprise." Brom leaned an elbow on his knee. "Maybe her killer was still in the building, after all. We do a sweep but if someone was to hide deliberately, we'd never know. Want to hear the real kicker? Our security cameras weren't working that night."

I bit my lower lip. "Did the police think someone tampered with them?"

"No. Mr. D'Angelo got fed up with the company we were using and cancelled the contract. He signed on with another company and the new install was yesterday."

I narrowed my eyes. "So Classy Kitchens essentially went without its usual surveillance for a few days."

"Uh-huh. It wasn't supposed to be like that. In fact, that's what Mr. D'Angelo told the police, according to Renata, who overheard him. Apparently the security company was ticked and cut off service immediately. Say, would that make them culpable in Tawn's death?"

"I'm afraid an attorney would need to answer something like that. Tell me, was Tawn having trouble with anyone? A cantankerous client maybe?"

He shook his head. "All of our clients are cantankerous but please don't quote me. What I truly enjoy about this job is the ability to design and create fantasy kitchen masterpieces that people can only dream of. What I absolutely loath is working with clientele who think they're above everyone else. Our clients have a monopoly on the word 'demanding.'"

I laughed. "I get it. I really do. But what if Tawn got pushed too far?"

"Not Tawn. Alexis, maybe, but not Tawn. She had a way of letting things roll off her back. Wish I could say the same."

"Renata didn't have the information but was certain you could help. I understand Tawn was working on three distinct projects. Can you tell me the names of her clients and their projects?"

Brom looked as if I was asking for classified information. He began to rub his hands together and pursed his lips.

"Listen," I said. "None of us would like to think it was a customer who could do such a heinous thing, but honestly, if my firm and the police can't figure out who killed your immediate supervisor, you'd always be walking on eggshells where clients are concerned. Bad enough to put up with vexing people who drain your energy. Imagine if you had to worry that one of them could actually—"

"Okay. Okay. I'll get you that information. Hold on a second. I need to print it out." He glanced at the credenza. "Help yourself to coffee or iced water. I'll only be a minute."

The last thing I needed was another cup of coffee but I couldn't possibly refuse iced water. My mouth felt parched and I seriously wondered how long I would've been able to keep questioning people without quenching my thirst.

Just as Brom came back and handed me a manila folder, the glass door opened and a tall blonde in a sundress and wedge heels bounded into the room. Her shoulder length hair had a natural flip reminiscent of those 1960s cover girls. She was carrying a large portfolio in addition to a crossover bag dangling from a shoulder. She gave me a quick wave. "Ugh. Give me a second. I've got to plop this stuff on my desk and I'll be right with you. Renata said Brom was meeting with a private detective about Tawn. Guess that would be you, huh? Renata wasn't too specific and I kind of pictured a more matronly-looking woman."

Is that a backhanded compliment or what?

With that, she walked into a small office on the right and was out before I could say a word. She took a seat next to Brom, muttered, "How's it going?" without waiting for a response from him, and gave me a smile. Perfect white teeth. "I'm Alexis Sumpter, one of Tawn's associates."

Brom rolled his eyes and gave her a nudge. "This is Marcie Rayner, a private investigator, and she knows we're Tawn's design assistants. *Were* Tawn's assistants. I told her we all left together the night Tawn was killed. The front door had to have been locked behind us. Renata always checks."

"It's true," Alexis said. "Renata's very anal about that sort of thing. Double checks the doors all the time."

I gave her a nod. "I asked Brom if he thought anyone else could have still been in the building when all of you left. What do you think?"

Alexis shrugged. "We always shout out that the showrooms are about to close in ten minutes, then five…you know. We give a final shout, dim the lights and head out."

"Do either of you remember seeing Tawn or saying anything to her when you left?"

"I do," Brom said. "I told her I'd double check with the Rossignols about the gloss on those subway tiles. I joked about finding her at that work desk in the morning. Oh geez!"

He put his head in his hands and took a few deep breaths. "Sorry. It's just that…who would've thought?"

"I understand. What about you, Alexis? Do you remember anything?"

"I left right from my office so I didn't see her. Brom was waiting by the concierge desk and we all walked out."

"What about Mr. D'Angelo? Any sign of him?"

Alexis looked at Brom and when she didn't get a response, she said, "Don't know. Didn't see him. Sometimes he locks himself in his office. Other times he's not even here."

Her observation jelled with Brom's. I had one last question for the both of them. "Why was Tawn working in that Tuscan kitchen when she had her own office?"

Alexis spoke up immediately. "All of the computers are

linked. Same programs, same access. It doesn't matter where we work. Lots of times if one of us is in a kitchen with a client and we start working at that desk, we just stay there. Why back out of a program only to boot it up again? Waste of time. And none of our computers can be used for personnel stuff. Absolutely *verboten* if you know what I mean."

Either Alexis was trying to make herself sound more worldly or she'd caught an old, old episode of Hogan's Heroes.

"I see. Do either of you know who she'd been working with at that time? Was it a new client? One who hadn't signed a contract yet?"

They looked at each other and shook their heads. Alexis widened her eyes but it was Brom who spoke. "We get so busy around here that unless there's an actual contract, we usually don't have time to talk about speculative projects. Too much on our plates dealing with the real customers, not the tire kickers."

Alexis gave his ankle a kick and he gasped. "I'm sorry. I shouldn't have put it so crudely, but it's not all that unusual to be stuck with time wasters. You know, people who have the dream but not the bucks."

"I understand. Listen, before I go, would either of you mind showing me her office?"

"Sure," Alexis said. "The police had a forensic team go through it but I don't think they found anything. Other than some photos on her desk and a few of the award trophies she won in design contests, Tawn kept the place pretty minimalistic. You can see for yourself. Nothing's been moved and the police didn't take anything with them."

Alexis was right. Tawn's office looked spotless, almost as if it had been staged. And the photos on her desk were of places, not people. A waterfall somewhere and a beach."

"Mind?" I asked as I opened her desk drawer.

"No problem," Alexis replied.

Minimalistic was definitely the word. The long front drawer had blank note pads, transparent tape, scissors, a stapler, highlighters and three vials of assorted paper clips. The two side drawers had realms of paper and a copy of *Office 2016 for Dummies.* No one, under any circumstances, was that neat.

I thought back to the timeline for a moment. Her killer could have easily cleaned out her office and fled the place before the security guard arrived.

Alexis must have seen the expression on my face when I peered into the desk drawers. "Told you that you wouldn't find much," she said. "Not that I've been through her desk but you can just tell from the way the top of it looks. I think the dust was even hesitant to land there. Now Brom's desk, that's another story. I've had to go in there when I needed something like post-its or tape. It's a hoarder's paradise but don't tell him I said so."

"What happens next? Will one of you take over as the lead designer?"

"One of us should, but who knows what Mr. D'Angelo's thinking. Knowing him, he'll hire some high profile designer who already has made a name for him or herself."

Just then, the glass door flew open and a middle-aged pencil-thin woman, whose white gauze dress appeared to be two sizes too large, flung her boney frame on the nearest couch and stretched out her arms. The fetish necklace she was wearing probably weighed more than she did. Renata, who was a few feet behind her and out of the breath, struggled to catch her breath. "Mrs. Pendleton, please! I told you not to barge in here. Our designers are otherwise occupied."

"Otherwise occupied?" she shrieked. "They can un-occupy themselves and deal with me. When were you going to tell me my kitchen designer had been strangled? Or was it choked? I had to find out on the beach in Barbados when I pulled up Facebook."

The woman inhaled and exhaled as if it was an Olympic sport. “Monroe was able to charter a plane within the hour and well, see for yourself. Here I am! Of course we’ll have the devil to pay for canceling our return trip with American Airlines but Monroe can deal with that.”

Brom stood up, walked to his office and returned with a bottled water. “Please try to calm down, Mrs. Pendleton, we’re all dealing with the shock of Tawn’s murder. The cause of death wasn’t strangulation or asphyxiation. She was hit over the head with a meat mallet.”

“How perfectly barbaric.” The woman unscrewed the cap to the water bottle and took a sip. “While I can understand that all of you are dealing with that shock, it doesn’t negate the fact that I’ve lost the only designer who understood the subtleties of innuendo when it came to selecting backsplashes. And don’t try to pawn off anyone else on me. I’m distraught and I intend to remain distraught until I can be reassured that John D’Angelo himself will find me an appropriate replacement. Heavens! Don’t you people understand? It’s like Leonardo Da Vinci dropping dead in the middle of painting the Mona Lisa.”

Yikes. Talk about hyperbole.

Renata approached the couch and sat down next to the woman. “Candace, I mean, Mrs. Pendleton, try to compose yourself. Why don’t we leave our designers to finish their conversation with the private investigator and you and I can discuss the matter at the concierge desk?”

The woman eyeballed each one of us and didn’t say a word. She stood up, adjusted her gauzy dress and followed Renata out of the room.

“Believe it or not,” Brom said, “Candace Pendleton is one of our easier clients.”

CHAPTER 5

When Renata and Candace left the room, I picked up the manila envelope Brom had given me and asked, "I take it she's one of the projects Tawn was juggling. Am I right?"

They nodded simultaneously. We could still hear the woman whimpering and wailing behind the glass door.

"It must be an easier project, design-wise," I said, "because nothing about that woman looks simple."

Alexis snorted and Brom let out a laugh before speaking.

"She and her husband, Monroe, have a lake home in Minnetonka," he said. "A stately older home that's under constant renovation. Not that it needs it, mind you, but she needs something to do. Monroe's one of the Cargill Salt executives so money's not a big deal. Candace decided that she wanted to tear out the existing kitchen and create a luxury lake retreat with natural woods, stone veneer and a plethora of high end appliances that would make Gordon Ramsey drool."

"Tell her about the hand carvings," Alexis said.

"Oh yeah, *that*. Tawn was working with an artist guild from Canada to infuse hand carved railings and other features into the kitchen."

"How did the contractors at McCellan handle that?" I asked.

"The project manager, who'd worked for McCellan for years,

had a major heart attack and died a few days before Tawn. That should tell you something," Alexis said. "The guy was only in his forties."

Brom shot her a look. "It doesn't mean Candace Pendleton was the cause. For all we know, the man could have had an underlying condition. Just because someone looks great physically, it doesn't mean something else isn't killing them internally."

Alexis shrugged. "If you say so."

I stood and stepped away from the couch. "What about Leo McCellan? Talk about stress. It would seem he'd be the one taking on the entire shebang."

Alexis took a hand and swept her hair behind one ear. "Leo gives stress, he doesn't take it. He puts the capital P in perfectionist but that's why McCellan gets the bids on all those high-end homes and that's why our reputation is stellar. He and Tawn were a good team. Good *work* team, I mean. I have no idea what their lives were like outside of that. If you want to speak with Leo, he's not too far from here on Rolling Green Parkway in Sunnyslope. I can give you the address if you want to speak with him. That's the work site I was coming from before I got here. Turn-of-the-twentieth-century remodel. Nothing outrageous."

"Was this one of Tawn's projects?"

Alexis shook her head. "No. Like I said, simple, but costly remodel. Tawn gave me full reins on this one. Hold on, I'll write the address for you. Leo should still be there."

She walked to her desk and began writing. I could still hear Candace Pendleton gasping from behind the glass doors. If I were Renata, I'd demand extra pay.

I turned to Brom. "Do you mind? While Alexis is writing the address, I'd like to take another look at Tawn's office."

"Not really much to go on, if you ask me. Tawn wasn't exactly very open when it came to her projects so I doubt you'll find much there. I always figured she worked out her plans, put them on flash drives or even a notebook, and then erased the one she had on the computer."

"She was that paranoid?"

Brom rubbed his chin and grimaced. "I wouldn't call it paranoid as much as *careful*. Don't get me wrong, she trusted Alexis and me with the scope of the projects. It was the nuances she kept to herself."

"I see. Anyway, I'd still like to take another peek. Especially at the framed awards she had on her wall."

"Sure. No problem. I'll be at my desk if you need me."

I went back into Tawn's office and had another look. I was fairly certain one of the frames contained a photo and not an award. I was right. There were at least fifteen or so people in the snapshot taken at a fancy hotel. The sign above them read, "Maricopa County Home and Garden Show, Phoenix, Arizona, and if I wasn't mistaken, the Property Brothers, Drew and Jonathan Scott, were standing right in front."

"Brom? Alexis?" I asked from the doorway. "Can one of you tell me which one of these ladies is Tawn?" I was pretty sure I recognized her but needed to be absolutely certain.

Alexis immediately rushed in from the outer office and handed me the address in Sunnyslope. "Sorry. I had to step outside for a minute. I left something in my car. It's parked next to yours, the Honda, right?"

I nodded. "Yep, my reliable old Honda."

"Oh, you asked which one in the picture is Tawn. She's the third one from the left. That photo was taken before she had her hair layered. Still the same color, though, honey-blond. Say, that's Leo McCellan over on the right, next to the heavy-set man with the mustache. That photo was taken last year in Phoenix. HGTV had a major thing going on and Tawn was invited. I would have killed to get asked to be on a show with the Property Brothers. OH MY GOD. I didn't mean it that way. MY GOD."

"It's okay, Alexis," I said. "I know it was only an expression. I can see myself out. If I need anything else, I'll call and please, if you or Brom think of anything that might help with this investigation, call my office right away."

I handed her a business card and told her I'd leave another with Renata at the concierge desk.

Candace was dabbing her eyes with a tissue when I stepped out of the designers' office. She looked up at me and then continued to wipe her eyes. Renata turned and I approached her desk.

"Thanks," I said. "I appreciate your time. Please contact me if you can think of anything I should know."

With that, I exited the concierge area and walked directly to the front door. Neil was greeting two women as I got closer to the door. I gave them a smile as they breezed past me into the corridor. Then I did the same with Neil.

"I should have introduced myself to you when I first came in," I said, handing him a business card. "I'm a private investigator looking into Tawn's murder. Renata and the designers were very helpful. Can you tell me, when was the last time you saw Tawn Hamlin?"

"You're an investigator? I had you pegged for a wealthy customer. Oh, about Tawn. I need to think for a minute."

It was as if his diction and poise evaporated in that split-second. "Um, it was earlier in the afternoon. Maybe around three when she got back from somewhere. She walked in, said hello and that was it. I left at five on the dot. I could hear Renata, Alexis and Brom right behind me in the corridor."

"Nothing out of the ordinary?"

"Nope. I was already outside when the three of them came out of the building. I could hear them talking and I turned around in time to see Renata double checking the door behind her. She always does that. Sometimes even triple checks."

"Okay. Here's my card. If anything else comes to mind, call me."

"Sure thing."

I felt like saying "you can go back to being prissy and affective now," but getting snarky doesn't get anyone anywhere. It was only ten thirty but I was starving. Coffee could only get me so far. I googled best breakfast restaurants and came up with the Edina Grill, not too far from my current location. I all but wolfed down the thick French toast with whipped butter and powdered sugar before taking off for Rolling Green Parkway and an impromptu meeting with Leo McCellan. Impromptu meetings had their advantage since no one has time to prep or come up with a story. In Leo's case, I didn't expect so much of a story as a reaction.

Rolling Green Parkway was right up there with Lake of the Isles in terms of large sprawling mansions and perfectly manicured lawns. I read somewhere that the median income in this area approached a million, and judging from the real estate, I was on target. If the make of cars parked in front of Classy Kitchens was an indicator of wealth, the size and number of attached garages on Rolling Green was its red-tipped pointer. Nothing less than three car garages.

I spotted the house without any trouble. It was the one with seven or eight trucks parked in front, each with a large silver toolbox in its bed. Yep, no shortage of carpenters, tilers and painters. Not to mention hand-carvers, if needed. I parked behind a dark Dodge Ram that was caked with dirt. One of the four garage doors was wide open and I could see a few men going in and out of the house.

When Alexis said, "turn-of-the-century remodel," she failed to mention the place made Edith Wharton's residence in Lenox,

Massachusetts look like a one-room schoolhouse. I slammed the car door behind me, took a breath and walked directly up the curved driveway to the open garage door. I stopped to take in the garage-turned-work area when the door to the inside of the house opened and I could hear a man's voice. "Don't touch the beams or move them until I've had a chance to check the diameters of the knots. She was insistent – nothing over three quarters of an inch."

Someone must've said something because I heard the reply. "I mean it. I'll be damned if there's as much as one knot that approaches an inch. She'll have us tear down the entire structure and begin again."

With that, the man bounded into the garage and all but collided with me. Jeans and a dark T-shirt. I recognized him immediately from the photo on Tawn's wall.

"This is a work area," he said. "You'll have to use the front door. The staff's here but the owners won't be back to check the progress until later today."

Up close, I got a good look at Leo McCellan. Average height but muscular. Late forties or early fifties with salt and pepper hair that looked as if it had been recently trimmed. Dark eyebrows and a few lines around his mouth that gave him some character.

"Actually, I was hoping I could have a few words with you, Mr. McCellan. I'm Marcie Rayner with Blake Investigations out of New Ulm. We're been hired by a private party to look into Tawn Hamlin's murder."

He furrowed his brow. "Have we met before? You seem to have the advantage."

"I saw a photo of you on Tawn's office wall. Looked like a fun time in Phoenix."

"Yeah, staged photos always give that impression. Actually, we were there on business. So, what is it you'd like to know?"

It wasn't the best spot for a conversation but since I pretty much ambushed the guy, I wasn't about to lose my momentum. "I'll try to be brief. If I need to follow-up, I have your contact information. The employees at Classy Kitchens were very accommodating."

Leo stood there poker-faced and widened his eyes.

"When was the last time you saw or spoke with Tawn?" I asked.

"I spoke with her the morning before they discovered her body. It was a quick phone call to find out when she wanted to take a look at the Pendleton residence with me. She had to check her calendar and let me know."

"How did she seem during your conversation?"

"Fine, I suppose. It was a quick business call."

"Other than work projects, did you ever socialize with her?"

"Socialize? Look, if you're asking if we were involved, it's a solid no. Even without the age difference, Tawn wasn't my type. Beside, she'd gotten married not too long ago. What about the husband?"

I felt my face warm and brushed one of my cheeks as if to swat a small insect. "What do you mean?"

"Nothing in particular."

He crossed his arms and looked away for a second. "Hey, I'm not making an accusation but usually it's someone close to the victim and Tawn and I weren't close. We worked well together but if you were to ask me anything about her, other than the projects we were handling, I'd pull up a big zero."

"Hmm, about those projects… Was there anything gnawing at her? Was she being intimidated by any of her clients?"

"Intimidated? No. Annoyed maybe and even exasperated at times but not intimidated. Frankly, I doubt her killer was one of the clients. Listen, I've got to be at another site. You've got my info if you need me."

"I do. And thanks for your time. I appreciate it."

I turned to walk back to my car when Leo called out, "Hold on a second," and I spun around. "I liked Tawn," he said. "It was pretty bad getting the news about her. Especially a couple of days after losing my project manager. He died of a sudden heart attack. Not foul play but shocking as hell. The guy was a marathon runner for crying out loud. And yeah, he had a family history of ventricular arrhythmia but still—. And as for Tawn, she didn't deserve to lose her life. I didn't want you walking away thinking I was some sort of cold-hearted ass. I tend to be pretty straightforward when I'm questioned, that's all."

"I understand. I did catch you off-guard. I came from Classy Kitchens and thought I could do a quick interview before getting back on the road. It saved me a trip. For now."

I reached into my bag and pulled out one of the remaining business cards I had. "Call me or leave a message if you hear anything. Okay?"

"Will do. Hey, one thing. Why a private eye if the police are on it?"

"Because we don't make things fit to close a case. We close it when it does fit."

As soon as I said that, I seriously wondered if it was a quote from somewhere. A novel I read maybe? A movie? It didn't matter. He got the point and I got in my car and drove back to New Ulm.

Angie handed me an overnight express envelope the minute I got back to the office. "It must be important. I would've opened it by now if it was addressed to the office and not you. I didn't recognize the return address so I checked our client database and guess what?"

She answered before I could mutter a syllable. "Jordan Rayner. It's his address."

Other than the two of us, the office was empty so I immediately pulled the long paper tab and opened the envelope. No letter, no note, just a flash drive.

Angie crinkled her nose and adjusted her glasses. “That’s very cloak and dagger, don’t you think? So now what are you going to do?”

“Give him a call while I scan the damn thing for viruses.”

CHAPTER 6

My call to Jordan went to voice mail so I left an explicit message for him to phone me at the office or on my cell. Then, I spent the next hour getting caught up on paperwork and touching base with my other clients.

At a little past four, when the virus scan was completed and the flash drive was deemed safe to view, he called the office. Angie announced it the way she usually does when the phone rings. "You have a call on line one." Of course we only have one line, but Angie had gotten so used to that refrain, especially when clients were within earshot, she refused to give it up.

"You got the flash drive, right?"

No hello. No "how's it going." Talk about cutting to the chase.

"Hi Jordan. Mind telling me what this is about? I haven't looked at it yet because I had to make sure it was virus-free."

"And?"

"It's okay to view. So, again, what's going on?"

Guttural noises emanated from Jordan's throat for at least five seconds before he spoke. "It's all of the files from Tawn's laptop. I downloaded everything yesterday and rushed it to you. Damn good thing because the police were over here first thing in the morning with a search warrant for her computer."

"Did you get an attorney like I asked?"

"I've got an appointment with one for tomorrow afternoon."

"Good. So tell me, what prompted you to download Tawn's files? Did she give any indication that she was working on something that could have put her in danger?"

"No. Nothing like that. Look, you may be the investigator but I've watched enough TV crime dramas to know that the police always come looking for whatever's on the victim's computer. It was only a matter of time. Whew! Close call, huh? So, what did you find out already?"

"That the project manager she worked with died a few days before she did from a heart attack. When were you going to share that tidbit with me?"

"It was a heart attack, not a bullet wound. I didn't think it mattered."

"It probably doesn't, but still..."

"Sorry. I should've said something. I've been a wreck if you must know. I can't concentrate, I can't eat without getting queasy. Heck, Tawn should've had a proper burial by now but instead her body's at a damn forensic lab getting cut up like chopped liver."

"About that. I never got to ask you. Does she have family? And before you say anything, I already did my homework. I know Tawn wasn't her given name."

"So you know she changed it from Mary Ann Locaste to Tawn Hamlin when she got into college. She wanted to graduate with a professional sounding name, especially in her field. Graduated top of her class from the same university where I'm teaching now. That's how we met. She was back on campus to give a presentation and we literally ran into each other at one of the coffee bistros. We shared a table and by the time we were done with our drinks, I'd asked for her number and—"

"Okay. Got it." *If I want a romance saga, I can search Amazon.* "What about her family?"

"No siblings. Her father died when she was fourteen and her mother passed away in her sophomore year. She pretty much had to fend for herself."

I was beginning to have second thoughts about Tawn. I would've done the same thing about the name change if I didn't think my mother would have gone ballistic. *What's wrong with Marcie Krum? It's a lovely name.* Lovely if you intend to sell fish or work for a government agency.

"No wonder she was so driven," I said. "By the way, I met her assistants today at Classy Kitchens, Brom and Alexis. Also Renata, the woman who handles the concierge desk. I've got some information to look over regarding the three projects Tawn was overseeing. Maybe something will pop out. Oh, I also had a quick word with Leo McCellan, the contractor that Classy Kitchens uses. Ever meet him?"

"No, but Tawn told me on more than one occasion she was glad Leo was at the helm. Same deal with the project manager, Josh Newburgh. She was stunned to hear he had a heart attack."

"I've got a lot of digging to do, Jordan, so don't expect a quick turnaround. This isn't crime TV. I'll review everything on that flash drive and if I have any questions, I'll call you right away. Same with the info I've got to pour through on those clients of hers. By the way, I'm glad you called a lawyer."

"Yeah. That was probably the second best decision I made."

No sooner did my call with Jordan end when Max rapped on my doorjamb. "How's it going, kid? Angie said you had one heck of a day trekking all the way to Edina."

"My head's still spinning from my visit to Classy Kitchens but I didn't leave emptyhanded. I've got a copy of Tawn's recent projects so it's a start. Plus, Jordan overnighted a flash drive with a download of her laptop files. Um, are you going to need the whiteboard in the workroom because I thought I'd plot out a crime organizer for the case."

"Knock yourself out, Rizzoli," he said as he walked into my office and grabbed the nearest chair.

"Very funny."

"Listen, I'm not in a hurry to get home. I could give you a hand. Doris invited her sister Camila for dinner and the menu is tofu turkey salad. I can't imagine anything worse. Unless she adds quinoa."

At that second, Angie gave the door frame a rap. "The deli just delivered your corned beef on rye, Mr. Blake. Do you want to eat it in here or should I put it on your desk?"

I burst out laughing. "Give me a hand! You just needed an excuse to devour a corned beef sandwich before facing that tofu turkey."

"Guilty as charged." Then he turned to Angie. "Thanks. Put it on my desk, okay?"

As Angie walked away with his meal, he said, "Give me five minutes and I'll meet you in the workroom."

"Take ten. Those corned beef sandwiches are enormous."

When I left the office at a little past five, Max and I had mapped out a crime web with more tentacles than a giant squid and when I groaned, he said, "It always looks like that. You should know by now. Deal with the tight circle and if that pulls up a dead end, widen the net."

"Widen the net" was one of Max's favorite expressions and one of his most prophetic. I hoped in this case, the net would be fine as is – taut and tight.

"First thing tomorrow, I plan to wade through Tawn's flash drive. Meanwhile, I'll see what I can turn up tonight with an internet search on her clients," I told him when we locked up for the night.

"Hey, it's not a marathon. Give yourself a break, too."

"Actually, it might be a marathon. The police confiscated Tawn's laptop and Jordan is convinced it's only a matter of time before they concoct something and charge him with her murder. He was worried enough to download the files ahead of time."

Max rubbed his chin. "I'll give my friend at the Edina Police a buzz and see if he can shed any light on their end of things."

"That would be great. Hope you still have room for that tofu."

When I got home, I kicked off my sandals, fed the cat and called Hogan. I told him everything about my day in Edina and all the miscellaneous information including Max's pre-dinner deli sandwich. "You know what the worst part was?" I asked. "Getting a load of those filthy rich, pretentious customers at Classy Kitchens. One woman's hired juried artists to hand carve the railings in her kitchen!"

"It's like a layer cake of income brackets, hon," he said. "You got a glimpse of the icing during that high-stakes poker game last year at Lake of the Isles. Now you're in for a real taste."

"Those people are untenable and any one of them could turn out to be Tawn's murderer. I swear, the woman I met, and only because she barged into my meeting with Tawn's assistants, was totally unhinged. I mean it. Unhinged."

"Take a breath. Try to relax. I'd give you a shoulder rub if I was over there but you'll have to suffice with the thought."

"The thought's good. Any chance you can make it over here one of these nights?"

"I'm aiming for Thursday. Got a full crew working Friday morning so if all goes well, tell Byron we're locking him out of the bedroom. He keeps walking across my head when I try to sleep."

"Then don't sleep."

Dinner was compliments of Marie Callender's frozen meals – Panko chicken with mixed vegetables and grains. One of her healthier choices. I finished it up with a few ripe plums I bought and bottled water. Byron had settled on the windowsill by the kitchen to check out the action in the courtyard below.

Living at Bayberry Apartments was its own form of entertainment from screaming kids to loud music, slamming doors, and the occasional police car. I had only planned to rent the apartment for a short time while I decided whether or not to stay at Blake Investigations or return to my former job in St. Paul. Once I made the decision to stay, it was much easier to renew the lease than begin another apartment search. Besides, the location was pretty darn good. The complex was off of North Broadway Street with a decent selection of fast food places and an easy walk to Johnson, Mueller, and German Parks.

It was way too soon in my relationship with Hogan to think about cohabitating but I knew eventually the subject would come up. Thank goodness he had a trusted brewery crew so he could drive here most weekends. And when he couldn't, I went to Biscay. The status quo was fine with me.

I changed into a long loose-fitting T-shirt and opened the manila folder Brom had given me. It was meatier than I had expected. Three separate client files were included, each with addresses, contact information and a detailed scope of the project they had contracted. By the time I was done reviewing each one, I was way too tired to boot up the computer and begin an internet search. I'd have to add it to my "to-do" list for the following day once I was done seeing what Tawn had on her files.

I turned the TV on in time for the nine o'clock news and went back to the kitchen to grab another plum from the fridge. That was the instant when I heard one of the anchors, "Police in Edina are close to making an arrest in the murder of celebrity kitchen designer, Tawn Hamlin. Ms. Hamlin was found bludgeoned to death in the showroom of Classy Kitchens less than a week ago.

We'll keep you apprised of any developments as soon as they come to light."

Close to an arrest? Jordan! What possible evidence could they have other than the fact he was married to her? I reached for my cell phone and dialed his number. No answer. Damn. Not good. I thought about calling Max but it was late and he was probably at wits end after an evening with his wife and sister-in-law. Everything would have to wait until morning. I just hoped the same could be said for the pending arrest.

My head hit the pillow before eleven but unfortunately, it didn't stay there. In the dim light emanating from the courtyard lights below, I could read the digital numbers on my alarm clock – three fifty seven. Wide awake, I decided not to wait another few hours to get working. Jordan might be in handcuffs by then and on his way to a preliminary hearing.

I threw the lightweight sheet off me, booted up my computer and began to see what I could dig up on the first name in the folder – Ernie Star. Underneath his name was the word "Realtor." That made it easy for a Google search. In less than five minutes, I had found his LinkedIn profile, his personal website that connected him to Mohn Realty, and his name on a site that listed the top ten Realtors in the Twin Cities.

A bit more internet plodding coupled with the notes from the file Brom had given me revealed Ernie was having a new home built on Lowry Hill in the prestigious Mount Curve neighborhood in Minneapolis. Classy Kitchens was contracted to design and construct an Italian Renaissance Revival kitchen in conjunction with the architectural style of his new dwelling. A side note said, "Kitchen plan from home builder is a bland, run-of-the-mill cookie-cutter design and nixed immediately. Builder was informed Classy Kitchens would be taking the lead for construction."

There was no mention of family on LinkedIn or on his website. I figured I've give Brom a call and see what he could tell me.

Next on my list was Daisy Jamos who owned a brownstone on 14th Street in downtown Minneapolis. The side note was handwritten. Tawn perhaps? It said, "Owner wants vintage charm look with twenty-first century technology."

Thankfully I didn't have to look too hard to find Daisy Jamos. Her contemporary art gallery was housed on Chicago Avenue and featured an eclectic array of poetry readings, musical entertainment and the occasional art book signings. This coming Friday was the reception for a debut watercolor artist from the Ukraine. Two weeks ago it was a mixed-media artist from Argentina.

Daisy's bio was available for all to read at the bottom of her website and not a single thing in it raised a red flag. The woman was in her seventies and worked in factories for a number of years before discovering her penchant for art. She made a name for herself with her bold and risky designs that "took the human form to new dimensions" according to a major art reviewer. Born and schooled in Pittsburgh, she relocated to Minnesota when she was in her thirties. The bio didn't say why. Failed marriage? It couldn't be on account of the weather. Minneapolis made Pittsburgh look like Nirvana.

Then there was Candace Pendleton whose performance at Classy Kitchens rivaled Gloria Swanson.

A wave of exhaustion hit me at four fifty-seven on the dot. I noted the time in the lower right hand corner of my laptop right before I logged off and went back to bed, hoping to catch another hour's worth of sleep. I made sure I hadn't inadvertently turned off my alarm clock although Byron does a pretty decent job of meowing his lungs off around six for food.

I wasn't any closer to exonerating Jordan by finding a viable suspect, but I'd gotten a lot of the legwork out of the way. With any luck, I'd either have an epiphany or find something on Tawn's files that would be equally impressive.

CHAPTER 7

"Late night?" Angie asked when I walked into the office the next morning.

"What makes you say that? I checked my outfit twice in the mirror before I left the apartment. Everything matches."

"The outfit, no. Try the giant Venti coffee cup from Starbucks you're holding. You couldn't even wait to pour yourself another cup once you got here. I've heard of two fisted drinkers but this is a first. So, what gives? And by the way, Max is running late. He called a few seconds before you got here."

"Aargh. I really need to talk with him. And yeah, I was up late. Actually, I woke up in the middle of the night and then stayed up late to do some internet searches on Tawn Hamlin's recent clients and their projects."

"And?"

"A great big zilch. For now. One wealthy Realtor. One wealthy gallery owner and one extremely wealthy nutcase. Gee, did I use the word 'wealthy' enough?"

"Oof! Do I detect a tad of distain in your voice?"

"Nah. More like frustration. Nothing whatsoever stood out. Not that I was really expecting anything. Not on the first go-round. I'll run some background checks on these guys and see if there are any connections one of them might have had with Tawn before she was hired to handle the kitchen design."

"Like someone holding a long-time grudge?"

I shrugged and took a sip of my coffee. "It's been known to happen. Geez, I hope Max hurries up. The news last night made it sound as if an arrest was eminent and the only person-of-interest is Jordan. He's sweating bullets right now and I'm not far behind. I tried his cell phone last night and again this morning. It went directly to voice mail both times."

"That doesn't necessarily mean anything. Men don't seem to be as obsessive about their phone calls like we are. For all you know, the darn thing could be turned off."

"I hope so. I certainly don't want to make a drive to Minneapolis to track him down. I know I've got a nine forty-five appointment with a new client but how does the rest of my morning look?"

Angie glanced at her computer monitor. "Free and clear until one thirty. You've got that birth parent case from Mankato."

"Right. The optician. At least she'll be getting good news today. Well, no sense wasting time when I could be delving into Tawn's files. With any luck, I might be able to pull up something useful. Let me know the minute Max walks in the door."

"Don't worry. You'll hear him the same time I do."

I wasn't sure what to expect when I put the flash drive in my computer and pulled up the files from Tawn's personal computer. It was impossible to resist scrolling through the photos that were taken of her and Jordan at various locations. Smiley faces… cozy kisses…I wanted to heave. Did they honeymoon on one of Minnesota's lakes? It looked that way. Other than the snapshots of her and my ex, there were a few photos that I presumed dated back a year or two given the change in her hairstyle. Those were taken with girlfriends at various restaurants and entertainment hotspots. Nothing out of the ordinary.

Next, I moved to the Word files. The folder marked "recipes" was exactly that – soufflés, crepes and quiche. The woman must've had a thing for easy French cooking. Another folder was marked "personal taxes" and it contained mileage records to and from medical appointments and business mileage along with a record of interest she had earned from dividends and bank accounts. If that was the only thing on record, no one could have possibly killed her for her money. Granted, she was doing well, but not *that* well. Like the rest of us, her interest income stunk, too.

There was a scanned receipt on the file for artwork she had purchased prior to marrying Jordan. It was a mixed media piece entitled, "Soulless Desire," by Margarida Tavares Branco and it cost her more than my monthly rent for Bayberry Apartments. The gallery name appeared to be smudged from the original notation on the painting but I could still make out the stylized initials – VFV.

I immediately did a Google search but it pulled up a blank. Just then, I heard Max's voice.

"I stopped by Cresci's for paczkis. Raspberry and cream."

"Paczkis?" Angie asked as I stepped into the main office. "I thought they only made those for Lent."

"Not anymore." Max took a giant bite from one of them and reached for a napkin from the coffee counter. "Don't give me that look," he said to me. "Doris's idea of breakfast was fiber twigs."

I snatched a raspberry paczki, which resembled a jelly donut, only square shaped, and took a giant bite. "That look had nothing to do with food. Which, by the way, thanks because I was starving. I caught the news last night and they said the police in Edina were close to making an arrest."

Max took another bite of his pastry. "Yeah, I caught it, too, and I knew you'd be a wreck. Relax. They're not any closer to making an arrest than you are to solving the case, unless there's something I missed in the last twenty-four hours."

"You didn't miss anything and how do you know they're not close?"

"You think I'd leave you out there to dangle? I made another call. The Edina Police want the media off their backs, that's all. But that doesn't mean you can dillydally. They're pulling out all the stops on this one and are zooming in on your ex."

"But they don't have any evidence."

"They have circumstantial evidence and they're looking for more."

"What circumstantial evidence?"

"Did Jordan tell you he's the beneficiary of a very hefty life insurance policy?"

The two bites of the paczki I'd taken landed like lead sinkers in my stomach. "No, he didn't say anything. The subject never came up. Damn! I should've asked him. How much of a policy?"

"Half a million."

"That doesn't mean anything," I said. "It's easy to get those large amounts when you're in your twenties and thirties and you're in good health. Term insurance is relatively cheap for young adults, unlike—"

"Don't go there," Angie said. "Better stuff another bite of the paczki in your mouth."

"Seriously, the police can't assume Jordan killed his wife for the insurance policy. What about him? Did she take one out on him?"

"They didn't say, but that's something you can take up with your ex when you speak to him."

"About that, I haven't been able to reach him. I figured I'd give him today and then, if need be, make a trek to Minneapolis tomorrow to hunt him down. Meanwhile, I'm going through Tawn's Word files to see if I can find any kind of a lead. You don't think something's happened to him, do you?"

Max tugged at his ear. "Hard to say. He could've gotten spooked and decided to hide out somewhere, but that would be really stupid on his part and I don't think Jordan's that dumb. Try some of his work contacts at the university if you're worried."

I was really thankful that the contract with Blake Investigations included a section on emergency and work contacts. Hopefully Jordan didn't leave any blank spaces. Angie was already a step ahead and began to type something on her computer. "I'm pulling up the contract now and I'll email it to you right away."

"Great. I'd better get back to Tawn's files. When my eyes start to blur over, I'll begin phoning any work contacts Jordan listed. Fall classes don't start for another two months and the spring session ended. I'm not sure if he's picked up anything for summer school or if he's using that time for research. Pray that when I'm done scrutinizing Tawn's documents, I can point a finger to anyone but her husband."

There were a few more folders in Tawn's files and I opened the one marked "HH." I closed it after a quick look-see. "HH" was her abbreviation for "Happy Holidays" and it was her holiday greeting from last year. She mentioned how much she liked married life and that she and Jordan planned on purchasing a home sometime soon. Then a lot of blah, blah, blah about the weather, the seasons, and the joy of it all. Yep, a real snoozer. Next was a folder that contained a few business letters to retailers whose products didn't match her expectations. Since most of them had to do with clothing and bedding, I closed that file as well.

Finally, I hit the mother lode – the client file. It was titled, "Notes from the Beyond," and for a moment I was almost positive she was drafting a sci-fi novel. That was until I saw the names and dates. Each separate word document detailed her personal notes regarding the renovation project. If Tawn was the quintessential professional in the office, her private files read more like a mud-slinging gutter snipe, beginning with her assessment of one Ernie Star.

"If that officious little bugger asks for one more 'teeny-weeny change' I swear I'll scream my lungs out. The last one extended the project time by two weeks. God knows when Leo will ever be able to finish this monster. Hell! It'll take longer than the entire Renaissance itself did! Revival my ass. This is a resurrection."

Underneath her comments were short phrases that detailed precise instructions. Phrases like "One inch crown molding. Must be exactly an inch." Only a few short sentences dotted the pages. Things like, "Who the heck really cares which way the sun beams come up in the kitchen? You're cooking food, not taking a snapshot."

I moved on to Daisy Jamos and when I saw the length of the file, I finished the rest of my coffee in a single gulp. Revision after revision. Single words with multiple exclamation points. Words like "witch," "hellcat' and "harpy."

"I'm going to need another cup of coffee," I called out to Angie as I strode past her desk to the machine. "Tawn may have been composed on the outside but she was seething from within. You should get a load of what she had to say about her clients."

Angie looked up from her computer screen. "Anything juicy like in a Danielle Steele novel?"

"Nah. More like venting."

"Okay then. I'll let you get back to your work. Remember, your nine-forty-five will be here in twenty minutes."

"Oh my gosh. I knew that and then it slipped my mind. I'd better try Jordan one more time and then call one of his university contacts."

Again, Jordan's phone went to voice mail. I pulled up the email with his contract and scanned it for the list of contacts. His mother's number in Chandler, Arizona, was listed but last thing I wanted to do was scare the daylights out of the poor woman. She was a sweet lady and didn't need any more drama. The other name was for a Barry Hayes in the fine arts department. I placed the call immediately, not knowing if I was going to get some university office or someone's personal phone line.

Instead, I got something completely unexpected – a recorded message telling me the number had been disconnected. Drat! My trip back to Minneapolis to meet with Tawn's clients would now include hunting down my ex. I'd wanted to set up those meetings in advance since it was too long a trek to pop in on someone. Now, advance meant a one-day warning. Unlike Classy Kitchens, which was a business and open to the public, I had no idea where these people would be and if they would be willing to meet at the last minute. Ugh. I dreaded the thought of wasting time and gas.

I was about to look up the university directory for Jordan's department chair when Angie buzzed my office to inform me that my nine forty-five had arrived a few minutes early. I closed the files and stepped into the office to greet my new client, a middle-aged woman who needed to find her birth mother regarding needed medical information. I took down the details and told her I'd get started with a preliminary search. Fortunately, Angie was conversant with many of the databases Max and I used so she could get it started for me.

It wasn't as if the woman was experiencing any medical issues but as she put it, "these things pop up out of nowhere and then you're left scrambling. I want to get ahead of the game and find out if there are any medical skeletons in my closet that could really haunt me."

She was able to provide me with the city and date of her birth as well as information provided by her adoptive parents. Unfortunately, the adoption agency they used was no longer in existence. I know because I recognized the name from a prior case. That agency folded in the early 1990s. Still, there was enough to go on. I explained to the client that I was expediting another case but that our office would begin the preliminary work right away. The woman seemed satisfied and I walked her to Angie's desk so that a contract could be drawn up.

Back in my office, I tried Jordan again. Lousy voice mail. Like it or not, I'd be on the road to Minneapolis in the morning. I figured I might as well see if I could persuade one or more of Tawn's current clients to see me, beginning with "the pompous Ernie Star." That meant a call to Brom at Classy Kitchens. Since Brom was familiar with the client, and my internet search made no mention of family, I thought Tawn's assistant might be able to fill in the gaps.

I caught Brom just as he was headed to one of his projects – a kosher kitchen. Thank goodness he answered my call.

"What is it you needed to know about Ernie Star?" he asked.

"Anything and everything about his personal life. The man plastered his professional image all over the web along with his penchant for fine dining but what about his personal life? Who's he dining with? Is he married? Kids? Those homes on Lowry Hill begin at three thousand square feet. That's an awful lot of space for one person."

"One person but four Maltese dogs and an in-house pet sitter who takes care of them. And before you ask, the answer is no. The pet sitter is not romantically involved with Ernie. I kind of stepped into it when we first got the contract and she answered the phone. Made it clear that Ernie's preferences did not include women. Ernie's kind of a man-about-town who prefers to remain single and continue dating."

"So no real relationships for the guy?"

"None that I'm aware of. Sorry I couldn't be more help."

"No, you've been great. I'm simply trying to see if anyone Tawn worked with, or any of *their* close contacts, would have had a reason to do her in. Guess I can rule out the Maltese doggies. Anyway, I'll be giving Ernie a call. Hopefully he'll be able to spare some time tomorrow."

Brom cleared his throat. "Sorry, allergies. About Ernie…in between showings and whatever else he does in that Realty office, he's at the jobsite driving everyone crazy. Maybe you'll meet him there. If nothing else, it will give you an idea what Tawn had to face on a daily basis."

I wanted to tell him that I read her personal notes and had a very clear picture of what the woman was dealing with but instead I thanked him and told him I'd be in touch.

Ernie Star answered on the second ring. He sounded disappointed I wasn't a perspective client but agreed to meet with me tomorrow at one in the afternoon when he would be "inspecting the progress on his Italian Revival Kitchen." He emphasized the words "Italian" and "Revival." Then he paused. I wasn't sure if he expected me to comment over his design choice or fawn over the fact it was bound to make the other kitchens in Mount Curve seem plain by comparison. Instead, I repeated the time and place before thanking him and ending the call.

Daisy Jamos also lived in Minneapolis and was having the kitchen in her downtown brownstone renovated. I figured she was either going be at her gallery or at her home. Both options would work for me. I dialed the most likely place, the gallery number, and waited for her to pick up.

"Visual fields of vision," may I help you?"

Visual Fields of Vision. Was that the VFV notation on Tawn's painting?

I introduced myself and told her I'd been hired to look into Tawn's murder. She didn't seem surprised and agreed to meet with me at her gallery on Chicago Avenue "around three." That would give me more than enough time to chat with Ernie Star and make my way downtown. As far as Jordan was concerned, I planned to hightail it over to his place in the morning, even if it meant an early wake-up call.

A strange nagging thought kept eating away at me and I tried to dismiss it. What if someone wanted him dead, too. But who? Or why? He and Tawn weren't into any shady business. I mean, it wasn't as if they needed the money. I pushed the thought aside and checked the address for that loony Candace Pendleton. Her renovation was at a lake home in Minnetonka but that didn't mean her actual residence wasn't closer. I checked the file again and smiled – Lake of the Isles. I should have expected as much. At least I was familiar with the area. Still, it was pushing it to schedule another interview for tomorrow, unless of course I managed to locate Jordan today, thus freeing up my morning.

For the time being, meeting with Candace would have to be put on hold. Same deal with John D'Angelo, the owner of Classy Kitchens.

A sudden rap on my doorjamb and I looked up. Angie was pointing to her watch. "If you don't grab lunch now, it'll get away from you. I'm making a deli run. Put in your order while you can."

"Ham and Swiss on rye with mayo and a bit of mustard. You're a life saver."

"Nah, I'm starving, that's all. The paczkis can only go so far."

"What about Max? Is he still in his office or did he go out on a case?"

"Left about ten minutes ago and said he'd be stopping for lunch. Something about fortifying himself with a meatball special before he does some surveillance."

"It's a good thing he and Doris have their own cars. One whiff of the interior of his Buick and she'd send him to one of those weight loss retreats."

CHAPTER 8

I inhaled my sandwich and all but washed it down with one gulp of Coke. As expected, the optician from Mankato who was hoping to find a birth parent was elated when I provided her with two names, her mother and her father. They were teenager parents when she was born and decided it would be in the child's best interest to be adopted by a loving family.

That being the case, the young woman who sat across from me at my desk still had a persistent drive to find out why she was given up at birth.

"What I don't understand," she said, "is why they didn't have an open adoption."

I shrugged. "Sometimes birth parents can't handle it and don't want to complicate the child's life. But years later, some of them want to meet the child they relinquished. I was able to make contact with your parents, who, incidentally, finished their schooling and married ten years after you were born. They were elated to hear about your successes and want to speak with you."

Tears welled up in the woman's eyes and I quickly offered her an entire box of tissues from my desk. "They live in New Jersey and plan to retire from Bausch and Lomb in a few years," I said.

"Bausch and Lomb? They're the innovators for vision and eye care. Oh my gosh! It must run in the family!"

I gave her the contact information and wished her well. At least I had one happy ending to chalk up at the end of the day. I wasn't as optimistic about tomorrow. The next few hours were spent with paperwork from other cases and a few more tries to reach Jordan. By now, I was convinced something horrific had happened to the guy and, even though there was no love lost between us, he was still part of my history. If nothing else, I owed him for giving me a decent last name.

The day ended the way it began, with me needing a cup of coffee. Iced, this time. A quick trip to the nearest Starbucks. Exhausted when I climbed the stairs to my apartment, I was counting the seconds until I could toss off my sandals and slip into shorts and a T-shirt. I reached into the pocket of my slacks for the keys and that's when I heard a noise in the apartment. Like someone setting something down on the counter or maybe moving a small piece of furniture. Byron's been known to jump all over the place and knock things over but that sound would be a crash, not a deliberate movement by a deft cat. I pressed my head against the door and listened. Music? It was faint but certainly discernable. And not a result of anything I'd left on in the apartment. It didn't appear as if anyone had broken in, and other than Spiderman, no one was going to scale the wall and use a window.

Slowly, I pulled my pant leg up and took out the Ruger LC9 Max had insisted I carry with me at all times. A few near calls had taught me the value of having a concealed weapon permit. With the gun in my right hand, I slowly turned the key in the door with my left and gave it a kick open.

The gun was drawn and I heard Jordan's voice before I actually registered it was him sitting on the couch with Byron in his lap. "Stop! Put that damn thing away! It's only me!"

My face was warm and I swore my pulse had all but doubled.

"I have a good mind to shoot you! Too bad the cat's in your lap. What the bloody hell are you doing in my apartment? And how did you get in?"

Jordan stood and took a step toward me. I had already placed the gun back in its ankle holster and he looked relieved. "Your landlord let me in. I knocked on his door, showed him my driver's license and told him I was your brother. Said I was invited for dinner but got here early and couldn't reach you."

"I'm going to have a good talk with that guy so this never happens again. Okay, you're here in my apartment. Tell me why."

Up close I could see small beads of sweat on his brow and I doubted it was from the heat. He rubbed his hands and took a few short breaths. "Someone tried to kill me. I didn't know what else to do."

"You didn't know what else to do? How about calling the police? Duh!"

"They wouldn't have believed me. They'd think I was making it up."

"You could've driven to our office. You had no problem finding it the first time."

"Hey, I got in my car and got the heck out of the city as fast as I could once the garage finished up with my car. I wasn't sure your office would still be open but I figured you'd have to come home sometime. I had your address written down."

Crap. I never should've given it to him when I moved but I figured he might as well have it in case he had to forward something to me.

"Garage? What are you talking about?" I asked.

"Look, can we please sit down for this conversation? I get the feeling you're going to whip out that gun again."

"Good!"

He looked up and wiped his brow.

"Fine, sit down." I said. "I'll get us some iced teas. Byron's still on the couch waiting for a lap."

I kicked off my shoes, walked to the fridge and came back with two iced teas. I handed one to Jordan and took the armchair next to couch. "Back up and tell me what's going on."

Jordan took a gulp of his drink. "I blew the first incident off but I'm not so sure of the second. Yesterday, when I was leaving my office and walking across campus to my car, someone on a bike drove straight into me. By the time I got up from the ground, they were gone. I have no idea who it was or what gender for that matter. Luckily, I got by with a few elbow and knees scrapes."

"Was anyone else around who saw it?"

"Two guys caught the aftermath and asked if was okay. No one else was there at the time."

"And the second incident?"

"That's why my car was in the garage. I had to have it towed there this morning. I got up early and parked it where I normally do on campus. I've got tons of work to do on a seminar I'm preparing for later this month. Anyway, when I got out, the rear passenger tire was flatter than a pancake. And get this. The newer cars don't have spares. Not that it would have mattered, when they got it into the garage, the mechanic found a huge chuck of metal in the front passenger tire *and* a roofing nail on the driver's side tire. He said it was only a matter of time before those would've been un-drivable, too."

"Yeesh."

"Marcie, this wasn't caused by any road debris. This was done on purpose. I'm positive. Someone is out to get me. According to the mechanic, I would've been dead meat if I'd been on the road."

"So again I'm asking. Why didn't you tell the police?"

"Flat tires and a bike collision on campus? Come on, you know they would've blown it off. Besides, it might've had the opposite effect. What if they thought I'd made it up to get the attention off of me as a possible suspect?"

"I get it. I do. But I think you're overreacting. By the way, why didn't you pick up any of my calls? I thought something terrible might've happened to you. For your information, I planned to drive to Minneapolis tomorrow to track you down."

He looked sheepish. "A collision with a bicycle and the flat tires *were* terrible enough. Say, you really were going to look for me?"

"Like I have a choice. You're my client." I paused for a moment and continued. "And what's with your emergency contact, Barry Hayes? That line was deader than a doornail."

"Barry dropped his landline service a few days ago and only uses his cell. He forgot to tell me so when I wrote down the contact number on the contract, I used the old landline. I'll make sure to give you his cell number."

"Great. That explains Barry. What about you not answering?"

"My cell phone was hacked. As if I didn't have enough to worry about. It's a real mess. Ever try dealing with Apple support? I'm still working on it. This morning, on my way to my office, I stopped at Walmart and bought one of those pay-by-the-minute jobs or whatever you call them. Here, see for yourself."

He reached into a pocket and shoved the phone at me.

"I've seen cell phones before. Just give me the damn number. Now!"

He read off the number and I entered it into my phone.

"I'm really freaking out over this, Marcie. In fact, I had an alarm system installed on my car while it was in the garage. If someone tried to kill me by wrecking the tires, they could easily cut a brake lining or something."

"At least that was one smart thing you did today," I said. "As for getting into my apartment, next time I'll shoot your toes off!"

"Cut me some slack, will you? Can't you see I'm one step away from losing it? Geez, the police called yesterday asking if Tawn and I had life insurance policies on each other. I told them Tawn had one and I was in the process of getting one."

I took another sip of my iced tea. "How far in the process were you?"

"Not far. I was reviewing different options like term, universal life, variable life..."

"It doesn't matter. There's no life insurance policy on you so it looks really bad. You were the only one to gain from Tawn's death. No wonder the police are eyeballing you."

Jordan put his head in his hands and I could see his fingers tremble. "I didn't kill her. For God sakes, we've been through this. Hell. My wife was found murdered, I've got the police breathing down my neck and now some maniac is out there gunning for me. I'm petrified to drive home. Who knows what the heck I'll find."

"Well, you're not staying here. Think for a moment, why would someone want to kill you and Tawn?"

"I have absolutely no idea. She got along with everyone and as far as I'm concerned, I haven't managed to piss anyone off."

"What about your students? Did you fail anyone who might want to get even?"

"A few Ds but no failures. No one came unglued if that's what you're asking. Plus, none of that would have had anything to do with Tawn."

"What about your one-night stand?"

"No strings. Over and done with. If you're thinking some sort of *Fatal Attraction* thing, you can forget it."

"Fine. Given the fact everything was hunky dory at your end, it has to be something else. I've been in contact with the clients your wife was working with and I've set up interviews with some of them. Same deal with the Classy Kitchens' employees. This is a process and it takes time."

"Yeah, about the employees, why aren't the police taking a closer look at them?"

"Actually, they looked at their alibis from the time they left Classy Kitchens to the time the night security guard arrived. No red flags."

Jordan rubbed his forehead and didn't say a word.

"Want another iced tea?" I asked.

He nodded and I walked into the kitchen for refills. This time I came back holding a pitcher. "One more thing that's come up. What can you tell me about Orlando?"

"What do you mean? Tawn was there on business."

"I heard there was some tension between you when she got back."

"We had one lousy argument and it had nothing to do with Orlando. Who gave you that misdirected intel? It had to be someone at Classy Kitchens, right?"

"It doesn't matter. Are you positive there's nothing else I need to be made aware of?"

"Other than the fact I think I might be next on someone's hit list, absolutely nothing."

"Driving all the way to New Ulm from the east side of Minneapolis was really pushing it."

"Like I said, I was totally unnerved and had to get the hell out. Heck, if you must know the truth, I'm even too nervous to turn the key in the door to my house."

"All the more reason for you to contact the police. Look, I know it's a long drive and maybe you would be better off waiting until morning. One thing for sure. Like I said, you're not staying here. There's a Comfort Inn two blocks down and a Springhill Suites another block away. Take your pick. I've got an appointment with one of Tawn's clients tomorrow at one so I can follow you to the police station nearest your house and you can tell-all when we get there. Sound okay?"

"It'll have to be."

Just then the phone rang. Hogan! Thursday! With all the craziness going on I'd completely forgotten he was planning on spending the night. We'd made tentative plans and he said he'd call if all went well at the brewery and he could make it.

"This is an important call," I said to Jordan. "I'm taking it in the bedroom. And if you know what's good for you, you won't utter a sound. Not even to the cat."

CHAPTER 9

No one in their right mind wants to have a relationship based on half- truths or lies. Especially me. I hit Hogan with the "You'll never guess who showed up at my apartment after work" line before he could even finish saying hello.

"You're kidding? The guy was *in* your apartment? The landlord let him in?"

"Not *was, is.* He's on his way out right now. Drove here because he thinks someone is trying to kill him."

The next few seconds were spent with me recanting what had happened to Jordan on campus and to his car. "Anyway," I said, "he's on his way out. He'll be staying at a motel here in New Ulm and then will head over to the police station near campus tomorrow. I told him I'd follow him since I've got to be in the city to interview some of Tawn's clients. And don't even think of inviting him to join us for dinner."

"Whoa. That never crossed my mind. The whole idea of your ex letting himself into your apartment without your permission is enough to put my nerves on edge. I'm not sure how I'd act around him."

"Like the perfect gentleman and knight-in-shining-armor I know you to be."

"Very cute. I'll let you show your ex the door and I should be there in less than an hour. Wherever you want to eat is fine with me. I'm not making the drive for the food. I miss you like all get-up-and-go."

"Me, too. Drive safe."

Jordan was leaning back on the couch and staring into space when I came back into the room. "You really need to get going," I said. "I'm expecting someone."

"By the tone of your voice, I guess it's not a girlfriend."

"Like I told you in an earlier conversation, I've moved on. Look, get checked into a hotel, order a meal from one of their delivery services and keep your doors locked. I seriously doubt anyone followed you to New Ulm. Meet me tomorrow at nine in the office. From there, I'll make a few calls and head over to Minneapolis. Regardless of whether or not the police think you're a person-of-interest, they still have an obligation to protect you."

"The Edina Police think I'm a person-of-interest. I'm not sure about the ones in Minneapolis. Hey, I almost forgot to tell you. I hired an attorney. Sean Rothberg from the Hazelton-Smith Law Firm."

"That's a pretty well-known firm."

"Yeah, well, this was one expense I wasn't about to skimp on."

"I didn't take a close look at your address in relation to the police precincts but we can do that in the morning or I can have Angie look it up at work."

"No problem. I live pretty close to campus and not far from one of the precincts. I never bothered to look and see which one. Anyway, my place is bicycling distance from campus. You know how I hated long drives to work. Funny, but Tawn never minded the commute to Edina. Half the time she was all over the place on job sites. Said it went with the territory. Said— Oh never mind. I'd better be on my way."

He stood and walked to where Byron had settled himself.

This time on a small end table near the kitchen. "I didn't mean to mess up your plans for the night, Marcie, but you can understand why I'm such a basket case."

"I do, or I would've booted you out of here immediately."

"Uh, you mentioned meeting with one of Tawn's clients tomorrow. Were you able to pull up any information from the flash drive? Maybe one of them had it in for her."

"Sorry, nothing like that. If she left a clue, I haven't found it yet. All I saw were her personal notes. Reactions, really. It appeared as if she really didn't like them. Frankly, given what little I know about the clients at Classy Kitchens, I can't say I blame her. Her assistants said she was the epitome of diplomacy when it came to dealing with those demanding customers. I think her flash drive notes were her way of blowing off steam. But the flash drive had other information, too."

Jordan's mouth opened slightly and he let out a breath of air. "Other, like what?"

"Photos. And before you let your imagination go berserk, they were ordinary photos of both of you plus some with her girlfriends. I repeat, *ordinary.* The kind of stuff people put on Facebook. If she put it in a video, it could appear on the Disney Channel, so relax."

"What else was on there?"

"Only one document that caught my attention. Prior to your marriage, your late wife purchased a mixed media painting entitled 'Soulless Desire.' Acrylic on canvas. It was quite costly, not that I'm all that familiar with fine art."

"Oh God! I hated that thing. Still do. Guess I'm just a straightforward person when it comes to art. I want things to look like what they're supposed to be, not a hodge-podge of texturized colors and shapes. For some reason, Tawn was mesmerized by that thing. It's hanging in our bedroom. If you want, I can snap a photo and email it to you but I don't think it has anything to do with her death."

"Probably not but I noticed it was from a gallery with the initials VFV. One of her clients, Daisy Jamos, owns Visual Fields of Vision downtown. It could be a connection. Maybe they knew each other before Daisy signed on to have her kitchen remodeled."

Jordan shrugged. "She never said anything about that to me but who knows?"

"I will. Soon enough. So, you'll meet me at the office first thing in the morning and then on to Minneapolis. When you leave my apartment, make a right hand turn and go down two blocks. You'll see the Comfort Inn. Keep going another block if you want the Springhill Suites."

"Got it."

Jordan walked to the door, opened it and turned to face me. "Thanks again. About everything."

He closed the door behind him and I let out a long, slow breath. Hogan would be arriving in less than forty five minutes and I needed to freshen up and change my clothes to something more casual. Fancy dining in New Ulm was not on our agenda. More like a homey Italian meal or maybe even Chinese.

I opened the window in the living room and the one in the kitchen to let in some fresh air. I didn't dare leave them open when I was gone. Not that someone would break-in, but Byron would be tempted to chew through a screen.

No sooner did I get into the bedroom and scour my closet for a top when I heard a loud "POP!" coming from the front courtyard. Loud enough to make the hairs on my arm stand up. A gunshot? That was the first thought that came to mind. My God! Maybe Jordan had been followed to New Ulm.

Without wasting a second, I bolted out of my apartment and raced down the stairs. My gun was still secure in its ankle holster and I prayed I wouldn't have to take it out for the second time in less than an hour. I reached the front door of the apartment building and again another "POP!" This time louder. I was closer to whoever was firing their gun.

Flinging the door open, I took a half-step and eyeballed the entire courtyard. I could see Jordan at the far end near the sidewalk and thankfully he was still vertical. "Duck down," I shouted, and next thing I knew he was out of sight. The courtyard was empty but that didn't mean someone wasn't aiming a gun out of a window. Last thing I needed to do was step out in front and make myself their prime target. My heart was racing and my mouth felt dry even though I had downed a full glass of iced-tea only minutes before.

I took a step back into the foyer and reached for my cell phone. A third "POP!" went off and this time it all but shattered my eardrums. In that split-second I knew Jordan didn't have a thing to worry about. I'd been practicing every week at the shooting range and not just with *my* gun. That ear-piercing pop wasn't from any gun. The miscreants who detonated it had moved closer to the building's main entrance.

"It's not the Fourth of July," I yelled. "Give it a week or two."

By now, other neighbors had heard the popping sounds as well and were shouting from their windows and balconies including one guy who was yelling so loud I thought he'd have a coronary. "If it explodes or flies in the air, it's illegal in this state! I could have you delinquents arrested."

One of the kids shouted back, "Get a life, you old geezer. It's a stupid party popper. We're testing them out."

The coronary guy screamed back, "Test them in your damn bathroom and leave the rest of us in peace."

My back was turned to the sidewalk as I scanned to see who was doing the yelling. Just then I heard Jordan's voice. "Party poppers my ass. Those kids are shooting off bottle rockets. I was positive it was a gun and I'd be lying face down on the pavement."

I swallowed and nodded. "I had the same thought. I ran out of my apartment on the first pop."

"So you were worried about me."

"I was worried I might have to take on two murders. Let's leave it at that."

"I'll take that as a yes."

Jordan turned and took a few steps toward the street.

"Leave me a voice mail or text me when you get to your hotel."

"Hah! I knew it. You *were* worried."

"I'm thorough, not worried." With that, I went back into my apartment, hung up my work clothes and washed the small beads of perspiration from my face. I slipped on a clean graphic T-shirt with matching capris and poured myself another iced tea. Four sips later and Hogan was at the door.

"You missed the excitement," I said. "Some kids shot off bottle rockets just as Jordan crossed the courtyard to the street. I heard the sound and was almost fooled thinking it was a gun but thankfully my training kicked in."

"What about Jordan?"

"Let's put it this way, at least he didn't wet himself but make no mistake, the guy's really frazzled."

Hogan came inside and plunked himself on the couch giving Byron a new lap to sit in.

"Hold on a sec, I'll grab you an iced tea. You must be thirsty from the drive," I said.

"Thanks. I'm still getting used to the early summer heat. So your ex thinks someone's trying to kill him, huh? What do you make of the situation?"

"Like I said, the guy's really a basket case. Not that I can really blame him considering his wife was murdered. But as far as I can tell, there's nothing that would connect the two of them to a killer. If Tawn had enemies, they were her enemies, not his. As far as that cyclist running him down, I doubt it was intentional. When I was running crime stats at the college, there were reports all the time about pedestrians getting knocked over by overly zealous people on bikes. The tire damage is also iffy. Iffy but disturbing. One tire with a slash or tear is understandable, but three? Unless he happened to drive over the remains from an auto accident on the road or a construction site, it does seem suspicious."

"Can't really blame him for wanting to get the heck out of the city for the night. It's no fun looking over your shoulder all the time wondering if anyone is out to get you."

"I know. Geez, I wish I were further along with this investigation but it's just getting underway. Once I get a sense of who all the players are, and by that, I mean Tawn's clients, I might have a better idea of who had it in for her. Meanwhile, Jordan can report the incidents to the police in his precinct tomorrow and I'll start my interviews. Got two of them lined up."

Hogan listened intently while I told him what I'd hope to accomplish the following afternoon. He brushed the soft wisps of hair from my forehead and gave me a kiss on the cheek.

"What do you say we continue this conversation over dinner somewhere? I don't know about you but I was starving an hour ago."

"Yikes. Why didn't you say anything?"

"Because you needed to talk and I needed to listen. Without interruption."

One Chinese food dinner later, followed by both of us crashing on the couch before climbing into bed, I realized it was getting harder and harder to have Hogan race out of here at the crack of dawn so he could be at the brewery on time.

"So, Saturday evening? I could drive to your place this time," I said, pulling the covers up to my neck.

"You've got a murder to solve and not a lot of time before your ex goes full-fledged loco. Last thing I want to think about is having him show up here again. Cyclists, tires or bottle rockets. I'll leave the brewery at five and head right over. At least we'll have Saturday night and all day Sunday to ourselves. Tom and Tyler will be fine running the place on Sunday. Tom's finally coming around after his brother's death. It's been over a year but each day he shows more interest in life. That's a good thing."

"I won't have time to cook but I'll pick up salad fixings."

"Sounds great."

I fell asleep pressed against his chest along with the cat. Morning was a blur and by the time I got into the office, Jordan was there waiting for me. Angie had already looked up the precinct number for us and had written the directions.

"Max won't be in until noon," she said. "He's meeting with someone in Mankato. A fraud case, I think."

I grabbed a coffee for me and one for Jordan. "That's okay, Angie. Tell Max I might not make it back until six. If he's gone by then, I'll give him a call. My appointment with Daisy Jamos is around three and I have no idea how long that will take. Plus, I've got the rush hour traffic on the way back to contend with. Ugh."

Jordan thanked Angie for her help and followed me out the door. Next time I saw him was south of the University of Minnesota in the outer office of the third precinct in Minneapolis. He filed a report with an all-business police officer who told him that it was most likely coincidental but to remain vigilant and notify them of anything unusual.

He kicked a small pebble from the sidewalk as we left the building. "What did I tell you? Even though I explained about my wife's murder in Edina, they're not taking this seriously."

"Right now there's no connection and I don't expect to find one, unless you're holding out on me."

"What? You know everything I do. More, probably. You've seen the flash drive."

"That reminds me, send me a photo of that painting she got from Daisy Jamos's gallery, okay?"

"I'm not sure how that could possibly be related to Tawn's murder, but sure. And if you tell me you think it's a fantastic piece of artwork, I'll know you're stretching the truth."

"According to the price tag, it must've stretched her wallet. I need to find out why."

"It probably appealed to her for some bizarre reason or another. Like new designer shoes. You can relate to that, can't you?"

I bit my tongue. "Where are you off to now?" I asked.

"Home and then my office. I've gotten over my case of nerves. For now."

"Don't forget, email me that photo."

"It'll be the first thing I do when I walk in the door. Promise."

CHAPTER 10

Mount Curve was west of the city and south of Kenwood Parkway. Its homes were described as elegant and historic by every real estate site I checked. Elegant, historic and worth a fortune. Ernie had to be doing more than well in the real estate market. I had no problem finding his estate/construction site given the line-up of work trucks parked in front of it. If I hadn't known any better I would've thought there was one hell of a garage sale going on.

I glanced at the small mirror over my visor to make sure there were no tell-tale signs of the drippy Chicago style hotdog I grabbed for lunch before driving over here. Once out of the car, I stood for a few seconds and stared at the massive structure. Mature pines and oaks framed the house on the grassy knoll. With its slate gray bricks off-set by white fan-shaped ones around the windows, the place looked as if someone had magically snatched it from a royal estate in England and set it in Mount Curve's Lowery Hill.

I walked across the lawn and wondered if Ernie planned to have a brick walkway as well. Of course he did. Anyone spending that amount of moolah on a home wasn't going to skimp on curb appeal. As I reached the recessed entry, I could hear hammering and pounding from inside the structure. Since the place was clearly under construction and there was no doorbell or knocker, I turned the door handle and let myself inside.

"Mr. Star?" I shouted above the cacophony of construction noises. "Mr. Star?"

"He's in the kitchen," someone shouted. "Walk straight ahead past the circular stairwell and look to your left."

What? No yellow brick road?

I did as directed and found myself face-to-face with Ernie Star who all but bumped into me on his way into the grand foyer. "Excuse me. Pardon me. You must be Marcie Rayner from that detective agency. I was about to step outside to greet you but it seems you're either early or I'm running a tad late."

Ernie was wearing a short-sleeved pinstriped shirt with matching light gray slacks. He was slightly built with dark black hair that looked as if it had been recently dyed to cover any gray. Same for his thin moustache.

I held out my hand. "Marcie Rayner. Thanks for agreeing to meet with me. Is there any place we can go to sit and talk where we won't be disturbed by the pounding?" I figured worse came to worse, we could always have a chat in my car.

"There's a lovely spot out back that will soon overlook the gardens I plan to have. I had some Adirondack chairs placed out there so I could contemplate the progress on my estate. Come on, I'll lead the way."

I followed Ernie through the house and out a sliding door that opened to a large expanse of land. Yep, Ernie was certainly reaping it in from the real estate business.

"I won't take much of your time," I said as I seated myself in the large, uncomfortable wooden chair. Adirondack chairs had never appealed to me. They were awkward to sit in and impossible to maneuver if you wanted to adjust your position. I chose to lean forward and do my questioning hunched over. "As you know," I went on, "I'm investigating Tawn Hamlin's murder and as such, I'm meeting with her current clients."

"I'd offer you something to drink," Ernie said, "but as you can see, with the exception of the exterior, my new home is still under construction."

"That's fine. Like I said, I won't be long. How long have you known Ms. Hamlin?"

Ernie gave a sharp nod, almost as if he could click his face. "I knew her by reputation first. That's why I chose Classy Kitchens instead of using my contractor. I'd read about Tawn and I even saw her on HGTV. That's when I knew I didn't want anyone else to offer as much as a single design sketch. No carbon copy designs for me."

"What will you do now?" I asked. "Without Tawn?"

"What do you mean? The design is already in place and as expected, the attention to proportion and symmetry is above reproach. The master carpenters at Classy Kitchens simply need to follow what she created." He slapped a hand over his chest and tilted his head back. "To think she could have been killed before completing my design. Whew. The timing. I signed off on the design only days before her death. A torturous process, mind you. The design. Not her death. I know nothing about her death except what I've been told by the Edina Police and what I've read in the papers."

"What exactly do you know?"

"That someone hit her in the back of the head with some sort of meat mallet while she was still at work."

"And when was the last time you saw her?"

"When we signed off on the kitchen design. I have that document but it's at my current home in Falcon Heights. If you'd like, I can email you a copy."

"That won't be necessary. The Classy Kitchens will have it on file. Tell me, you saw Tawn a few days before she died. Did she seem distraught? Worried about anything?"

He shook his head. "No. She was composed and professional as always. I might add, relieved. The design process was grueling and I'm afraid I wasn't always my cordial self."

Officious little bugger to be exact. At least according to Tawn.

"Was there anything in particular that made your kitchen design so challenging?" *Other than you.*

Ernie clasped his hands together and smiled. One of those smug self-serving smiles. "In an expression, trompe l'oeil."

"I'm not sure I understand."

"Trompe l'oeil. It's French for 'fool the eye, or deceive the eye,' something to that end. In creating a piece of art, or in my case, the kitchen design, it makes the viewer believe they are seeing one thing when they are really seeing another."

"Like an optical illusion?"

"Exactly. We've all seen those painted arches in fancy Italian restaurants where it appears as if the outdoor garden is only a few feet from us when in reality, there is no outdoor garden."

"What kind of possible optical illusions would someone want to have in their kitchen? If I'm walking to the refrigerator, I want it to be the refrigerator and not the stove."

"Ah-hah! But does it have to be so obvious? Refrigeration units today can be concealed to look like cabinets. Same for dishwashers. That's something any seasoned contractor can do. But Tawn was able to take things to the next extreme with subtleties of design and an understanding of color pallets in conjunction with form and space. Again, I hold my breath and give thanks that she was murdered after she completed my design."

Dear God! This man is reprehensible. But that doesn't make him a killer.

"Um, one more thing before I head out, Mr. Star. Did you ever notice Tawn having words with any of the construction workers on your site? Or with Leo McCellan, the contractor?"

"Once and a while she'd get into it with Leo, but it was strictly design and construction stuff. You know. She'd say something like, 'The interior pilasters mustn't be over six inches in diameter' and he'd say, 'eight inches if you want the damn place to remain standing.'"

"So that was it? Design differences?"

"As far I knew. I never heard them talk about anything personal. Like I said, she was the consummate professional."

"Thank you. I appreciate your time. If you can think of anything else, anything at all, please call me. Feel free to leave a message if I'm not in my office."

I handed him my business card and he escorted me through the house again. I glanced to my right where the kitchen stood only this time something was off and I froze. Ernie caught my reaction and immediately responded. "Oh, did I fail to mention the carousel? It functions for the grand part of the kitchen but not for the ovens. Gas hook-ups and all that."

My brain kicked in and I remembered Jordan telling me something about carousel kitchens when he first approached me about solving his wife's murder. My eyes widened and I took in the entire scene in front of me. Granted, the place was still under construction but there were enough solid structures for me to notice that the island had shifted its position. Ernie was still talking while I stood there like a preschooler at Disneyland.

"Interesting about the plumbing, huh?" he asked. "The island moves around a stationary faucet. You'll have to come back in a few months once the house is completed. I expect it to be one of the showcase homes for the area. Once you see the completed kitchen, you'll understand why I was so adamant that Tawn be the one to design it. Too bad all her secrets went to the grave with her."

Ernie's last sentence sounded like something out of a horror novel. "Secrets?" I asked.

By now we had moved past the kitchen, through the grandiose foyer and on to the recessed porch with its arched columns. I didn't bother to check their width. Ernie looked straight at me and replied. "Design secrets, that's all. The kind competitors kill for."

"Is there something else you'd like to tell me? Did Tawn mention competitors?"

"What? No. I was only saying— Thinking out loud. That's all. Hey, if I knew anything, I would've said something to the police. They phoned my home a few days after the murder. Guess they were too lazy to drive from Edina to Minneapolis. I told them I sure as hell didn't kill her. I wanted her to finish the job. Now I'll have to be on Leo like nobody's business to make sure he follows her instructions and doesn't deviate by even an inch."

Just then Ernie's cell phone buzzed and he retrieved it from his pocket. "Got to take this call. Whoever it is. Business, you know."

I thanked him but I wasn't sure he heard. He launched into his spiel with a rehearsed Realtor voice that could almost make me forget what a self-centered, self-indulgent ass he was.

"Good afternoon. This is Ernie Star from Mohn Realty. And to whom do I have the pleasure of speaking?"

I was halfway down the lawn when I turned to have another look at Ernie's estate-in-progress. He was no longer standing in the entryway. I got in my car, turned the key in the ignition and looked at the clock on the dashboard – 1:57. More than enough time to hop on the highway and be at Daisy Jamos's gallery by three. I figured if I got into the city early, I'd stop at a Starbucks for an iced coffee. Anything to wash down the sour taste in my mouth from my extended conversation with Ernie Starr.

No sooner did I merge into the highway traffic when my phone rang and I immediately pushed the little green button at the bottom of my steering wheel. One of the neat features about having a newer car was that it linked to my smartphone via Bluetooth. Unfortunately, it didn't come with a screening mechanism and next thing I knew, I was speaking with my mother. Well, she was speaking. I was trapped.

"I'll never chide you again for divorcing Jordan. One of my neighbors is from St. Paul and she still gets the newspapers delivered to her. A few days later, but still, the local news from Minnesota. She phoned me the minute she read an article about some kitchen designer who was found bludgeoned to death in Edina. The woman was married to Jordan Rayner – a person-of-interest in her death. How many Jordan Rayners can there possibly be? My God, Marcie. To think you were married to a homicidal maniac!"

"Whoa. Slow down. Person-of-interest does not translate to homicidal maniac."

I stepped on the gas and passed a slow moving Prius as my mother continued her rant.

"Did you know about this? Why didn't you tell me? Your brother didn't say a word either but I can excuse him, what with having a toddler and all. But you? I shouldn't find these things out from the neighbors. It *was* that cheating ex-husband of yours, wasn't it? Thank goodness he's out of your life. Let him be someone else's problem. It's a darned good thing you didn't go in for a whole lot of cooking or he might've used one of those heavy duty utensils to do you in."

"Enough! Jordan may have been a lousy philandering spouse but he was no killer. It's an open case. The police are scrutinizing all kinds of evidence."

"How do you know?"

By now I was only a few miles from Route 94 and a faster way into downtown. I moved to the exit lane and cleared my throat. "Blake Investigations is also working on the case." *Technically not a lie, but not exactly upfront and honest.*

Unintelligible sounds preceded my mother's response. "Tell Max you are not to be involved. Let him deal with it. You can chase after lost dogs or missing roommates. Something safe. If you want, I'll call Max myself."

"NO! If you must know, Jordan came to me in the first place. His late wife was dealing with all sorts of temperamental and eccentric clients. Not to mention over-the-top wealthy. I have a feeling one of them might have been responsible."

"Then why is Jordan the person-of-interest and not the temperamental customer?"

"Come on, even you've seen enough crime shows to figure out they always go after the spouse. Look, I promise you, I won't be alone with Jordan and I'll keep my cutlery under lock and key."

"Very funny, Marcie. I'm serious. I don't want to get the three-day late news from Minnesota and find out you're missing or God forbid, worse."

"Three days? You hardly go three hours without calling." *Okay, maybe three hours is an exaggeration.* "I'll be fine, Mom. Honest."

"All right. Talk to you soon."

The call ended as I passed the first Route 94 exit and headed for the second. Fortunately traffic was light at this hour and I had ten glorious minutes to enjoy an iced coffee at a nearby bistro before turning on to Chicago Avenue in search of Daisy Jamos's *Visual Fields of Vision.*

CHAPTER 11

Chicago Avenue was an eclectic mix of old mid-century buildings, modern complexes and standalone residences that had long been converted into businesses. It was also home to the Chicago Avenue Fine Arts Center and a plethora of art galleries. South of downtown and smack dab between Lake Calhoun to the west and the Mississippi River to the east, it was its own focal point. The art galleries on the avenue were easy to spot with their flags, vivid murals, and banners that called out to every passerby, art connoisseur, college student, and bargain hunter.

I snagged a great parking spot down the block from her gallery and got there a few minutes before three. The green VFV banner that hung over the entry had the same letter design as the one I'd seen at the bottom of "Soulless Desire." I stepped inside and perused the gallery. An entire wall featured the watercolor paintings by Ukrainian artist Pavla Andruko. Her biography and photograph were prominently displayed off to the right of her artwork. I took a step closer to read the print when someone approached me and whispered, "Her vision reaches out and touches the soul, don't you think?"

Before I could answer, the tall woman in a black caftan reached out her hand. "I'm Daisy Jamos and you must be Marcie Rayner."

"That obvious?" I asked.

She looked at my shoes and then the rest of my outfit. "Most definitely."

I knew the woman was in her seventies but with jet black curls that hung to her shoulders, full dark brows and Kohl eyeliner, she could have easily passed for someone who was in their fifties. Maybe it was the ageless way she dressed. Artsy with no boundaries.

"I don't usually show watercolors but Pavla Andruko's work was so compelling I had to make an exception. My gallery is known for its contemporary mixed media. Varied textures. Bold lines. Oils and acrylics. But there's something so ephemeral about watercolor that once in a while I'm smitten. Well, enough about my gallery. You didn't drive all this way to discuss art. We can chat over there at the far end of the gallery. That's where my desk and work area are."

Daisy ushered me into a small corner and took a seat at her desk, a large mahogany work desk that was cluttered with papers, used cups, magazines and an ashtray filled with paperclips. "Did you want anything to drink? I've got bottled water in a small fridge in back. Sorry I can't offer you anything stronger."

"I'm fine, thanks."

She seemed nice enough to me, unlike the words Tawn had used to describe her. Harpy. Witch. Hellcat. Then again, I wasn't doing a kitchen remodel for the woman.

"Forgive this unruly work area of mine." Daisy brushed a few items aside. "You know what they say about messiness being a sign of genius? Well, in my case, it's a sign of not straightening out since I got back from Brazil not too long ago. I wanted to meet with some new artists. Then, a few days later, I got the word about Josh. Then, Tawn, of all things. Talk about dark clouds."

"I know. It's heartbreaking really. I don't know much about

the project manager, Josh, but Tawn was your kitchen designer. According to the information I have, your project is in the final stages of renovation."

"Thank God for that. I mean, the project being in its final stages. We agreed on the basic elements like flow and function. Tawn was in the process of infusing the more subtle ones like illusion when it came to space utilization."

That was the second time today I'd heard the word "illusion" used. Whatever Tawn could create, it most likely couldn't be duplicated easily.

"Did anyone else understand what she did, about...um, illusion and stuff?"

"Brom and Alexis to some extent, yes, but they were neophytes compared to Tawn. At least her original sketches and the implicit directions for Leo are intact. If he doesn't install those handmade tiles to specification, all will be lost."

If Daisy Jamos or Ernie Star, for that matter, had issues with Tawn, it would make no sense at all to do her in before their projects were completed. Still...someone hit that woman over the head.

"I understand," I said. *At least I think I do.* "Did you and Tawn get along well?"

"If you're implying 'did I kill her,' the answer is no. And for the most part, we got on fine."

"How long were you acquainted with Ms. Hamlin?" I asked.

"When I signed on with Classy Kitchens for my brownstone remodel. A few months back, I suppose."

"Hmm, you didn't know her before? Maybe from your gallery?"

"She might've come to one of our openings or even stopped by to see the artwork but I never met her and I would not have known who she was. Why do you ask?"

I took out my phone, held my breath and prayed Jordan remembered to email me that photo. Sure enough, it was there. I showed Daisy the image of "Soulless Desire" and waited for a response. Nothing.

"You recognize the painting, don't you?" I asked. "It was one of yours. Margarida Tavares Branco is the artist, right?"

Daisy crinkled her nose, lifted the black reading glasses that hung on a beaded chain around her neck and took a close look at the small screen. "Ah yes. 'Soulless Desire.' It was one of my favorites. The clenched teeth and the tightened fist… what imagery."

Clenched teeth? Tightened fist? What on earth was she seeing that I wasn't?

I waved the iPhone screen in the air. "Tawn Hamlin purchased that painting. For quite the tidy sum, too, I might add. You had to have known her or at least conversed with her about the piece."

Daisy shook her head and I caught a glimpse of the most stunning earrings I'd ever seen. Dark blue hues with a hint of pink in the center. When she moved her hand to adjust them, I noticed a matching ring. "I'm afraid not," she said. "That piece was sent to auction along with another of Margarida's works and a few from other artists who've displayed their pieces here."

I felt as if I'd been hit over the head with a sledgehammer. I had one good reason to zoom in on Daisy and it evaporated in midair. Puff! Just like that. "It went to auction? Can you explain that?"

"Of course. Buyers are really funny when it comes to making a purchase. If they think someone is after the same piece they've shown interest in, they're often times more willing to jack up their offering price so that the other person doesn't acquire the work. Hence, the auctions. True, I've got to pay a commission but the truth is, I wind up with more money than if I'd sold the piece off the floor."

"Can you give me the name of the auction house?"

"I'll need a moment. My memory's good but not *that* good. Margarida's showing was eons ago. I'll need to look that up. I use three auction houses, all Minnesota-licensed, and offhand I can't recall who sold her pieces. Why don't you have a look around the gallery while I find that information?"

"Sounds good."

I walked around the large rectangular room taking the time to read the small cards underneath each of the paintings. A few people who had entered the gallery while I was talking with Daisy, were doing the same. I tried not to be nosey but it was impossible to escape their conversations.

"Eight thousand dollars for that thing? Looks like the wallpaper you find in old bathrooms."

"Shh! I knew I shouldn't have asked you to join me."

Most of the patrons seemed to be quite taken with the watercolors. I liked them, too, but not eight thousand dollars' worth. I continued to mosey around the room when I caught Daisy giving me a wave. I immediately returned to her small enclave.

"Benningworth Galleries out of St. Paul. Raymond Benningworth is the owner. I've written down the information for you."

She handed me a gallery business card with the auction information scrawled on the back. I slipped it into my bag. "Thanks."

Daisy gave me a quizzical look. "I'm not sure I understand why the auction house I used would be of interest in Tawn's murder investigation."

"Like you said, maybe she outbid someone and they were seeking revenge. We've dealt with stranger motives. It's a longshot, granted, but I might as well consider the possibility if nothing else pans out."

"What about the husband? I heard the police thought he might be the one who killed her."

"Right now it's an open case. Without ironclad evidence, it's all hearsay and innuendo. Daisy, did Tawn ever give you the impression she was nervous or afraid of anything?"

"No. Not at all. She was self-assured and knew how to approach a project like nobody's business. This isn't my first remodel. I had a house near the university before I decided to purchase my brownstone. I had to practically refurbish that rat trap before putting it on the market. Of course, that was strictly a fix-up, not a living work of art like I expect my kitchen to turn out."

"Well, thanks again for your time. If you think of anything, anything at all, call me." I handed her my card, stood up and walked to the door. The gallery had filled up during our brief two or three minute conversation. "Is it always this busy so late in the day?" I asked.

Daisy nodded. "Some people go to bars after work, others head straight home, and still others, the true art lovers, know where to unwind and refuel their souls."

And others, like me, contend with rush hour traffic to get back to a dark office so they can put in a few more hours of work.

I had to update the crime profile that I left mid-stream on the whiteboard in our workroom. It was the typical graphic organizer I had come to rely on in order to have a visual of the salient points in the investigation. From a distance, I could almost pass it off as modern art, especially after viewing some of Daisy Jamos's gallery pieces.

Max and Angie had gone for the day and, as expected, the office was quiet and dark. I went in, turned on the lights, locked the door behind me and headed straight to the workroom expecting to be there for less than an hour. The new information I'd gleaned about Tawn would plague me no end if I didn't include it with the rest of the outline so I wrote it in the form of questions.

Could her murder have anything to do with that gallery painting? Daisy told me that Margarida Tavares Branco's works had appreciated in double digits. Maybe someone was really ticked.

Then, there was the master illusion comment that Ernie made and Daisy substantiated. Tawn certainly had a talent no one else did, at least according to them. Could that talent have gotten her killed? Why?

The motives I had were sketchy at best. On the far left of the whiteboard, I had written the names of the most likely suspects – her co-workers, her boss, and her clients. Next to each one, I added new information as it came my way. And, as much as I didn't want to do it, I added Jordan's name as well. Like it or not, he had the most to gain.

From the profile, I moved to the timeline and that's when I realized something. Renata, Brom, Alexis, and Neil all left at about the same time the night Tawn was killed. According to the police, all of them had solid alibis. But what about the owner? John D'Angelo. It was downright odd that he would be informed of his designer's death and not make a single phone call to let his employees know. They found out the next day, crime tape and all. In my book, that pushed John right up my suspect list. I circled his name in red and left myself a post – Call him ASAP.

I was already getting worn-out driving to Minneapolis. Road glare coupled with traffic were getting the best of me. At least Edina, where John D'Angelo lived, wasn't as rough as driving into the city. I figured I'd try to see him the beginning of the week. *If* he was amenable to the idea. I didn't want to put it off until later because Jordan was probably chewing his fingernails by now.

That left the looney Candace Pendleton and her dream kitchen somewhere on Lake Minnetonka, fifteen miles west of the city.

I dreaded the thought of making two long drives. Then, a thought occurred to me and I grabbed the phone. Hogan answered on the second ring. "Hey, is everything all right? I didn't think I'd be speaking to you until later tonight."

"Everything's fine."

"I hated the kiss and run deal this morning. At least we'll have more time tomorrow night and Sunday," he said.

"Um, about Sunday…how do you feel about a nice trip to Lake Minnetonka or perhaps a familiar spot - Lake of the Isles?"

"Is this some kind of a test? Because if you were thinking about a boat rental, I know someone who works at a marina in Wayzata."

"I'm not exactly sure which place. It would depend on Candace Pendleton."

"Ah-hah! That's the nutty client of Tawn's right? I knew it. The real reason slips from your tongue. You want me to do some sleuthing with you. As long as it doesn't involve going through another creepy mansion like that Mystery Castle a while back, I'm game."

"I don't think it'll be creepy but the owner's a high-strung eccentric prone to sudden outbursts and sobbing."

"Terrific. I always want to spend my days off with challenging people."

"Very funny. I'll have to call her and see if she'll agree to meet with me on Sunday. The big question is, where? She may be staying at their vacation remodel on the lake. Tawn's assistants told me her husband is way preoccupied with his executive position at Cargill Salt so she has lots of time on her hands."

"Like I said, either or, I'm in. Anything in particular you want me to bring?"

"Yeah, earplugs."

"I was thinking more like a flashlight, compass…that sort of thing if we wind up on Lake Minnetonka."

"Slow down, MacGyver. We're interviewing a suspect, not escaping from Devil's Island."

"Ah, you're taking all the fun away."

I gave the whiteboard another look when I got off the phone with Hogan and called it a day. It was past seven and I was exhausted. The case felt as if it was dragging and frankly, it was. The information gathering part of any investigation can be slow and tedious but this one felt especially long. That's because, like it or not, there was an emotional stake involved. I locked up and drove home.

Byron was yowling for food the second I got in the door and I immediately opened a can of grilled salmon for him. Far better than the leftover turkey salad I had in the fridge. I had no sooner kicked off my sandals and changed into lightweight sweats when the phone rang. Jordan! Not again.

I picked up the receiver but before I could say a word, Jordan's voice exploded over the phone.

"My apartment was broken into! Ransacked! The place was fine mid-morning after you and I left the police station. I was only in there for a few minutes to snap a photo of that painting and change clothes. Then I left for my office and didn't get back until late in the day. I knew something was wrong the minute I got to my door. It looked like someone pried it open with a crowbar. Damn it! The place was trashed."

"Oh my God!"

"Yeah, well, like I said, I saw the door and I immediately dialed nine-one-one. I waited out front until a police car arrived and then I followed two officers inside. When I gave them my name, they pulled it up immediately and one of them said,

'Weren't you in the precinct this morning to file a report?' Before I could answer, they told me to wait outside while they checked the premises. They were back in minutes and announced the place was clear but obviously had been torn apart."

"Are they going to send a forensic crew over to dust for prints or anything?"

"Nope. They told me to go through my valuables, fill out another report and notify my insurance company if anything was stolen and I needed to make a claim. They went on to tell me that there had been a number of burglaries in the area with a similar pattern of trashing the place. Like that was going to put my mind at ease. They left a few minutes ago. I gave the place a quick look-see but it doesn't appear as if they took anything. TV's still here. So is the computer. And the—"

"Quick! Go touch the top of your computer tower. See if it's still hot. You do have the same computer as before, don't you?"

"Yeah, give me a minute."

I held the line while Jordan went to check the computer. I wanted to believe this was a random burglary but if the thieves didn't make off with anything, what were they looking for?

"I'm back," he said. "Yeah, it's warm."

"Okay. Whatever you do, don't touch the keyboard. Disconnect it from the computer. Maybe the police won't dust for prints but Max and I can take care of that. Go to any Best Buy or Walmart and buy another keyboard to use. I've got to be back in your area to meet with more of Tawn's contacts so I'll get in touch and pick it up the beginning of the week."

"You should see this place, Marcie, it looks like hell. Random burglary my you-know-what. This was personal."

"You don't know that. *Yet.* When you say trashed, what do you mean? Did they tear up the couch cushions, dump furniture all over the place? What?"

"They opened all my desk drawers and the drawers in the bedroom and dumped the stuff on the floor. Moved some stuff around in my closets but I don't think they took anything."

"What about that painting of Tawn's? Is it still hanging?"

"God yes! Thieves know hideous when they see it."

"You may want to start using another adjective to describe 'Soulless Desire.' I met with Daisy Jamos today and that thing's doubled in value. Maybe more."

"Good. When this is all said and done, maybe I'll sell it back to her."

Just then I heard a knocking sound from Jordan's end of the line.

"That'll be the landlord. He said he'd be right over to put in a new lock."

"Make sure it's a deadbolt. I'll talk to you later tonight."

CHAPTER 12

Candace Pendleton answered on the third ring. I called her as soon as I got off the phone with Jordan.

"I'm sorry if I'm calling you at a bad time," I said. "This is Marcie Rayner, the private investigator who was at Classy Kitchens the other day. We weren't exactly introduced given the circumstance. So, I wondered if I could arrange to meet with you regarding Tawn Hamlin's death."

"Me?" Candace screeched into the phone. "Why me? I didn't have anything to do with it."

"Um, we're not accusing anyone, Mrs. Pendleton, we're simply trying to gather sufficient information about Ms. Hamlin to give us a good idea as to who might have had a motive to kill her. Our investigative firm will be interviewing all of Ms. Hamlin's current clients."

"Well, it wasn't me. With Tawn out of the picture, I'll be forced to contend with those neophyte designers and God knows who else Classy Kitchens drums up. At least the design plans are in place for the contractor. Still, I'm not sure Leo McCellan fully grasps the concept of deep illusion. There's more to it than cabinets and sheetrock, you know."

Deep illusion? I'm not sure I'm grasping any of this, either.

"Deep illusion? I understand about the trick-of-the-eye to

make some things appear closer or farther, but I'm not sure what you mean."

"I'll spell it out for you, honey," she said. "Tawn Hamlin could disguise a kitchen so that it could resemble something entirely different. She could do for kitchen design what the French artist Pierre Delavie could do with canvas."

That's a big help. And how do you spell that name?

I scrambled for a pen so I could jot down the name by syllables while Candace continued to speak. "As I was saying, Tawn was a genius. Think mazes and labyrinthine structure in conjunction with form and function."

My eyeballs spun around in their sockets. "Uh, getting back to meeting with you, would it be possible if I drove to your home in Minneapolis this Sunday so we could talk? I know it's the weekend but I have a pressing schedule and this investigation can't wait."

Candace hummed for a moment before she responded. "I suppose that would be all right. I was planning on checking the progress on the lake house on Sunday but I can shift my schedule and do that on Saturday. It's not as if the contractors would be there. Heavens. It's Monday through Friday or not at all. Do you happen to know where I live? I imagine the address is with the information Classy Kitchens gave you and they should not have done that without my permission."

"Rest assured, Classy Kitchens didn't provide me with your personal information other than a phone number."

The line went quiet for a few seconds before she spoke. "I live at 2415 Lake of the Isles Parkway. Are you acquainted with that area?"

More than you think.

"Yes, I am. Can we meet in the early afternoon? Say one or two?"

"Two would be perfect."

"Rest assured, this shouldn't take more than forty minutes or so. Oh, and before I forget, I'll be joined by an associate. I hope you won't mind."

"That should be fine. I'll pencil in an hour for you, although I have no idea what possible information I can provide."

"Sometimes it's the little observations that bring investigators closer to the answers they need. Thanks Mrs. Pendleton, I look forward to seeing you."

I hung up the phone and took a long breath before grabbing some pre-cut veggies and chopped ham for a makeshift dinner salad. When I had rinsed off my plate and silverware, I fired off a quick text to Hogan – "Boating another time. Lake of the Isles it is. (cute heart shape). See U tomorrow."

I spent the next morning cleaning the apartment and picking up a few things at the supermarket. Mostly salad stuff, cold cuts, breads and assorted snacks, not to mention cat food. Then, even though it was Saturday and the office was closed for clients, I headed over there to study my profiles again and continue with the background checks I had started. It had been five days since Jordan showed up in my office and it felt like fifty. I had to get moving.

I'd left Silvano (John) D'Angelo out in the cold in comparison with the attention I paid to the other suspects, namely Tawn's clients. But unlike Brom, Alexis, Renata, and Neil, no one was really certain of John D'Angelo's whereabouts the night in question. That concerned me. He could've easily hidden somewhere in the building and then quietly snuck up behind Tawn. Still, the police were satisfied with whatever explanation he gave and as far as motive was concerned, there was none. Nevertheless, background checks often find hidden gems. And unlike the tangible ones my mother seemed to be obsessed with, I was hoping to uncover facts and connections, not facets and color hues.

The TV shows make background checking look exciting with stunning revelations that pop out of nowhere. However, the actual process is time consuming and often boring as was the case with John D'Angelo's information. I used the sites that Max had suggested beginning with government sites and moving on to social media. Not a single eye-popping notation on criminal background, judgements, liens and public records. The only thing of consequence, and I'd hardly even call it that, was a divorce fifteen years ago. Welcome to the club.

Out of curiosity, I widened my search to real estate tax records, something I was becoming more and more proficient with. No surprises there, either. He owned a home in Edina and his taxes weren't delinquent. BORING.

I don't know what I had hoped to find but at least on the surface, Silvano (John) D'Angelo looked clean as a whistle. Then why wasn't I convinced to leave it alone and look elsewhere? Maybe the face to-face meeting I planned to have with the guy would yield better results. Maybe he'd have a slip of the tongue followed by a hasty cover-up. It was late and I was letting my imagination get the best of me. Not a particularly good trait for a detective.

I left the office at a little past three and went straight home to unwind. I intended to call John D'Angelo first thing on Monday to set up a meeting. Two items were top on my list – his whereabouts during the timeline of Tawn's murder and any information he might have regarding ruthless business competitors. Brom and Alexis didn't mention anything but they were Tawn's assistants, not her boss. If anyone was privy to that kind of knowledge, it most certainly would be the business owner.

Hogan arrived at a little past six and I literally gave him the biggest bear hug I could muster. "I know you were only here a day ago but it feels like forever."

"No kidding. Too bad the highways come with speed limits."

We opted for a meal at Applebee's followed by couch cuddling and late night TV. The subject of my investigation kept coming up like bubbles on a soft drink. Especially Jordan.

"I still can't believe he drove all the way over here instead of going to the police," Hogan said.

"Yeah, it freaked me out no end. I suppose I should cut him some slack considering his wife was found murdered, but he's really going off the deep end. You don't suppose someone is gunning for him, too, do you?"

Hogan gave my shoulder a pinch as he moved me closer to him. "Hmm, hard to say. From what you told me his place was messed up but not vandalized. There's a difference. Someone was looking for something, not trying to give him a message."

"That was my take, too. But what? What were they after?"

"It had to be something of Tawn's. Something her murderer didn't find when he killed her at Classy Kitchens. Are you sure you went over everything on that flash drive?"

"Pretty sure. Unless some of the titles for her files weren't what they appeared to be. Okay, you opened this can of worms, might as well deal with it." I got up from the couch and booted up my computer. "Let's take another look, Joe. Or do you prefer to go by Frank?"

"Whoa! Someone's read the Hardy Boys."

I laughed. Hogan pulled up a chair next to my desk and leaned over my shoulder.

"Same files," I said. "Photos, holiday message, business mileage, tax information, that dreadful client diary of hers, and of course, those French recipes."

"What about the file marked 'to do list'?"

"I glanced at the text but it was only a list of things she wanted to do. Call so and so. Have Brom return swatches to Designer Linens. That sort of stuff."

"Keep reading. I have a funny feeling about that list."

I shrugged and scrolled farther down the page. "Still things she needed to do. Highlight touch up with Sylvia. Nails. Have Alexis pick up the variated subway tiles for ES's backsplash. Run light tests on tiles."

I turned to Hogan. "ES must be Ernie Star and she was probably checking out the subway tiles with different types of lighting. Not sure, but it's my best guess."

"If you say so. Keep scrolling."

"Too bad there are no dates next to the items on her list."

I kept my hand on the mouse and read the text. Nothing unusual. And certain nothing I'd want to do. Then I noticed something odd. The text read, "Call insurance agent ASAP. Need collector's policy for the Branco work."

"How do you like that?" I said to Hogan. "Tawn must've really be smitten with that mixed media painting Jordan can't stand."

"Smitten or did she know something he didn't?"

"She probably knew the piece went up in value. Daisy Jamos told me that when I talked with her at the gallery. Anyway, I doubt 'Soulless Desire,' was what the thief or thieves were interested in when they broke into Jordan's apartment or they would've taken it. But get this – she put ASAP in bold. It must've been a top priority, huh?"

I finished scrolling down Tawn's list and came up emptyhanded. If Tawn was hiding something, it wasn't on her flash drive.

Hogan rubbed the back of my neck as I exited the file. "Guess we can call it night, huh? Maybe we'll get a better idea of what got Tawn killed when we meet with that Pendleton woman tomorrow. From what you told me, she could rival the female cast members on most Telemundo shows."

"Rival? She can direct them."

I had started to drift off to sleep when Hogan gave me a slight nudge. "You don't suppose it was a rival kitchen designer who did her in, do you?"

"Huh? Wha—"

"Sorry, thought you were still awake. My mind's been bouncing all over the place. I know those restauranteurs are notorious for rivalry and downright cutthroat behaviors but maybe it's the same deal with high end designers. After all, they're in it for thousands of dollars if not more with some of those extravagant homes."

The sleepy fog evaporated from my head and I was able to think. "Funny you should mention it. I was so preoccupied with the upfront suspects like the employees and her clients that I only began to think of a possible competitor yesterday. I made a note to ask her boss, John D'Angelo, about it next week. I can't put off meeting with him."

Hogan leaned over and kissed me on the neck. "It's scary, you know."

"What is?"

"The fact we're beginning to think alike. Next thing you know we'll be completing each other's—"

"Sentences?"

He gave me a light kick on my ankle before turning away and giving the blanket a tug.

CHAPTER 13

"It looks different in daylight," I said as we drove down West Lake of the Isles Parkway outside of Minneapolis the next day. It was one thirty and I'd told Candace we'd be at her house at two. Glad she could accommodate me on a Sunday.

Hogan, who was behind the wheel because he insisted we take his truck, gave me a quick glance. "How so?"

"The houses. In the daylight they seem even more enormous and the lawns aren't even lawns. If I had to come up with a description, I'd call them 'sweeping grounds,' like something out of a gothic novel. Of course the same could be said for Ernie Star's mansion-to-be on Lowry Hill. Geez, I wonder what it must be like to have money like that…"

"Hey, maybe you'll solve the case of the century and wind up rich and famous, or my brewery will take off like nobody's business and I'll beat you to it. Either way, we'll enjoy our newfound wealth." He paused for a moment and squeezed my knee. "Truth is, I don't need wealth to be happy but that doesn't mean I'd want to be destitute just to prove a point."

"I don't think either of us has anything to worry about. Say, isn't that number twenty-four fifteen on your left? It looks like the image I googled this morning."

Hogan's truck came to a crawl. "It looks like sixteen hundred

Pennsylvania Avenue, only twice as large and slightly more imposing. My God!"

"It's her house, all right. The driveway has to be at least a quarter of a mile."

"Well, not quite that long but long enough that I don't want to walk it from the street. Yeah, I'm pulling in."

"Candace told me the house was a center-hall colonial and went on to explain how its style reflected the very roots of our heritage."

"Oh brother."

"Hey, at least she wasn't crying, sighing or swooning because Tawn was out of the picture regarding her other place."

"Yet! We're not in the clear yet."

The driveway curved around the house ending at a massive four car garage in the rear that looked larger than most residences. We got out and walked along a paved path bordered by colorful annuals until we reached the front entrance. It was larger than my bedroom with wrought iron benches and colorful planters. A chandelier hung from the ceiling of the structure and I wondered what lucky person got to dust that thing.

"Well, here we go," I said. "Don't say I didn't warn you." My finger pressed the bell but before I heard the ring, Candace had opened the door.

She brushed some flyaway hair from her brow and studied us. "Don't you simply love these home monitoring systems? I saw your truck pulling into the driveway while I was at my computer. It comes up on my screen. Not one of those garish Ring devices. Might as well announce you're on the lookout. Anyway, do step inside."

Before I could say a word, Candace motioned for us to follow her into the sitting room immediately to our right. Two creamy yellow loveseats and two sage wing chairs with a solid coffee table in the middle of the room. A brick fireplace, adorned with summer flowers in glass vases, was the focal point. "This is the day room," she said. "Lovely, isn't it? Have a seat, please."

I took a seat on the couch and Hogan grabbed the wing chair to my left. "I know we haven't been properly introduced," I said as Candace took the seat on the couch opposite mine. "except of course over the phone. I'm Marcie Rayner with Blake Investigations and this is Hogan Austin."

Hogan stood and reached out his hand. Candace gave it a shake and he sat back down.

"I might as well get started," I began. "As you know, we're investigating Tawn Hamlin's death."

Candace suddenly got up. "My goodness. I don't know what I was thinking. Can I offer you something to drink? Iced tea? Iced coffee? Lemonade?"

"Iced tea would be nice," Hogan said and I nodded. She immediately left the room and we both caught our breath.

"Hit over the head with a mallet, right?" Hogan whispered. Before I could answer, he gave me a wink. "She wasn't poisoned so our drinks should be fine."

"Very funny. I need to be serious with this interview."

Candace stepped back into the room and handed each of us an iced tea. "I can bring sweetener if you'd like."

I reached for my tea. "This is fine. Thank you."

The only sound was the overhead fan as I took a sip of my tea. Candace leaned toward us from her spot on the creamy yellow couch. "I told those stodgy Edina police officers everything I knew," she said. "Can you believe it? They phoned my house the day after I stopped by Classy Kitchens. Someone in that office must have informed them I was a client. And, as if badgering me on the telephone wasn't enough, they wanted me to stop by their station. I said 'absolutely not.' Frankly, I wasn't about to drive all the way over to Edina unless they had a warrant for my arrest. Next thing I knew, they sent an officer to my house."

Candace stopped long enough to arch her back before resting her shoulders on the large couch cushions.

"They were following protocol," I said. "It doesn't mean they suspected you of anything. Same reason we're here. We need answers. Tawn's killer is still at large and that's a pretty disturbing thing. So, any little detail or bit of information you might have would certainly be a help."

"If you say so."

I smiled. "Tell me, were you acquainted with the other clients she was working with? Daisy Jamos and Ernie Star?"

Candace bit the bottom of her lip and fidgeted with the tennis bracelet she was wearing. "I only know Daisy Jamos from reputation. Not hers, her gallery. It's always featured in one article or another in the Sunday papers. And as far as Ernie Star is concerned, if anyone deserved to be bopped over the head with a hammer or whatever it was, it should've been Ernie. What an annoying self-centered pest! Like I said, I certainly had nothing to do with Tawn's murder, but if I were to wield a heavy instrument over someone's head, it would have been Ernie's."

Hogan shot me a look and I gave him a slight nod before turning my attention to Candace. "Um, that almost sounds personal."

"Personal? I wouldn't want to be within two feet of that man. Let me tell you a little bit about Mr. Star. First of all, he felt his project should come first. Called Tawn constantly when she was conferring with me. One time he insisted she drop everything and drive straight away to Lowery Hill because, and I quote, 'The overcast clouds are moving. The kitchen space needs to be defined during transitional weather movements.' Damn office phone was on speaker and I heard everything before she turned it off. Transitional weather movements my ass. Pardon me, but that pompous buffoon is insufferable. I can't even bear to watch those Mohn Realty commercials."

"Would you know if Mr. Star and Tawn were on good terms?"

Candace shrugged. "I can't say but I'll tell you this much, even if they were on the worst possible terms, he wouldn't have been so stupid as to kill her. Not before his kitchen was completed. Unlike my kitchen at the lake house, which, by the way was designed to emanate the vast expansive style of the Northern Pacific, Ernie wanted something completely different. That crazy man insisted his kitchen be the next Disney attraction. Can you imagine?"

"I, er..."

"I know. Looney huh? I'll stick with the basics. My kitchen was carefully thought-out with its vaulted beamed ceilings, intricate wooden carvings that reflect our native tradition, and deep illusion so that my guests will feel the same way Lewis and Clark did when they saw the Pacific Ocean for the first time. Granted, we're on Lake Minnetonka, but illusion is illusion. I doubt Ernie Star would even understand the concept of time and space. Not every feature needs to move around like a merry-go-round. Fluidity of design gives the kitchen its soul."

I didn't want to let on that I'd seen Ernie's carousel feature and it was astonishing so I motioned for her to continue.

"As I was saying, Mr. Star wanted his Renaissance Revival to be more of an attraction than a kitchen. You know, movement and all that."

Hogan, who'd been taking it all in, propped his head on the elbow that was resting on the wing chair and asked, "How do you know all this?"

I was wondering myself. It didn't seem very professional for Tawn to share Ernie's plans with Candace but then Candace gave a laugh and rolled her eyes. "Unfortunately, Mr. Star and I found ourselves in the concierge waiting room at the same time a few weeks ago. He all but gave me a dissertation on his project."

"I see," was my response. "Other than Mr. Star, were you acquainted with any other clients of Tawn's?"

"Not personally, no, but I did see some of her finished projects in Architectural Digest. Enough to whet my appetite. That's why I hired her in the first place."

"So it wasn't necessarily Classy Kitchens you wanted, but their designer?"

"Indeed. And now I'm in a terrible fix. Two quasi designers, wet behind the ears with absolutely no idea of how to define space and movement. Honestly, it's almost as if someone wanted to sabotage my project all together! This is unbearable. Simply unbearable!"

At that instant, Hogan's eyes widened and his mouth opened slightly. I swore I knew exactly what he was thinking. What if, for some strange reason, someone really did want to make sure one of those clients of hers would never have their kitchen completed as they envisioned it? But why?

All three clients had signed on for Tawn's unique ability to fool the eye. That's what she was known for. Her other kitchens must've exemplified that trompe l'oeil maneuver as well. Candace, Ernie, and Daisy weren't all that unique when it came to utilizing deep illusion or whatever the heck they wanted so that dishwashers could pass as fancy cabinetry and someone could starve to death trying to locate the refrigerator.

So, again, why would someone go to all that trouble to commit murder in order to halt a project? It had to be more than that. These were kitchen designs for heaven's sake, not top secret nuclear codes.

I was so lost in my own thoughts I didn't realize Candace was still talking.

"...and if that's doesn't put the kibosh on everything, I got an email from Leo McCellan this morning telling me they won't be able to send the crew to the lake house tomorrow because something unexpected came up. I'll tell you what came up. That miserable Ernie Star. I'll bet he pitched a fit and carried on shamelessly until Leo had no recourse but to send two crews over to Lowery Hill. Well, I've got news for you. First thing tomorrow morning, I intend to take a little drive over there to see for myself."

"Um, that's probably not such a good idea, Mrs. Pendleton," I said. "Maybe you should call Classy Kitchens first and let them deal with the matter."

"All they'll do is to try and placate me. Especially Renata. She treats me as if I were a two-year old."

Given that display of yours the other day in the office, can you blame her?

"Oh, I suppose you're right. Ugh. Too bad that husband of mine is stuck in New York on a business matter. Did you know Cargill Salt has plants all over the place?"

"They're a huge conglomerate," Hogan said. "Agriculture, food, beverage… I imagine it's quite a demanding job for your husband."

"He has secretaries and more underlings than you can possibly imagine. Meanwhile, I'm left here to undertake this kitchen project all on my own. Talk about demanding."

"Well, we've taken up enough of your time," I said, "and we should be on our way. Would you mind terribly if I used your restroom before getting back on the road?"

"Not at all, go straight past the grand foyer and into the corridor. If you get to the kitchen, you've gone too far but if you do, please take a moment to enjoy its subtleties."

What the heck is a kitchen subtly?

I thanked her and gave Hogan one of those looks that said, "Sorry to leave you in the lurch with her."

CHAPTER 14

Candace wasn't kidding when she used the term "Grand Foyer." It was actually a large sitting area with lovely carved benches and enough assorted greenery to rival most hothouses. Colonial lantern sconces framed the walls. I kept walking. Figuring I must be in the corridor, I glanced at either side of it for a restroom. No luck. At least I hadn't gone past it into the "feel-free-to-take-a-look kitchen."

Behind me I could hear Hogan speaking but couldn't make out the words. I kept going, pausing once to take in the small work area to my left. Lovely oak desk complete with computer and printer. Candace's office, I imagined. More greenery and two coach lamps on the wall. The only thing missing was a door. It took me a moment but I realized it was there after all – a pocket door, hidden from view. With only Candace and her husband, I presumed, the need for privacy wasn't a must.

I paused to take another look and realized I could actually see the stack of papers she had on her desk. It was a haphazard pile that teetered on the edge of the desk and looked as if it would hit the floor at any moment. Without giving it much thought, I took a step inside and gently moved the papers away from the edge. The sheet on the top was a form from her doctor's office and the only thing filled in was her birthdate – December 7, 1971.

Pearl Harbor Day, thirty years later. Next, I noticed three stylized initials on the sheet of paper that was second from the top of the pile. I froze. There was no mistaking the VFV design that served as the logo for Daisy Jamos's Visual Field of Vision Gallery. No way could I step back into that corridor without taking a peek.

Muffled voices were still audible and I prayed Hogan would keep Candace's attention long enough for me to lift the top sheet and read what was on that paper. My hand was shaking as I slid the top sheet off to the side and leaned over to read what else was on the page with the VFV initials. At first, I thought it might be an invoice or a receipt but instead, it was an actual letter. Not an email but a letter. So much for Candace Pendleton not knowing Daisy Jamos.

Damn! I left my iPhone in my bag on the couch, squelching any chance I had of taking a quick photo. It didn't matter. I could read and the letter was clear and succinct. Well, maybe not clear, but certainly succinct. It read, "I have one MTB with two and one with three. Flawless. I must know by the end of the week."

She must know what? No time for guesswork, not now. I left the office as quickly as I had walked in and continued my jaunt down the corridor. The restroom was eight or nine feet past the office and on the same side. Pedestal sink complete with a swan basin nickel-brushed faucet, straight out of HGTV. I was careful not to leave any smudge prints on the metal.

Candace's kitchen would have to wait for another day. I walked briskly back to the sitting room and cut in to the conversation as soon as I approached the couches. "Oh, sorry if I interrupted. Lovely grand foyer, especially all those plants."

"These interiors practically beg for greenery, especially in winter when everything is suddenly dismal and drab," Candace said. "That's why it's paramount Classy Kitchens does not screw up the lake house renovation. I made it explicitly clear to Tawn that the illusion I wanted to create was one in which the grandeur of the Pacific Northwest would eclipse the everyday moods that drift over Lake Minnetonka like fumes from a factory furnace."

Hogan and I exchanged glances. Then he looked at her. "I doubt they'll mess up the beamed ceilings or the picture windows."

"It's not *that,*" she said, "it's the entire feel of the place when one steps through the door. It must invite nature in. And if you're thinking hackneyed picture windows, think again. Ours will open to the world."

Tell me how that works out for you when the first bat flies through it.

I stood and motioned for Hogan to do the same. "Well, we've certainly taken up enough of your time, Mrs. Pendleton. Thank you for meeting with us and for your hospitality."

"I wish I could've been more help regarding the investigation, but as I said, I don't have any idea who could've possibly benefited from Tawn's death. Except of course her husband. It always turns out to be the spouse, doesn't it?"

Unless he's the universal scapegoat.

"Then again," she said before I had a chance to respond, "as much as I like that Brom fellow and Alexis, I wouldn't put it past *any* aspiring assistant to, well, you know."

I had to admit, that thought had crossed my mind on more than one occasion but according to the Edina Police, their alibis checked out. That didn't mean I couldn't do a bit of double checking myself. And as for Candace's alibi, she was in Barbados. I was able to verify that shortly after our encounter at Classy Kitchens.

Ernie Star had a solid alibi, too, and Daisy Jamos's alibi was plastered all over social media with a gallery showing. Candace was right about one thing, even though she lied to me about not knowing Daisy – it wouldn't make any sense at all for one of them to kill off the only person who had the panache and ability to pull off the kind of kitchen magic that only Tawn Hamlin could accomplish.

"Again, we appreciate your time. If there's anything else you can think of, here's my card. Please feel free to call."

She escorted us to the front door and we heard the smooth latching sound the moment she closed it behind us. I grabbed Hogan by the wrist and squeezed. "I need to tell you something but not here. Wait until we get into the car."

"Walk fast, then. The suspense is killing me."

As soon as we were buckled in and he started the engine, the words flew from my mouth. "She lied. She absolutely lied. A boldface, right-in-my-face lie!"

"About what?"

"She knows Daisy Jamos. She *more* than knows Daisy Jamos."

"What are talking about?"

"When I went to use the restroom I sort of stuck my nose into her small office."

"You really are quite the Nancy Drew sleuth, aren't you?"

"Very funny. I didn't do it on purpose. Well, not really. I glanced at her desk and saw that a stack of papers was about to land on the floor so I—"

"Went through them?"

"If you weren't behind the wheel, I'd give your leg a kick."

"Remind me not to take my hands off the wheel."

I chuckled and went on to tell him what I had discovered. "VFV. What else could it be but that gallery? And then the reference to MTB. That has to be Margarida Tavares Branco. You know, the artist who created that dreadful 'Soulless Desire,' at least according to Jordan. But what I don't get is the cryptic bit about having one with two and one with three. I do get the part about having her make up her mind quickly. So, what do you think it is?"

"Geez, I'm the last person who would know anything about modern art. Are you sure that's what it said?"

"Absolutely."

"One with two and one with three, huh?"

"Both flawless. She said that, too."

"Hmm, flawless is kind of a strange way to describe a painting. Then again, she could have been talking about the technique."

"Maybe. I couldn't very well have blurted it out and asked her because I had no right to snoop around her office. But nothing prevents me from giving Daisy Jamos a call. Candace refused to acknowledge she knew Daisy and that's a red flag in my book. By the way, what did you two chat about while I was out of the room? Anything that would help with the investigation?"

"Unless it was Ernie Star who turned up dead, I'd say no. Candace looped right back to complaining about him. She did mention something interesting, though. It was sort of an afterthought or a passing reflection. She said, and I quote, "They'd better make sure the doorways were wide enough to accommodate that growing paunch of his."

"I'll be darned. No wonder she referred to Ernie's project as Disneyland. I'll bet he was having some sort of secret passage or cubby built. Maybe he has a wine stash he doesn't want anyone to find. And yet, he couldn't help blabbing about his kitchen plans to Candace. What a braggart."

"She leans toward the pompous side, too, you know."

"Leans? One breath from a passerby and she'd keel over. Brom was right about the kind of customers that sign on with Classy Kitchens. But wealth and snobbery don't equate to murder. So far, I have so many loose ends I could scream. And oddly enough, the only common denominator connecting some of Tawn's clients has to do with that artist from Daisy's gallery. Strange, don't you think?"

"Not really. You're dealing with people who have lots of money and some of them obviously enjoy investing in art."

"But the same artist? Think about it. Tawn's only extravagant purchase, made before she and Jordan tied the knot, was a Margarida Tavares Branco mixed media piece. It originated in Daisy's gallery even if it was sold by auction. Then, that baffling letter I came across on Candace's desk that referenced a possible purchase of Margarida's work as well. It's too tight a connection for coincidence but you're right, it doesn't exactly shout 'foul play.'"

I rubbed my temples and stared into space. Hogan took his right hand off the steering wheel for a split second to give my shoulder a squeeze. "Hey, you've got one more key player to deal with and that may tie everything together."

"I sure hope so. First thing tomorrow I intend to call John D'Angelo and firm up a meeting time with him. Looks like I'll be making the drive back to Edina either Tuesday or Wednesday. I really can't put off having a conversation with him. Even though no one at Classy Kitchens could vouch for the guy's whereabouts the night Tawn was murdered, he must have a decent alibi or the police would be hauling him in and not badgering Jordan."

"You sure about that?"

"Uh-huh. Max has been amazing about eking out information for me from his contact at the police so if John D'Angelo was on their radar, we'd know about it."

"I'll tell you what's on my radar – food! I'm starving. What do say we find a decent restaurant before we hit the highway?"

"Sounds like a good plan to me."

Monday morning arrived like a firecracker on the Fourth of July. Both of us overslept and raced around my apartment to make up for the lost hour. We didn't. Hogan called Tyler and told him to get in early in order to set up the brewery and I left a message on Angie's email telling her I'd be a bit late.

"Angie's email?" Hogan laughed. "Not Max's?"

"First of all, by the time he reads it, it'll be noon, and second, he's on a case in Mankato. So there!"

I poured some kibble for Byron, refilled his water dish and locked the door on my way out. Hogan had left only a few minutes before and the long sweet kiss he gave me still left some moisture on my lips.

"Next Saturday I'll make the drive to Biscay," I told him. "You've been a regular road warrior and it's my turn to give you a break."

"You sure about that? What about your case?"

"It won't matter whether or not I'm in New Ulm, Edina or Biscay. As long as I have my notes and my phone I'll be okay. Unless I pull up another dead end with John D'Angelo. Yeesh. There's got to be some tiny crack or fissure that brings me closer to finding that killer. Meanwhile, I'll keep digging deeper into Tawn's past while I'm at the office today. My other cases are downright routine."

Angie was on the phone when I walked into the office but she gave me a wave and I mouthed, "talk to you later." I booted up my computer and put the cup of Starbuck's Blonde Roast on my desk.

I dialed Classy Kitchens and asked for John D'Angelo before taking a sip. Renata was at the other end and asked how my investigation was coming along.

"Interesting," I told her and cited my experiences with both Ernie Star and Candace Pendleton.

"Hold on, I'll put Mr. D'Angelo on the line, and good luck."

It was a brief call. The Classy Kitchens owner agreed to meet with me on Wednesday. Preferably at eight-thirty "before things got rolling."

For me, it meant I'd have to get rolling by five in order to make the drive, grab coffee, and be prepared to interview him as if I was a litigator. I figured if I survived Leo, Ernie, Daisy and Candace, I could manage another round, this time with the head honcho.

Thankfully it was a slow day at the office and that meant plenty of time for me to dig deeper into Tawn's past, study the crime profile I had diligently charted on the whiteboard, and tackle some miscellaneous searches related to other cases. Angie ordered out for lunch and we chatted over deli sandwiches.

"Do you happen to know anything about artwork?" I asked her.

"I can name the masters, if that's what you want to know. And I know the difference between classical and modern, but that's the extent of it. Why?"

"Something I came across at Candace's place yesterday."

"Came across?"

"Came across...stumbled upon....happened to see by accident...."

"Oh brother. What was it?"

"A letter from Daisy Jamos about a piece of art. Well, actually, more like a note. It said she had one with two and one with three and that Candace needed to make up her mind ASAP. What do you suppose that means?"

"Hmm, I'm not sure. If it said, "one of two" or "one of three" that would make more sense, especially if it was a print or a lithograph."

"Ah-hah! You know more about art than you let on."

"Not really, but I do know that lithographs, prints and serigraphs are numbered and the numbers are usually much higher than two or three. Are you sure you weren't in a hurry and misread the note?"

"Positive. Anyway, it couldn't be a print. The artist, Margarida Tavares Branco, works with oils and acrylics. Those can't be reproduced and numbered."

"Buyers? Could she have been referring to other potential buyers? That would make perfect sense."

"Oh my gosh, you're right! How dense of me not to think of that. Geez, up until now I never heard of that artist, and all of sudden, she's a hot item. And you know what the real kicker is? She's the only thing in common that links three people in this entire investigation. And it's real loosey-goosey. I'm as frustrated as hell."

"Don't beat yourself up. You said you still had one more important interview. Maybe that will tie things together."

"Let's hope."

Late in afternoon, when I had totally exhausted my search into Tawn Hamlin's past, I stepped back into the main office and pulled a chair up to Angie's desk. "Pheromones," I said. "It had to be pheromones. Nothing else would explain it."

"Huh? What are you talking about?"

"The only possible reason that Tawn Hamlin, aka Mary Ann Locaste, would get hitched to Jordan Rayner. Not to say he wasn't a good catch, but she was eons out of his league."

"I'm listening."

"After graduating from the University of Minnesota – Twin Cities, she went on to obtain a Master of Interior Architecture from Boston Architectural College and from there an internship with a kitchen designer in St. Paul before landing her job at Classy Kitchens. But that's not all. Want to hear what her thesis was about?"

"You'll tell me anyway, so sure, knock yourself out."

"Utilizing fractals to conceal entities and fool the eye."

"Come again?"

"You heard me. Tawn was all into creating illusion. That was probably the big selling point that landed her the Classy Kitchens job. But could it have been the thing that got her killed? You'll have to pardon me; I'm thinking out loud. It's what I do when I don't have answers."

"Do like the rest of us do – start making them up."

CHAPTER 15

The next day wasn't much better when it came to finding out who knocked Tawn over the head with that mallet. I did, however, have much better luck tracking down the birthparent of the woman who wanted family medical history. By noon I felt as if I had at least earned part of my paycheck.

I dove deeper into Ernie Star's background on the off chance he might have been hiding something but it seemed Ernie was one of those people who lived his life out in the open for everyone to see. Dear God! The man even posted what he ate for breakfast on Facebook. And Candace wasn't much different. She wanted the whole world to know about every little nuance in her life but unlike Ernie, she preferred to do it with photos on Instagram.

Max breezed in a little past three and I caught him up on my progress or, lack of it. One good thing, though. He told me, "In spite of the rumblings from the media, the Edina Police are no further along than you are but you've got the advantage."

I was incredulous. "I do?"

"Yep. They're so focused on your ex-husband they're not paying serious attention to anything else."

"There's no real evidence, you know. I mean, so what about an insurance policy? Everyone gets one. And someone's reference to an argument? Name one married couple that didn't argue.

Weren't they at least a little taken back when they heard about Jordan's apartment being ransacked? And the near miss with the bicycle? Not to mention his car tires. The police officer in Minneapolis told Jordan that the department would share that information with the Edina Police."

"They shared it according to my contact but the Edina Police have another take on the matter. They think Jordan trashed his own apartment to make it look as if someone was after him."

"What??? And would he be stupid enough to slash his own tires? And he certainly didn't run in front of a bicycle!"

"No, but until they hone in on someone other than Jordan who would've benefitted from Tawn's death, he's still numero uno."

I cringed. "Tomorrow morning I'm meeting with John D'Angelo, the owner of Classy Kitchens. Maybe he'll have an idea of who wanted her out of the way. Sure, there's Brom and Alexis, but neither of them was ready to step into her Manolo Blahniks. Besides, they were both pretty sure their boss was going to find a well-known interior designer to take her place. Come to think of it, Neil mentioned something of the sort when we first spoke."

"Any connections among her clients other than their kitchen remodels?"

I shook my head. "Not really. Except for that artist of Daisy Jamos's."

I told Max what I had discovered and even confessed my information gathering tactics. All he did was chuckle. "You're lucky Candace didn't find you with the letter in your hand."

"Hogan said a similar thing."

"I knew I liked that guy."

"So," I said, "you don't think the Margarida Tavares Branco artwork had anything to do with Tawn's murder, do you?"

"I don't see how it can. Jordan's painting wasn't stolen and other than the fact this Daisy woman wanted Candace to decide upon a purchase, nothing links back to Tawn."

"That's what I thought, too. But it *is* odd, isn't it?"

Max crinkled his nose. "Nah, not really. Lots of these wealthy people are always looking for investments and fine art tends to be a solid choice. That's all. What did you say that artist's name was?"

"Margarida Tavares Branco. Brazilian artist. Mixed media."

"Never heard of her."

"Oh come on, Max. What artists have you heard of?"

"The good ones."

We both laughed and I asked how his workload was coming along.

"If I'm lucky, I'll be able to wrap things up in Mankato by the weekend. Doris and her sister have some sort of picnic planned. Fortunately for my brother-in-law, he's still in Chicago at some architectural symposium. He'll be spared the lemon-infused kale and God knows what else."

"Wallis! Oh my gosh! Wallis! I completely forgot he was an architect! Max, do you have his cell phone number? He might be able to help me with this case."

Wallis had helped me out before on another case involving a wealthy heiress who was found dead in her iconic landmark home in Mendota Heights. The place was a tourist attraction with secret grottos and passageways. If it wasn't for Wallis, Helena Heatherbrae's death would remain a mystery. If anyone knew about the kind of architectural designs Tawn created, Wallis was the one. I knew I had to get a hold of him but it would have to wait until he returned from that symposium. Meanwhile, I had to focus on John D'Angelo and that's exactly what I did the following morning.

I was up before the sunrise and on the road to Edina by seven. Fortified by a Grande mocha latte that I picked up on the way,

I was energized and poised for my conversation with the Classy Kitchens' owner.

The front doors were still locked when I arrived since the showrooms wouldn't open until nine and it was eight twenty. I imagined Neil wouldn't be at his post until eight fifty-seven. He struck me as one of those "adhere to the work hours only" kind of employee.

To the right of the doors was an ornate bronze bell and I pushed it. A few seconds later, I was face-to-face with Silvano (John D'Angelo). Fifties or even early sixties, tall, dark hair, heavy set and dressed to the nines in what looked like a designer shirt and trousers. No tie but I chalked that up to the summer weather.

"You must be Marcie Rayner. Come on in. I'd offer you coffee but Renata's the one who knows how to fiddle with the machine so you'll have to wait I'm afraid. I can get you a bottle of water though."

"I'm fine, thanks. I had coffee on the drive over."

"No sense standing here in the foyer," he said, "might as well mosey to my office and get this over with."

I remembered his office was cattycorner to the concierge desk and followed him as he took some shortcuts through kitchen showrooms. Like the designers' workspace, John's was tastefully decorated. That's where the similarity ended. A massive mahogany desk in the center of the room, coupled with a huge oval table and four wing chairs, made it look more like a command center than a business office. John waved his hand and motioned for me to take a seat in one of the chairs.

"Thanks for agreeing to meet with me," I said. "Our firm was hired by a private party to look into Tawn Hamlin's murder."

"The husband, right? Look, you don't have to tell me but it stands to reason. If the guy's innocent he'll want to prove it, and if he's not, he'll want to make it look as if he is. So, what can I tell you that I haven't already told the Edina Police?"

"I'm not sure about the details you may have shared with them," *or anything for that matter,* "so we might as well begin with the timeline. Tawn was working late the night she was killed. Your employees all left at the same time and locked the building. Security arrived a few hours later." I took out my iPad and glanced at an empty screen. "According to my notes, no one could ascertain if you were still in the building when they left. So, were you?"

"Nothing like a pointed question to get things moving, and no, I wasn't. I had my Town Car driver pick me up a little past four. That's one of the perks in my old age. I get to have a driver."

No wonder none of the employees made any mention of seeing or not seeing their boss's car when the left because he used a service and wouldn't have parked one. He was off the hook as far as the Edina Police were concerned.

"I see. So, how did you learn of Tawn's death?"

"A visit to my home from two Edina Police officers at a little past ten. I gave my wife some cock and bull story about a break-in at the showroom and left with them. Had to identify the body along with Roger, from Top View Security. Then answer a litany of questions. Finally, at a little before one, a police officer drove me home. I was told the forensic crew was going to be on scene the rest of the night and that I needed to be back early in the morning. I was so dazed, tired and beside myself, I never thought to call Renata or anyone else for that matter. It was only when I told my wife the truth in the morning that she asked if I had notified the employees. At that point, it was too late. Everyone found out when they got to work."

The air conditioning in his office picked up and I buttoned the Boer & Fitch shrug that was my "go-to" sweater for changes in summer weather.

"Thanks," I said. "It must have been awful to see her like that."

"If you must know, I still see her like that when I close my eyes to go to sleep. The police officer who drove me home that night said those images can last in the mind for months. Years even. Nice thought, huh?"

"I'm sorry. Her reputation as a designer was stellar. Tell me, were all of her clients satisfied with the work she did? I've met with three of your customers who have projects in the works but I wondered about the jobs she had completed prior."

John threw his neck back and rolled it around before looking at me. "Let me tell you a little bit about Tawn. In all my years in this profession, I never had a designer who was as highly rated by our clients as she was. It was instinctual with her. She had a good grasp of what they wanted and delivered it as such. Once in a blue moon, she had style or design issues with Leo McCellan and his project manager, Josh Newburgh, but they worked it out. Talk about a shocker. Josh died of a massive heart attack out of the blue. Not the first time I've heard of those things where someone in tip-top physical condition suddenly had a coronary. Guess Leo will have to roll up his sleeves for a while until he finds a replacement."

"Is that the only construction company you use?"

"Yep. I work with the best and intend to keep it that way."

"So Tawn didn't work with any other carpenters or companies while she was doing your projects?"

"That's correct. Only Leo McCellan's."

"Do you know if Tawn had any close friends who'd stop by and visit? That sort of thing."

"I didn't monitor her day to day activities but I doubt it. She was very focused and single minded when it came to her work. She didn't let in a whole lot of people. That's why I was astonished as hell when she announced her engagement to that professor in Minneapolis. Never did catch the name. And once she was married, she still kept her professional name."

Whoa. That was a close call. Nothing like a bit of nepotism to squelch an investigation.

"And you mentioned that her former clients were satisfied. All of them?" I asked.

"Absolutely. As you've surmised, Classy Kitchens deals with a rather specific cliental - customers with money to burn and fanciful, if not downright disturbing, ideas about kitchen remodels."

It was the first time I'd heard the word "disturbing" used in any context related to Tawn's work. The tiny hairs on the nap of my neck seemed to stand at attention and it wasn't due to the air conditioner. "Disturbing? Can you expound on that?"

"Not disturbing as in horror movies or that sort of thing, but disturbing as in elements that visually upset the senses. Weird angles, insistence upon cabinetry features that made no sense, and materials that didn't convey the warmth or feel that most kitchens strive to obtain."

"Avant-garde?" I asked.

"Yeah, I suppose. But it was more than that. It went beyond style and purpose as most of us think about kitchens. It was as if purpose overshadowed everything and style had to compensate. I'm not sure if I'm making any sense so let me give you an example. One of our clients wanted a carousel for dishes, like those old Lazy Susans, but she didn't want it to be obvious. Anyhow, Tawn had to design a cabinet that looked immobile when in fact, it could swerve on a dime. Want to know what I think? The woman wanted a hiding place for something and who would suspect her kitchen?"

"Fascinating. You're going to have a difficult time replacing her. Are Brom or Alexis up to the task?"

John ran a hand through his hair and sighed. "I wish. They're good, don't get me wrong, but they're far from what I need at this point. Don't think me callous but I have a business to run. I already called Boston Architectural College and spoke with her advisor, hoping to see if there was anyone else on the horizon who had the background and skills Tawn did."

"And?"

"In a nutshell - no. Her advisor all but hyperventilated over the phone. In retrospect, I could have handled that call better, but like I said, I have a business to run."

"One more thing, Mr. D'Angelo, and I won't take up much more of your time. Does your business have any serious competitors who would—"

"Commit murder to further their own profits?"

"No graceful way to put that, huh?"

"Anyway, your answer is no. Modern Kitchens in St. Paul specializes in contemporary designs. Lots of glass and industrial features. Simply Stylish Kitchens in Falcon Heights offers more styles but less imagination. Classy Kitchens has never considered either of them to be our competition. Lowes and Home Depot might, but not us."

If I had a theory brewing about a competitor who wanted to get Tawn out of the picture, it dissipated as soon as John finished his sentence. I stood and thanked him for his time. I also handed him my card and gave him the party line - "If you can think of anything else that might be a help in this investigation, please call me."

As I stepped out of the office, I noticed Renata at her desk and on the phone. She gave me a wave and I did the same. Neil was at his post when I approached the front door.

"Marcie, right? The private eye."

"Yes on both descriptions. Good morning Neil. How's it going?"

He looked around to make sure no one was within earshot.

"Okay, I suppose, in terms of foot traffic but I'm not sure how many of those people signed on the dotted line for kitchen remodels. With Tawn gone, it has to put a dent in the business. Especially since her murder hasn't been solved. That's got to make customers a bit wary, don't you think? It makes me wonder if the new faces in the door might think one of us had something to do with it."

I hadn't really considered that observation but Neil had a point. Funny, but he didn't seem at all snobby or affective like he did when I first met him.

"This business rests its reputation on certain skills that aren't all that common," I said. "If that's what clients want, they'll come here."

Neil scratched an ear before answering. "Hope you're right. I need this job. I'm in a Flex Choice program at Rasmussen College in Eden Prairie. Going for my business degree. It's a quick drive on the 494 and I can take night classes as well as online ones."

So that's why he bolts out of here at five on the dot.

I was about to tell him to have a nice day and head for my car when something unsettling popped into my head. Something I probably should have broached with John D'Angelo. Then again, Neil would have nothing to hide. I took a breath and looked directly into his eyes. "Neil, you've got a good handle on the kind of people who visit this place. In the days leading up to Tawn's murder, did you ever notice anyone who didn't fit the usual mode?"

"Whoa. That's a toughie to answer. Usually, it's couples who come in here. Gay, straight, it doesn't matter. Once in a while we get an Ernie Star who's flashy and over-the-top or an artsy type like that Daisy Jamos, but I can't say I've noticed anyone I wouldn't expect to notice. Not recently anyway."

"But you have? In the past?"

Neil nodded. "Months ago. One of those steely business types with no humor and no time for small talk at the door. The only reason I remember is because the man was here all the time. I nicknamed him 'Fancy suit guy.' Figured he was working with Tawn but it wasn't my business to be nosey. I was hired to greet customers and usher them into Classy Kitchens. Why? Were you thinking it was a customer who killed her?"

"I'm open to the possibility it could have been anyone."

I thanked Neil for his time and wished him good luck with his studies. I didn't dare tell him what I was thinking because I was too horrified to even say it out loud. If Tawn Hamlin was a master at illusion and knowledgeable about architectural design when it came to secret passages, stairwells and carousels, then she could have easily found herself working for someone who had something to hide and given the extent of Tawn's expertise, I wasn't thinking money, jewels, or artwork. I was thinking something much worse and on a far grander scale –drugs or human sex trafficking, the two subjects that seem to be plastered all over the news. What if Tawn found out about such a clandestine enterprise and paid the price? She might have had information about it and that's why Jordan's place was ransacked. I really needed to have a conversation with Max and see if the Edina Police might have been aware of something, even if it wasn't in their city.

The screen on my dashboard said ten seventeen and I was famished. Even a decent latte could only go so far. I'd had good luck with the Edina Grill before so that's where I headed. No sooner did I pull into a parking spot when the car phone rang and gave me a jolt. I still hadn't gotten used to the fact that it linked to my cell phone.

"Hello?"

"Marcie, it's me. Jordan. I found something. You need to drive over here. If you hurry, it shouldn't take more than an hour and a half. It's mid-morning. Traffic should be light. Please! This is really important. Important enough for you to cancel whatever appointments you have and get over here."

"Okay. Slow down and tell me what you found."

"I'm not sure. I accidently dropped that hideous painting and something came loose. Look, I don't want to talk about it over the phone. You really need to see this. I don't think it can wait."

"What I really need to do, is to have something to eat. I've been working your case since dawn and I'm in Edina. And unless we're talking an explosive device, in which case you should hang up and call nine-one-one, it can wait long enough for me to get breakfast."

"Edina? That's great. It's much closer. If you eat fast, you can make it in an hour."

"I'll get there when I get there. Whatever it is, leave it alone and make sure your door's locked. All right?"

"Don't worry. It is."

CHAPTER 16

I couldn't possibly fathom what on earth Jordan had uncovered in that painting of Margarida's but whatever it was, it had him on edge. I pictured an airtight envelope with some sort of white substance that was on the underside of the backing or maybe even a key with a letter, but when I got to Jordan's place and saw firsthand why he was so concerned, I had to admit, I was, too.

The moment he unlocked the door and let me inside, he secured it again. The blinds were drawn as well, not that it mattered since he wasn't on the first floor, but still, it was a precaution.

I put my bag on the coffee table in his living room and with hands on my hips, demanded to know why he insisted I drop everything and make the trek into downtown Minneapolis.

"Okay, okay," he said. "I think I may have found out what got Tawn killed. Maybe even who did it."

He was talking a mile a minute and rubbing his hands as if they were frozen. I held my palms face up in front of him, the universal language to slow down. "Take a breath and tell me everything from the beginning. In fact, what do you say we sit down for a second? I'm not going anywhere and neither is that painting. So what happened?"

Jordan moved to the couch. "I had just gotten off the phone with First Memorial Mortuary to make arrangements for Tawn's cremation. Her body is going to be released this week. The forensic lab called me this morning and I had to make the arrangements. Cremation now and a memorial service next month."

I nodded and let him continue.

"It felt as if everything was spiraling around me so I went into the bedroom to stretch out on the bed. For some reason, the sight of that painting was more than I could take. I decided to get it off the wall and put it in a closet. I guess I was more nervous and more wound up than I thought because I stood on the bed instead of getting the small step ladder from the kitchen."

"And the painting dropped?"

"Not right away. It's a heavy sucker but I managed to balance it. Then, my hands started shaking and it slipped from my grip. It hit the headboard and landed on the nightstand before sliding off to the floor."

"I see. And when it fell off, did something come loose from the back of it or did it break entirely?"

"Come on, you can see for yourself. It's still exactly where it fell, only…never mind. Follow me."

Jordan's bedroom was neater than I expected. The bed was made and there were no dirty clothes lying around. Maybe Tawn had been a better influence than I was.

"Before you take another step," he said, "look at the floor around the painting. Look carefully."

The floor was a hardwood floor and it was easy to see what he was talking about. I gave him a shrug. "All I see are white dust chunks. The painting must've taken a good whack when it fell."

"Not dust chunks."

Ah-hah! Right on all counts! Drugs.

"Cocaine? Heroin? Are you sure?" My voice sounded shrill. "Mixed media artwork my butt. Margarida was using her talent to traffic drugs into the country. I was afraid of something like this."

Jordan looked at me as if I'd lost my mind. "It's not drugs. I picked up a chuck and the white clay or whatever it is, came apart. This is what was inside."

He opened the drawer of his nightstand and held out a small gemstone. "Diamonds are my guess. That artist probably coated them with a watercolor paint or something. Her paintings are highly textured and full of bumps and uneven canvas. Holy crap! She had to be smuggling the diamonds into the United States and somehow Tawn found out. Or…Oh my God, I hate to say this. What if Tawn knew about it all along and that's why she bought the painting? As an investment. Either someone tipped her off or she stumbled on something and it got her killed."

I looked at the gemstone and my eyes widened. Of all things, this couldn't be what I thought it was. "Jordan, take that stone to the sink and make sure the stopper is in place. See if the watercolor paint comes off of it."

I was inches behind him as he went to the small sink in his bathroom and ran warm tap water on the stone. "Nothing's coming off," he said. "This thing is deep greenish blue. Almost iridescent."

"That's because it's not a diamond. I think it's a tourmaline and if the rest of what I'm thinking is true, then you might have blundered into the jewelry heist of the century. I don't know the details because, to be perfectly honest, this information came from my mother."

"Iris? What does she know about jewel thefts?"

"She doesn't. She listens to the news or whatever gossip wafts her way and repeats it. Or embellishes it. Darn! I should've paid more attention. Anyway, it happened decades ago. Some sort of tourmaline theft in Brazil. And we're not talking a little theft, we're talking a major international jewel thief ring. Interpol has never been able to figure out how the gems were getting out of Brazil and into the United States. Or so I've been told."

"At least it's not drugs. Imagine the thought of going to bed with enough cocaine over your head to stone an entire city."

"Well, this isn't much better. From what I understand, the police are dealing with highly dangerous individuals who'll stop at nothing to move their illicit goods out of Brazil and into the states."

"And that artist?" Jordan was all but stammering. "Margarida what's-her-name?"

"Tavares Branco. She had to have been paid to coat those tourmalines and work them into the oils. That white cakey stuff is most likely some sort of polymer like Sculpey for crafts and jewelry making. That's why her paintings are so texturized. It's all beginning to make sense. And the conduit for all of this – none other than Daisy Jamos, the gallery owner who introduced Margarida to the art world in Minneapolis. But I'm really jumping the gun. I'm no gem expert. That being said, I'm pretty sure those are tourmalines but a gemologist would need to verify. Look, if it's all right with you, I'd like to take one of them and have it checked out."

"No problem. You can take them all. The painting, too."

"Hang on. I'm not walking out of here with a painting. A small concealed gem is one thing, a large oil piece is another."

"So now what? Now what do I do?"

My first instinct was to tell him to call the police but I held off. That simple act might put a target on his head. I bit my lower lip and tapped the floor with my right foot. "Gather up those chalk-covered gems from the floor. Looks like there are four or five of them, counting the one I'll need. Put them in a safe place. You have a fire safe box, don't you?"

"Yeah, I had to buy a new one. Those vandals smashed the small one Tawn and I had. They managed to bust it open but didn't take anything. We only used it for our marriage license, my teaching certificates, my car loan information, that sort of thing. Nothing tangible. Tawn kept her expensive jewelry in our safe deposit box at the bank. Geez, I'm lucky they didn't smash up the walls with whatever they used."

"They were interested in finding something specific, not vandalizing. Look, cover the painting and put it in the back of a closet. Or better yet, hang it back up. You haven't done anything wrong in the eyes of the law." *Except of course, concealing evidence.* "Tawn purchased that piece of art legitimately. And, it was acquired before you even met her."

"I don't get it. If this stuff is so valuable and those thieves will stop at nothing, then why didn't they steal the damn thing from off the wall?"

"Maybe they figured you already knew about the tourmalines and had removed them from the painting. Maybe they were looking for the gems. 'Soulless Desire' was merely the packaging."

Jordan lifted the painting from the floor. "This is unbelievable. Un-freaking-believable. Take a look. I thought for sure with all those chucks of white stuff and dust on the floor that the painting would be damaged, but look closely. It appears as if Margarida painted the same colors underneath where she affixed the gemstones with more coats of paint. 'Soulless Desire' still looks the same. You can't tell the different. When it dropped, it loosened up the gems but everything else is fine."

"Good. Forget the closet. Put it back on the wall. No sense raising suspicion should the police decide to interview you again and for some reason, ask to see the bedroom."

"What are you going to do?"

"What I'm *not* about to do is barge over to Daisy Jamos's and demand answers even though that's exactly what I feel like doing. I need to find out more about her and her connections. If she's really behind these tourmaline thefts, she's not acting alone and heaven knows who we're up against. I need to run this by Max and have an expert examine the stone. If it turns about to be a valuable tourmaline, then I've got to find out what the Minneapolis police know about this international gem theft. Your ex-wife's murder appears to be more complicated than I imagined. Can you give me a minute? I need to check on something."

Jordan shrugged. "Sure, take all the time you need. Want something to drink? Coke? Gatorade?"

"Yeah, Coke would be great."

Jordan walked to the kitchen and I immediately googled Bennington Auction Galleries in St. Paul. Thankfully my case notes were easy to access on the iPhone because, although I recalled the auction house name, I couldn't remember the owner. Raymond Bennington. Of course. Thirty seconds later, I was placing the call."

"Hello," I said. "This is Marcie Rayner from Blake Investigations in New Ulm and I'd like to speak with Raymond Bennington."

"At your service. I'm Raymond. What can I do for you?"

"My firm is investigating a homicide. The victim, a woman, had purchased a piece of art from your auction house."

"Goodness. Was it a theft and they killed her? How awful. When? What painting?"

"The homicide was recent, within the past ten days, and the painting was a mixed media piece by Margarida Tavares Branco. It originated at the Visual Field of Visions Gallery in Minneapolis."

"Hmm, Margarida Tavares Branco, you said?"

"That's right, why?"

"The purchase had to be quite a while back. We haven't acquired any recent works of hers."

"It was. I mean, the purchase was a while back."

"What was the name of the painting?"

"'Soulless Desire.' Were any other works by that artist sold at the same time or close to it?"

"I'll need a few minutes to check my records. Paintings are cross-filed by artist name, name of the piece and date of purchase. If you give me your number, I can call you back, or you can try me in about ten minutes. Would that be all right?"

"That would be fine. Thank you so much."

Jordan came back to the room and put a can of Coke on the coffee table. "What was that about?"

"I called the auction house where Tawn bought that painting. I need to find out if there were others. The owner is going to call me back."

I sipped on my Coke and kept tapping my phone to check the time. "According to my mother," I said, "Dear God, I can't believe I'm quoting this as gospel, but anyway, she told me this was a huge covert operation with far-reaching tentacles."

Jordan rolled his eyes.

"Her words, not mine and most likely not from any news source. Still, she probably got the gist of it right. For all we know, Daisy Jamos was in cahoots with that auction house."

My eyes looked down at the iPhone. Nine minutes had passed. "I'm calling back," I said.

The tips of my fingers tapped the small screen wildly and I held my breath until Raymond Bennington answered.

"Precise timing," he said. "But I'm afraid there might have been a miscommunication."

"Miscommunication? What do you mean?"

His voice sounded clear and calm. "It appears our auction house never sold the painting titled 'Soulless Desire.' Are you sure that was the title? We did auction off three other pieces by Margarida Tavares Branco – 'Withered Passion,' 'Flameless Heat,' and 'Stinging Embrace.' Maybe it was auctioned by another gallery house. You might want to check with Visual Fields of Vision again."

Oh believe me, I will.

"I don't suppose you're at liberty to give me the names of the buyers of those other works."

"I wish I could help, but no. That information is confidential. You'd need a warrant, I'm afraid."

I knew what he said was true, but still, it was worth the try. "Um, you mentioned other auction houses. Would you happen to know which ones in Minneapolis handle fine art?"

"That information I can gladly give you – Farlington's Auction House in Falcon Heights and Twin Cities Auction House in Minneapolis proper."

I thanked him profusely and shushed Jordan while I placed two more calls. I already knew the answers I would get but I still went through the process. Neither auction house sold 'Soulless Desire,' nor any other paintings by Margarida Tavares Branco.

"What does that mean?" Jordan asked.

"It means someone is lying."

CHAPTER 17

Jordan promised to hang the painting back up, secure the rest of the gems in his fire safe and not say a word to anyone about his discovery.

"I'll call you once Max and I have spoken. In the meantime, just go about your business."

"Go about my business. That's funny. I feel like the life blood's been sucked out of me and worse yet, I might be the next victim."

"Don't be so dramatic. I'm sure you'll be fine. Keep your doors locked, stay in public places…you know the drill."

"Aargh."

I slipped the colorful gem into the aspirin container I carried in my bag. "I'll talk to you tonight, okay? I've got to get going."

It felt like days since I'd eaten that mid-morning breakfast after my meeting with John D'Angelo but I didn't want to waste time at another restaurant. I figured I could pick up a burger at any of the fast food places off of the highway.

The traffic on 35W heading south was fairly light. Rush hour wouldn't start for another two hours. I stayed in the right hand lane in case my hunger pangs got worse. Every exit ramp displayed signage for food, gas, and lodging so I pretty much had my choice. I stuck to the speed limit since the last thing I needed was to be pulled over.

My mind raced with thoughts of smuggled gems, unscrupulous art dealers, and those wacky clients at Classy Kitchens. Wacky and maybe even dangerous. At first I didn't pay much attention to the black Dodge Charger that pulled alongside of me. I was probably going so slow a golf cart could have passed me.

It was only when the car slipped over the dividing line and all but slammed into me that I sat up and took notice. And by 'take notice,' I meant swerve to the shoulder until he passed.

"Jackass," I said out loud and in that moment, the driver slowed down until I was a few yards ahead of him. Then, he got into my lane and picked up speed. Enough speed to scare the crap out of me. *Damn it! That guy's about to run into me.*

I signaled left, moved to the next lane and stepped on the gas. Luckily, the cars in front of me were *way* in front of me. The Dodge Charger didn't give up. Again, the driver got behind me, this time so close on my tail I was positive he'd slam into me. *If* it was a he.

Up ahead I could see the half mile sign for the exit but instead of moving into the right lane, I held my ground in the left and waited until I was just about at the exit. Then, pulling a stunt I never thought I was capable of, I crossed the lanes at breakneck speed, and slammed on my breaks only feet from the stop sign. My heart was beating wildly and my hands were shaking.

My move was so quick and so unexpected that the Charger couldn't make the exit in time. It was no coincidence and it certainly wasn't a case of road rage because the only one raging was me. I pulled into a McDonald's on the right and looked around. The next exit was at least four or miles down the road but I wasn't taking any chances I'd be spotted. I drove my car to the back of the McDonalds and pulled up next to the Dumpster.

I grabbed my phone and dialed Jordan.

"Marcie? What's going on?"

"Listen. Listen carefully. I was nearly run off the road and I'm positive it was deliberate. Jordan, don't freak out on me, but I think your apartment might have been bugged. Maybe when it got trashed. I'm going to turn around and head back to your place. Whoever was tailing me probably thinks I'm on my way back to New Ulm. Let's hope so."

"Holy crap!"

I followed a Subaru into the drive-through and ordered two hamburgers, small fries and a Coke when it was my turn. Much easier reaching for hand size portions while driving. Sure enough, the Dodge Charger was nowhere in sight. Still, I was uneasy the entire way back to Jordan's. At least I wasn't starving when I got there.

I knocked on the door and when Jordan answered, I motioned him into the hallway. "Mouth your words," I whispered. "No speaking out loud. When we get inside, we need to look for a device. Chances are they didn't have time to install anything into a smoke detector since that would involve a ladder. Grab a screwdriver and start checking your light switches and outlets. Then check your surge protectors. Those seem to be popular for small bugging devices. I'll look at lamps and the obvious places like behind books on shelves."

We didn't say another word to each other and went about the task systematically. First, in the living room, then the bedroom and finally the kitchen. Nothing. An hour and a half had past and I was tense and exhausted.

Jordan kept shaking his head as he moved from one outlet to the next. I was beginning to wonder if I had made a mistake and maybe it was some nutcase on the road who had one too many. Then, I realized something and motioned for Jordan to follow me into the bathroom.

"I'm overthinking it," I said, no longer mouthing my words. "If whoever did this was so high tech, they wouldn't have wasted time trashing through your stuff. They would have planted serious devices and waited. I think we might be looking for someone with a basic knowledge and a short attention span. My guess is a nanny cam."

"Like those teddy bear inserts?"

I nodded. "But they've gotten more sophisticated now. Go back to the living room and take a good look on your bookshelves, especially knickknacks. See if there's something you don't recognize that you didn't notice before. And we can speak out loud because it's video. They know what we're up to."

Jordan charged into the room and studied his entertainment center. Everything looked normal to me. There were some fancy glass bowls on a few shelves and hard covered books on the others. Suddenly he reached for a book and I stopped him.

"Don't pick it up without using a tissue. Maybe there are fingerprints we can salvage."

Seconds later, he handed me the book and I took it gingerly using a paper towel. It was a burgundy tome with gold leaf on the cover.

Jordan shook his head. "I don't know why I didn't notice the damn thing before."

"It's fairly innocuous," I said. "Like most hard covered classics. Besides, how often do any of us scrutinize our stuff? "

Using the paper towel, I took the small black device from the plastic insert and removed the battery. "Grab a freezer bag. If we're lucky, there might be usable prints on it. One of Max's contacts at the police department can help with that."

"Glad you didn't give it back to me. I would've stomped on it."

"Then we'd lose evidence."

Suddenly Jordan's jaw dropped. "Geez, I looked behind the

books in our bedroom but not at them. I kind of shoved them aside with my hand. You don't suppose—?"

Before I could answer, he raced into the bedroom and eyeballed his bookshelf. "Pay dirt. We hit pay dirt. The bogus book is anchored by my Tom Clancy collection."

Again, I was careful to grab the thing with a paper towel and remove the battery. "Grab another freezer bag, will you?"

I followed Jordan into the kitchen and looked at the clock on his oven. "What time does your bank close?"

"Huh? The ATM's open all the time. Why? You need some cash?"

"No, but you need to put the remaining gemstones in your safe deposit box at the bank. Forget the fire safe. Whoever's behind this will undoubtedly know we found the hidden gems. I'm going with you just in case we get tailed."

"Wonderful. I'm glad you carry that concealed gun of yours."

"Max would have my head if I didn't."

"We'd better get a move on. The bank closes in half an hour."

"I don't think the Dodge Charger followed me back and my car's close, I'll drive."

Then, something occurred to me and I felt like the idiot of the century. "Oh my God! My car! Get a move on!"

Jordan and I picked up the pace until we were all but jogging.

He was almost out of breath. "What's the matter? What's going on?"

"You'll see," I said, without stopping to explain. When we reached my car, I bent down and looked above the driver side tire to the underside of the car body. Nothing. I did the same with the rear driver side. Still nothing. But I went I got to the rear passenger side I reached my hand underneath and yanked out a GPS tracking device. "Damn it! It was deliberate. Whoever planted those devices must have been watching and saw me put the gem in the aspirin vial. In fact, they probably thought I was putting all of them in. Come on, we'd better get to your bank before they lock up."

If there was any chance of getting a print off of the small tracker, I made sure it would be impossible. I was in so much of a hurry that I didn't bother to use protocol. Time trumped procedure and I was sure Max would understand.

Fortunately, Jordan's bank was only a few blocks away and I was lucky to find a parking spot in front. We got in just as the security guard closed and locked the door behind us. Jordan was able to put the gems in the vault without incident while I used that time to phone Hogan.

"You're where?" he asked.

"At Jordan's bank. In Minneapolis."

"I thought you were going to be in Edina."

"I was but, oh geez, it's a long story so I'll give you the CliffsNotes."

When I was finished, the only thing Hogan said was "Double check your car again. Hell Marcie, I don't like this at all. It's getting much too dangerous."

"Relax, I'll call you as soon as I get home. I'm sure no one's tailing me now. And if they were, they'd figure out the gems are not in my possession." *Except of course for the one I need to show Max.*

Jordan came out from the vault just I ended the call. "So, it all boils down to those tourmalines. How damn valuable are they that my wife was killed over them?"

"Hey, we don't know that yet and we don't know if they're the tourmalines in question. I'd hate to put everyone on high alert only to learn they were made of glass or something. With Max's list of contacts, a trusted gemologist wouldn't be too hard to find."

By now, Jordan and I were standing in front of the bank. He looked tired and numb.

"You hungry?" I asked, more out of concern for him than anything else. Those little burgers I devoured sat in my stomach like mini-lead sinkers. "I could go for something to eat. Anything around here?"

"There's a Greek place around the corner. The gyros are decent."

"Good. Let's walk. My car should be safe in front of the bank."

"If you must know, I'm one step away from being a total basket case over this."

"Yeah, I've got to admit, I'm a little un-nerved over things, too. When I told you I thought you'd be fine in your apartment, that was before the GPS tracker deal. Any chance you can call your friend Barry Hayes and stay with him for a day or so? I don't want to bring the police into it until I'm certain about the gemstone I'm carrying. Of course we'll have no choice if it turns out to be what I think it is. However, Max and I work fast. We don't have to sift through lots of red tape to get things done. We'll have those prints analyzed and a verdict on the gem in a few days."

"I'll call Barry when we get to the restaurant."

Jordan and I didn't say much more until we were seated at Mediterranean Pitas, a cozy little Greek place with aromas that made me forget about the burgers I had eaten. We ordered from the counter, poured ourselves drinks from the machine and took a booth in the back. The place was bustling, Greek music was playing, and our voices blended into the other twenty or more conversations that were going on.

"I got a passing look at the license plate on that Charger when he came up behind me. Minnesota plates but I only got the last few letters. I'm going to call Emily McLoughlin at the public safety building at St. Paul Community College to see if she can find a match for a black Dodge Charger."

"Think she'll do it for you?"

"Oh yeah. I ran more favors for that girl than you can imagine. Tracking that plate will take time though. Still…"

"I know. It's better than nothing. Our food should be here any second. I'd better give Barry a call."

While Jordan was on the phone, I made a quick restroom stop and my own call. This time to Max. His voice was loud and chipper so I figured his case must be going well.

"Hey kid, what's up? Everything okay?"

"Yes and no. I'm in Minneapolis and I don't want to get into it on the phone. Any chance you could meet me in the office around eight or eight thirty. I hate to ruin your night but it's important."

"You're not ruining it. I'm still in Mankato with a few things to tie up. I'll see you between eight and eight thirty. Don't drive like a maniac if you run late. I've got enough stuff to keep me entertained at the office."

I thanked him and walked back to the booth in time to watch the waiter place our meals on the table.

Jordan shoved his phone off to the side of his drink. "It's a go as far as Barry is concerned. Said he'd enjoy the company for a few days."

"Great. As soon as we get out of here I'll go back to your place while you round up a change of clothes and I'll follow you to your friend's house."

"I'll be okay, Marcie. You don't need to escort me. Barry's walking distance from my apartment."

I didn't say anything and bit into my gyro instead. We ate in relative silence, at least for the first few minutes. My mind was offering up theories but my mouth was too busy chewing to verbalize any of them. I figured whoever killed Tawn knew she posed a risk regarding their clandestine operation. Either she was part of it or she knew too much. And she most definitely would not have left those gems in that painting. With Tawn out of the way, why not retrieve them for themselves? Since their search was unsuccessful, they planted those nanny cams.

I was deep in thought when Jordan cut in. "When do you suppose they planted that GPS tracker on your car?"

"Huh? Oh, the tracker. Not so much a *when* but a *who.* I've already ruled out Candace, Ernie and Daisy, the three clients of Tawn's because they were with me the entire time I interviewed them. Same deal for Leo McCellan, the contractor and John D'Angelo, who owns Classy Kitchens. Of course that doesn't mean one of them couldn't have used a worker. Especially in Leo's case. Still, it's not adding up."

"So who does that leave?"

"Brom, Alexis, Neil, and Renata, the employees. But none of them strike me as having the money or connections needed to mingle into the fine arts world. Frankly, it had to be someone who knew about our connection and knew I was investigating the case. Someone who wanted me out of the way."

We finished our impromptu meal a few minutes later and left the restaurant. My car looked no worse for wear in its spot in front of the bank. I dropped Jordan off at his apartment and told him I'd call as soon as I found out about the little gemstone tucked in my aspirin vial. He grabbed me by the wrist and looked directly into my eyes. "Watch your back."

"You, too."

My ride home was uneventful, if not annoying with all the rush hour traffic. It was moments like that when I had come to appreciate living in New Ulm and not the city. As I got farther and farther away from Minneapolis, I became more and more apprehensive about Jordan. Had I put him at risk by not contacting the police? Should I have been insistent about driving him to Barry's? I was literally torturing myself with horrific scenarios. Most likely a trait I had inadvertently picked up from my mother.

I knew if we had notified the police in Minneapolis, it would take an inordinate amount of time for them to analyze the stones from the painting and decipher the fingerprints on those nanny cams. Max and I could work quicker with his police contacts at home. Nevertheless, I couldn't help but wonder if I had made the mistake of the year.

The lights in our office were on when I pulled up in front and I looked at the dashboard. Eight fifteen. I parked, locked my car, and opened the door. Thankfully Max didn't reset the alarm like he had done on prior occasions.

"Thanks Max," I called out. "I wouldn't have dragged you in here if it was something that could wait."

He stepped out of his office and hit the light switch. "Don't want anyone to think we're open late. Come on, let's head to the workroom. If nothing else, you can add to your crime profile on the whiteboard."

The moment we stepped into the room I took out my aspirin vial, opened it and handed him the colored gemstone. "This may be why Tawn was murdered."

CHAPTER 18

Max crinkled his nose and took a close look. "What am I holding?"

"It could be a rare tourmaline from Brazil. It was ensconced in a painting that Jordan's late wife purchased. The details are sketchy."

"A rare tourmaline, huh?"

"Believe it or not, I first heard about this from my mother."

"God help us."

"There was a major tourmaline heist in Brazil years ago and the thieves were never caught. Now it seems more of these gems are being routed out of the country. My mother actually used the word 'leached.'"

Max chuckled at the word "leached" but I kept talking. "If what you're holding happens to be one of those stones, then I know how they're doing it. Before Tawn and Jordan were married, she bought an oil painting entitled 'Soulless Desire.' Horrible thing according to my ex but I didn't think it was all that bad. Weird, maybe… The artist was Margarida Tavares Branco. From Brazil. Daisy Jamos, one of the clients from Classy Kitchens, runs an art gallery in Minneapolis. Visual Fields of Vision. The receipt Tawn had for the painting lists Daisy's gallery as the seller. Except Daisy told me it was sold at auction."

"And?"

"The auction house has no record of it. None whatsoever."

"Then it's a no-brainer. It had to come from Daisy's gallery."

"She denied it. Insisted it was sent to auction. Max, if that gem turns out to be one of those tourmalines, then it's quite possible Daisy Jamos is trafficking in stolen gems. And who the heck knows how Tawn figured into the mess. I've got to find out. Do you know any gemologists who could verify what kind of stone it is and maybe even take a gander at its value?"

Max plopped himself at our worktable and rolled the gem between his thumb and forefinger. "Yeah, I know someone. Aargh. I'll be paying big time for this. It's Camila's brother, Maurice. He's been with Fantasy Jewelers in Mankato for years."

"Mankato. That's where your current case is…Max, you don't suppose—"

"Like I said, I'll be paying big time for this. Look, our best bet is to lock it up in our safe for the night. First thing tomorrow I'll pick it up and get it over to Maurice. Doris has his number and I'll call him when I get home. Last time I saw him was at one of those godforsaken family gatherings at Camila's. Looks like we'll wind up having to host the next one."

"Max, you're the best!"

"Yeah, yeah. Don't say anything until we know what we've got. By the way, what about the other stones from that painting? You said there were more."

I told him I had insisted Jordan put them in his safe deposit box at his bank and Max nodded in approval. Then I told him about my encounter on the road with the Dodge Charger and my subsequent discovery of the two nanny cams at Jordan's and the GPS tracker on my car. His eyes widened, his hand flew to the bottom of his chin and he shook his head slowly. *Very slowly.*

"You're damn lucky you managed to evade whoever it was. Did you get a license?"

"A partial plate. Who knew learning to read things backwards when I was in seventh grade would come in handy. I've got a contact in St. Paul who'll try to run the plate."

"Good. Might as well hand over those two recording devices. Good thing some of the police officers in New Ulm owe me lots of favors. Maybe we'll get lucky and score a print from one of those things."

"I should've done the same with the tracker but I was in a major rush to get it off of my car."

"It's all right. Don't beat yourself up. You're doing great so far. To be honest, I thought Tawn's case had more to do with an ambitious co-worker or a disgruntled client."

"It's funny, isn't it? I mean nanny cams and an unsophisticated GPS tracker. It all but screams amateurs and yet—"

"Marcie, these may be clumsy and awkward attempts on the part of the thieves to get their hands on those stones, but make no mistake, they're the landing party, not the pilot. Whoever is orchestrating this deal has to be clever and slippery. How else could they go undetected for so long? Assuming of course, I'm holding a real gem in my hand."

"I know. I know. That's why I insisted Jordan get out of his apartment and stay with a friend for a few nights."

"Good idea. You *do* realize that we'll have to notify the Minnesota Police Department if Maurice tells me I've got a real rarity on my hands."

"Our case will just get swept up in police bureaucracy - local, national and global. They'll be so focused on closing in on a high profile jewel theft ring that Tawn's murder will be an afterthought."

"It makes no difference. You and I both know that but it

doesn't mean you can't continue with your investigation. And I use the word *investigation*. If you think you've got ironclad proof this Daisy Jamos was behind everything, then we need to let the police in on it."

"No problem. Last thing I want to do is fly solo against some international smuggling ring. I read enough Andrew Gross and Ken Follett."

Max laughed. "And here I had you pegged for gothic romance."

"Very funny."

"Look, if all goes well, we should have some answers pretty soon. Meanwhile, continue delving into your suspects."

"You've read my mind. If I wasn't so exhausted, I'd be in my office doing that right now."

"Do it tomorrow. We'd both better hit the road. If I'm lucky, Doris didn't leave a plate of food for me."

Max and I left the office together and like Renata, he double checked the lock on the door. Fifteen minutes later I was back at my own place scrambling to open a can of food for Byron.

"Quit yowling. It won't make things go faster," I told him. The response was a bump on my wrist and more yowls.

My day had been beyond exhaustive. It was like one of those sweater threads that kept on going and going even when the person trying to pull it off thinks they'll win. I couldn't believe I had started the day with a trek into Edina to meet with John D'Angelo. It seemed like days ago, not hours. I was tired and wired at the same. Not a terrific combination. And the hodge-podge of junk food and gyros sitting in my gut wasn't helping. To make matters worse, I felt as if I had been living in the same clothes for eleven weeks, not hours. I tossed my top and slacks into the laundry bin and turned on the shower. The day that had reeled around me like a coil loosened slowly under the lukewarm water.

I dried off and threw myself on the bed to stretch out. It was a little before nine and no sooner did I begin to doze off when the landline rang. Hogan! I completely forgot I promised to call him as soon as I got in. It had been that kind of day — way too stressful.

"Everything's fine," I said as soon as I picked up the phone, not giving him a chance to say a word. "The tracking device is off my car."

"Tracking device? Why do you need a tracking device?" My mother's voice was like an electric shock from a toaster.

Before she could launch into a full scale interrogation, I broke in. "I thought you were Hogan. I called him earlier from Minneapolis and thought it was him on the line. Tracking devices are routine in our line of work. No big deal. So, what's up? Is everything okay in Delray Beach?"

"It's summer in Florida. What do you expect? Heat and humidity. At least the snowbirds are gone and we can finally get a good parking space in front of Denny's."

Dear God, please don't tell me she called to complain about something.

"Um, I meant with you. Is everything all right? Usually we talk on the weekends."

"Usually, yes. But you've been so busy lately with all that detective work, we haven't been able to have a decent conversation over the weekend so I thought I'd call tonight. Besides, there's nothing but reruns on TV."

I didn't want to give my mother the brush-off, because, in a way, she was right. I had been harried and preoccupied, but who wouldn't be? Yikes, I was knee deep in a murder investigation that had more tentacles than the calamari at Olive Garden. So, I listened for a good five or six minutes while she droned on about her bridge club, the mahjong ladies and how the bagel places were all skimping on the lox. Somehow she managed to mention my brother, his wife and the baby but it wafted over me.

Finally, she ended the call and that was only because she didn't want to miss the 'Breaking News' that was about to come on.

"I'll call you on Sunday, Mom. Honest," I said. "Love you."

"Love you, too! Remember – a nice, safe desk job."

As soon as I hung up, I dialed Hogan's number and he picked up right away. "Please tell me you're calling from home and not somewhere in Minneapolis. Like Jordan's apartment."

"Don't tell me you're jealous."

"Jealous, no. Concerned, yes."

"I'm home, I'm fine, and all my doors are locked. I got stuck on the line with my mother. When the phone rang I thought it was you and I picked up. I really have to start using that caller ID."

"No troubles on the way home? I had awful visions of you being followed."

"No troubles. Max met me at the office and I gave him the gem I took so he could get it authenticated. Hey, remember when we were at Candace's and I found that note about one with two and one with three? Well guess what? We aren't talking other interested buyers for Margarida's artwork. We're talking gemstones encased in the textured oils. I'm positive. One of Daisy's newest acquisitions must have two stones in it and other, three. The artist must indicate it in her signature or something."

"Hmm, that makes sense. Looks like our drama queen, Candace, was in on the gem trafficking."

"I'll know more when Max comes back with a verdict. Meanwhile, I'll be focusing on more background connections for this growing list of suspects."

"At least I'll sleep easier for a day or two knowing you'll be working at your desk and not being chased by God-knows-who."

"Yeesh! You sound like my mother. Look, you really don't have to worry. If it turns out we're dealing with international gem thieves, the police will be on it like nobody's business. Max and I will be butting elbows to get in on the action. Meanwhile it's a sit and wait kind of thing. Ugh. So frustrating."

"Maybe your paperwork chases will lead you to something."

"I sure hope so. These drives to Minneapolis are wearing me out."

"Does that mean—?"

"It certainly doesn't. I plan to hit the road for Biscay Saturday afternoon. Besides, that's country driving. It's a whole different thing."

"I'll have a home-cooked meal for you when you get here, how's that?"

I laughed. "By home-cooked, you mean takeout from the Triangle Diner?"

"Hey, home-cooked is home cooked."

I went to sleep that night thinking of comfort food and the comfort of Hogan's arms. I wouldn't feel that safe again for days.

CHAPTER 19

The next morning there was a note on my desk from Max.

"Left for Mankato with the roosters. I'll call later with Maurice's verdict."

Fortified with two cups of coffee, I studied the crime profile on the whiteboard and began looking for possible links between suspects. It was grueling. So grueling that I actually heard myself groan. Then, at a little past eleven, Angie rapped on the doorjamb.

"There's a call for you on line one. I needed the exercise so I got up."

"Who?"

"Edina Police Department. Officer Conroy."

Conroy. Gary Conroy. That was Max's friend at the Edina Police Department. I immediately picked up the receiver and introduced myself.

"I wanted to give you and your boss a heads-up," he said, "but Max isn't answering his cell phone. On the road, huh?"

"On a case in Mankato." I tried not to sound too anxious about the heads-up. "Are you calling about the Tawn Hamlin murder?"

"Quite possibly. If they're related. I'm calling about another murder. Seems Ms. Hamlin worked with a project manager by the name of Josh Newburgh."

"That's right. He died of a sudden and massive heart attack a few days before she was found dead."

"That's partially true except for one thing. In cooperation with the Minneapolis Police Department, we reviewed the toxicology report that came back from the lab. It was an extended report because the medical examiner had some suspicions from the autopsy. Anyway, seems our Mr. Newburgh's cardiac arrest was caused by high levels of potassium chloride, possibly injected according to the M.E. She noted a small blister on the nape of his neck. It could be the injection site or merely an insect bite."

"Oh my God. Does your department believe the two murders were related?"

"Too early to tell. We've got a team on the road now. They need to speak with Mr. Newburgh's boss, Leo McCellan, as well as the owner of the house where Mr. Newburgh succumbed. I thought Max would want to know since your office is investigating Ms. Hamlin's death. And before you ask, the answer is yes. I emailed Max a copy of the medical examiner's report."

"Can you tell me where it happened? Whose house? Who was the client?"

"He was on the property of a Mr. Ernie Star on Lowry Hill in Minneapolis. Got the nine-one-one report, too, and I'll shoot it over to Max."

"Who made the call?"

My God. I'm beginning to sound like an owl with all my questions.

The line was quiet for a moment until Officer Conroy spoke. "Sorry about that. I was looking at my notes. Call came in from Mrs. Candace Pendleton who resides at—"

My mind was all over the place trying to make a connection. "I know where she resides. She's a Classy Kitchens client."

"Look, these cases don't solve themselves so if you come across anything, we'd appreciate a call, too."

"Absolutely. Absolutely." I didn't want to tell him what we uncovered regarding the painting but I felt as if I should say something.

"I've interviewed the owner and employees at Classy Kitchens but didn't turn up anything. Same with the three clients that Tawn was juggling and of course, Leo McCellan. Everyone seems to have an alibi. I'm delving deeper into their histories for any possible connections."

"Sounds like a viable plan. What about the husband?"

Suddenly I felt a lump in my throat and the muscles tighten in my neck. I swear my pulse had picked up in a matter of seconds. "We're looking into all of Tawn's close contacts. Um, is there something you feel we should know?"

"The husband's been on our radar ever since we learned of a high-benefit insurance policy he took out."

"Is that the only reason?"

"It is right now."

I felt the muscles in my neck begin to relax and my breathing slowed a bit. Apparently Max hadn't told his friend we were hired by Jordan and I wasn't about to divulge it either.

"Thanks Officer Conroy. I really appreciate your call."

"No problem. Tell Max he owes me a corned beef sandwich and I intend to hold him to it."

"I sure will."

The second I got off the phone I scurried around my desk for Candace's phone number. My fingers were poised to start dialing when I remembered something. Didn't she burst into the Classy Kitchens showroom telling everyone she had to make a sudden return trip from Barbados? If Josh was killed a few days before Tawn, how could Candace have been in two places? I distinctly remembered her going on and on about her relaxing week on the beach. Maybe she wasn't in Barbados after all. Then why mention American Airlines? I took a deep breath and let it out slowly.

Sometimes when people lie, they infuse that lie with enough real information to make it seem plausible. There was only one way to find out and I knew it would be grueling – call American Airlines and start my own lie.

I shoved my chair back from my desk, walked to my door and shouted to Angie, "This is going to be a long day. If you're ordering out, get me something. Anything. I'm not particular at this point."

"Ham and Swiss okay?"

"Yep. Mayo, not mustard."

I spent the next hour and a half pretending to be Candace Pendleton. I told the airline I had inadvertently left my new bifocals on the plane and had unfortunately thrown out my boarding pass. I needed to know if the glasses were turned into their lost and found. I insisted they were in a case with my name written inside. Then I threw a date out at them. When they couldn't find Candace's name on the manifest, I offered another date telling them maybe I had the date wrong.

The customer service representation, who had been very patient, began to show signs of exasperation. "Mrs. Pendleton, to expedite this process, simply provide me with your social security number and your date of birth. I can conduct a search with that information."

"I most certainly am not going to give anyone my Social Security number but you can have my birthdate. It's December 7, 1971." *And thank the gods I remembered it from seeing that medical form in Candace's home office when I sort of snuck in there.* "Surely you can conduct a search with my name and birthdate." If I were the woman at the other end of the phone, I'd be doing mental eye rolls.

"I need to put you on a brief hold," she said.

I straightened my back, stretched in my chair and tapped my foot. Her brief hold lasted longer than most TV commercials. Finally, she was back on line.

"Mrs. Pendelton, did you say Barbados? I must have gotten it wrong and I apologize. According to our manifest, you flew to Barreiras, Brazil. Let me give you the date and flight time."

My hand was all but shaking as I wrote the information on one of my many pieces of scrap paper. The customer service rep went on to say that no bifocals were found when the flight crew cleaned the plane but they would make a note of it and contact her.

While I wanted to thank the woman profusely, I had to remind myself I was playing Candace so all I did was snivel and sniffle before hanging up.

"Brazil!" I shouted to Angie as I got up from my desk and went into the office. "Barreiras, Brazil, to be exact!"

"Is that supposed to mean something? And by the way, the delivery guy will be here any minute with our lunches."

"It sure does. Candace Pendleton was in Brazil about a week before Josh and Tawn were murdered. And if I'm not mistaken, so was Daisy Jamos. At least Daisy didn't lie about it. You know what this means, don't you?"

Angie opened her mouth to speak but I didn't give her the chance. "It means they were most definitely in cahoots with that illicit tourmaline trade. Oh my gosh, *please* tell me the gem I gave Max will prove I'm right."

"When will you know?"

"As soon as his sister-in-law's brother, the gemologist in Mankato, can verify it. I'm so wired up over this I'm practically twitching. This *has* to be the reason Tawn was murdered. She knew about their operation. And somehow, so did Josh Newburgh. I just don't know how yet but I'll flush it out."

My ham and Swiss arrived a few minutes later and since there were no clients in the office, Angie and I moved to the workroom for a quick lunch break. We were interrupted by a phone call for me and it set the tone for the afternoon.

"Ever hear the expression one step forward and two steps back?" I asked Angie when I got off the line.

"Of course. Why?"

"I'm now taking a half dozen steps back. That was my friend Emily McLoughin from the public safety building at St. Paul Community College. She ran the plate for that Dodge Charger I told you about."

"No luck?"

"Oh, she had luck all right. The plate belongs to Judith Anwroy, a retired school librarian who lives in a suburb of Minneapolis with her niece. It appears as if the plate had been removed from Judith's car a week ago when she was shopping at the Mall of America, not to mention at least a half dozen other places."

"Aargh. So that means no luck with parking lot surveillance?"

"None whatsoever. For all I know, the person behind the wheel of that Charger could have a stockpile of license plates that he or she uses. What the heck. Maybe I'll have better luck with the fingerprints from those nanny cams."

"Nanny cams?"

I forgot I hadn't clued Angie in on everything related to the case so I took a breath and tried to fill in the blanks.

"So, essentially," she said, "whoever broke into your ex's apartment is still out there. At least they know those gems are no longer stashed in there. Still, if I were Jordan, I'd be on edge. In fact, I'd be getting myself a guard dog."

"I don't think he wants the work associated with owning a dog. Anyway, he's staying with a buddy of his for a few days. I sort of told him I thought I could get the case wrapped up by then."

"Hah! And you complained Candace Pendleton was a liar."

"That's different. I'm trying to get the case closed. Candace is merely covering her butt but let's see how far she gets when I give her a call. I'm about to do that right now."

"Let me know how it goes."

It didn't. Candace played the role of Candace better than my performance on the phone with the rep from American Airlines.

"You lied to me, Candace," I said. "About being in Barbados. You didn't rush back from Barbados when you heard about Tawn's death because you weren't there."

"What? What are you talking about? Of course I was. And what makes you think I wasn't?"

"I checked with the airline. You were in Brazil. Barreiras to be exact."

"Oh my goodness. Did I say Barbados? Slip of the tongue. I happened to be vacationing at a private beach an hour or so from Barreiras. And why does any of this matter?"

"Because I was given to understand that you were out of the country when Josh Newburgh succumbed to a massive heart attack."

"Josh Newburgh? The projector manager? What does that have to do with Tawn's death?"

"More importantly, how did you come to be the person who phoned in the nine-one-one call about Josh? And take your time, I'm not going anywhere."

"Is this line being recorded? I have a right to know. In fact, I plead the Fifth Amendment."

"You're not standing trial. There's nothing to plead."

"Oh. In that case I'll tell you."

CHAPTER 20

Candace claimed she called Josh to discuss an important matter regarding her renovation and when he told her he was tied up at Ernie Star's house on Lowry Hill, she drove there to meet with him in person.

"I recognized his truck in that never-ending line-up on the street so I knew he hadn't left," she said. "The major entrance was wide open and I walked inside. I half expected that dreadful Ernie Star to appear and insist I leave the premises but he wasn't around. Then again, maybe he was. After all, it's a huge monstrosity of a house. Anyway, I saw Josh coming out of an alcove or butler's pantry and I called out to him."

"Then what happened?"

We stepped outside and I started to tell him about my idea for revolving window treatments when all of a sudden he began to sweat profusely and grab his chest. At first I thought he was acting rather dramatically at my suggestions but when he fell to the ground I knew it was for real. That's when I screamed. Of course no one heard me. Not with all that clamoring going on inside. I immediately took out my phone and called nine-one-one."

"Did Ernie Star ever show up on the scene?"

"If he did, it was well after the EMTs took Josh to the hospital. And after I left."

"When you and Josh were talking…before he grabbed his chest, did you notice him doing anything else? Like rubbing or scratching the back of his neck?"

"Huh? No. One minute I was explaining about the need to have window treatments adapt to the moment and not the season when all of sudden, he was clutching his chest."

"Why didn't you tell me any of this the other day at your house?"

"Because I thought you were investigating a murder, not someone's heart attack."

Candace may have been a liar and an exaggerator, but in that brief second I believed her.

"Was there anything else unusual? Anything at all you remember?" I tried not to sound as if I was pleading.

"Come to think of it, yes. Josh kept licking his tongue as if there was some sort of aftertaste on it. Why?"

"Nothing really. I'm trying to piece together the details. Was he drinking anything? A cup of coffee maybe?"

"He was holding a paper coffee cup. Starbucks. Hard to miss. You think the caffeine could have caused a heart attack? I've heard of those things you know. People have all sorts of sensitivities."

As much as I wanted to delve into Josh Newburgh's demise, I knew I would have plenty of time later, but right now I had to press Candace regarding that tourmaline business.

"Did you and Daisy Jamos plan to stay at the same hotel in Barreiras?"

"What? Where did you hear that? Did she tell you?"

"Give me some credit for being an investigator."

"It was purely a coincidence. I can't help it if there are only a handful of four star hotels in that city. I was only there for a few days before embarking on my coastal vacation. What did Daisy tell you?"

"Um, nothing of consequence really."

"Oh. I see. Daisy goes to Brazil to scope out burgeoning artists. Latin American artwork is hot right now."

Not as hot as those gems you're probably trafficking.

"What about Tawn?" I asked. "Did she ever travel to Brazil as well?"

Candace hummed for a minute and then responded. "Seemed she did a lot of traveling for her work but she never mentioned Brazil to me. Why? Why all this interest in Brazil? Do you think it was one of those cartels who killed her?"

"Unless she was involved with the kind of nefarious businesses they conduct, I'd have to say no. Those gangs usually stick to drugs, money laundering, and sex trafficking. Sometimes stolen artifacts. Things of that sort. You know, those gangsters will stop at nothing to get their goods. Human life is valueless for them. And the way in which they kill people...sometimes the body parts aren't even recognizable. I don't even want to think about it. Once they know who screwed them over, it's curtains for that person."

Candace all but tripped over her own words. "Er, um, ah... how would they know? Suppose whoever took their goods was really good at sneaking them out?"

"No one's *that* good. It's only a matter of time. Anyway, Tawn's murder might have been a bit more personal. That's why I asked about Brazil. She might have been seeing someone there."

The line got suddenly quiet for a minute. Then I swore I could hear rapid breathing at her end.

"Candace? Are you still there?"

"Yes. Yes. I'm still on the line. I was thinking about Tawn, that's all. If you don't mind and if I've answered all your questions, I really need to get going."

I was right. It sounded as if she was out of breath and scared.

"Of course. Thanks for your time. I'll be in touch."

I was positive Candace's fingers were frantically tapping out Daisy's phone number. If nothing else, Candace was now on high alert and that's exactly where I wanted her to be. When people are nervous, they tend to slip up. If she planned on purchasing one or both of those Margarida Tavares Branco's paintings, she might back down. But what if the purchase wasn't for her? What if it was for a client *she* had? Like those salespeople for Avon, Gold Canyon Candles, Pampered Chef, and a multitude of stay-at-home businesses where you try to get more people to become consultants, Candace might indeed be one of Daisy's protégés. If so, she and Daisy were going to move that artwork quickly.

It was too late for me to drive to Minneapolis to stakeout Daisy's gallery. Besides, Daisy Jamos was probably storing that artwork in her own brownstone. Unnoticed and unobtrusive. And no client was about to show up at night for the transaction. Tomorrow was a different story. I didn't need the final verdict from Maurice in Mankato to tell me Jordan had uncovered something extremely valuable. I sensed it in my gut and had to go with my instincts.

I stepped into the office and walked toward Angie's desk. "Did anyone schedule any appointments with me for tomorrow that I don't know about?"

Angie tapped her keyboard and looked at her computer screen. "Nope. No appointments until the beginning of next week. You said you needed time to work your cases."

"I did. I mean, I do. But I have to drive back to Minneapolis tomorrow to stakeout Daisy Jamos's house. I think she's going to unload some Margarida Tavares Brancos in a hurry. If I'm right, Candace Pendelton is part of the operation and I put the fear of God into her. Well, more like the fear of a bloodthirsty Brazilian cartel."

"But you said yourself you didn't know if those gems were real. Not until Max gets the word from Maurice. It *is* Maurice, isn't it? It's hard keeping all your contacts straight."

"It's Maurice. Max's sister-in-law's brother. And why hasn't Max called yet? It can't possibly take that long to authenticate a tourmaline if you're a gemologist."

"Slow down. The man wasn't expecting Max on his doorstep and probably has a boatload of work to do. Like setting diamond engagement rings or resizing stuff. Whatever it is they do."

"Ugh, I suppose you're right, but after speaking with Candace, I'm convinced of two things – someone put that potassium chloride into Josh Newburgh's coffee and Candace wasn't in Brazil to get a good tan."

I went back to my office and called Jordan. I needed to know that he was all right and he needed to know I was devoting every second to his case.

He sounded tired but otherwise okay. "So, uh, have you gotten anywhere? Was that gemstone what you thought it was?"

"Max is having the stone checked right now. He's in Mankato with it. I called to make sure you were all right."

"I've haven't gotten any death threats and no one's tried to bust into Barry's place if that's what you mean."

"It's a start. Look, you'll just have to hang in there for a few more days. I think I'm getting close but I can't say anything yet."

"Can't or won't?"

"Both. Remember, keep a low profile and call me if anything seems unusual."

"Oh hell, Marcie. All of this is unusual. It's freaking insane if you must know."

"I meant anything new. Catch you later."

I was off the phone in record time and adding new arrows and side notes to the whiteboard. My mother and my seventh grade English teacher would have given me gold stars. I had just put the dry eraser down when Angie called out her usual refrain, "There's a call for you on line one. The caller ID is the New Ulm Police Department."

"Miss Rayner?" The voice at the other end of the phone was a woman's. Older. "This is Officer Demora, I'm a friend of your boss. He asked me to call you directly about those nanny cams he dropped off this morning as well as a keyboard. Wish I had good news for you but I don't. Not a single viable print. Although, there was something that might be of use."

Wow. Max sure was working overtime for me on this one.

"What? What was it?" I tried not to sound like a high school cheerleader but I was anxious.

"Whoever inserted those nanny cam devices into the hardcover book jackets must have recently run their fingers through their hair. Our lab detected film from styling gel or mousse."

"Can your lab tell which styling gel? Which mousse?"

"I'm afraid not. We're not that sophisticated but the lab in Minneapolis is and I took the liberty of sending those nanny cams their way. I hope that's all right with you."

"Absolutely. That's great. Do you know when they'll have an answer?"

"I put a rush on it but nowadays so does everyone else so it's hard to tell. I'll let you or Max know as soon as I hear anything."

"Thanks so much, Officer Demora. I really appreciate it."

"Tell Max he owes me a pastrami on rye."

I laughed as soon as I got off the phone. First Officer Conroy and now Officer Demora. If nothing else, they shared Max's penchant for good deli food. The time at the bottom of my computer monitor read four fifteen. *Come on, Maurice, identify that damn gemstone.*

Since I had made up my mind I was going to stakeout Daisy's residence tomorrow, I figured I could tackle some of the smaller, less complicated tasks related to my other cases. It was amazing what I could accomplish in forty minutes of solid internet searches. I had just closed the tab on one of my sites when I thought of something. I had promised Hogan I'd drive to Biscay on Saturday but if my stakeout didn't go well, I'd have to extend it to the weekend. I figured I might as well clue him in now and not wait until tonight.

Tyler, their apprentice brewer, answered the phone, asked how I was, and told me to hang on while he got Hogan on the line.

Hogan sounded as if he'd made a fifty yard dash to the phone. "Hey, is everything all right? I was in the tank room when Tyler gave a shout you were on the phone."

"Everything's fine. Take a breath. I called because I'm really on to something. I'm certain Daisy Jamos and Candace Pendleton are the tourmaline thieves."

"Whoa. Can you prove it?"

"Not without a stakeout. That's why I called. I'm driving in to Minneapolis before sunup tomorrow to do a little covert surveillance on Daisy's residence. If I'm right, those two paintings she mentioned in that note to Candace are going to be moved out of there in a hurry. I think Candace is getting cold feet. Long story."

"Will Max be with you?"

"Huh? No. He's tied up with a case in Mankato. I was able to piece together all sorts of information to get me to my conclusion. Hogan, I'm positive I'm right."

"You can tell me tonight. In person."

"In person?"

"Yeah, you heard me. I'll drive to New Ulm as soon as I get out of work."

"And then rush back in the morning?"

"Not exactly. If you're going on this little covert operation on your own, I intend to keep you company."

"Don't be ridiculous. I'll be fine."

"If what you've told me turns out to be true, you're dealing with thieves and a murderer. If they've killed one person, they won't think twice about killing another."

"Uh, about that...they did, or *someone* did. Kill another person. Josh Newburgh to be exact. The medical examiner did a double take with an in-depth toxicology report and it turns out his heart attack was caused by potassium chloride."

"Geez. Now I'm definitely driving to New Ulm tonight."

"What about the brewery?"

"Tom and Tyler will be fine tomorrow. They'll be fine all weekend. I'll do double duty come Monday. Besides, the busy season doesn't really begin for us until late August as far as tourists and tasters are concerned. As for the bottling, we've got that under control as well."

"You sure?"

"I'm sure. See you later tonight. We'll grab a pizza or something."

"Or something."

CHAPTER 21

"I hope Max is okay," I said to Angie as she began closing things up for the day. First, shutting the coffee maker, then the printer. "It's five of five and no phone call. This is nerve-wracking. Aargh."

No sooner did I finish moaning when the phone rang and Angie grabbed the receiver.

"See? That's probably him right now."

I stood over her desk with my feet tapping a mile a minute. She shook her head and gave me a thumb down with her right hand.

"That was our cleaning service calling to let me know they'll be late tonight."

She turned off her computer and opened her mouth to say something when the phone rang again. This time I snatched the receiver before she could answer. "Blake Investigations. Marcie Rayner speaking. How may I help you?"

"You can begin by telling me what happened to Angie."

"Max! Did you find out? Is it one of those priceless tourmalines? And Angie's right here."

"That figures. You were probably chomping at the bit, weren't you?"

"I've already chomped. So tell me. What did Maurice say?"

"Maurice is in a state of shock. I've never seen the man so dumbfounded in my life."

"Oh my God! So that means—"

"Okay, don't get too excited, but here's what he was able to ascertain. That gem happens to be a Paraiba, one of the rarest tourmalines in the world."

"I knew it! I knew it! So, um, how rare? How much does he think it's worth?"

"Maurice estimated the value to be between seventy and a hundred thousand but before you go jumping off the rails, listen carefully."

"I'm listening. I'm listening."

"Maurice had no problem identifying the gem. Tourmalines have certain qualities. Characteristics. And Paraiba tourmalines give off a color hue that makes it nearly impossible to not recognize what they are. Don't ask. I'm not a gemologist. Anyway, the moment he realized what I had brought him, he immediately went to his files. When the original tourmaline heist took place a decade ago, Interpol and our police agencies sent all certified gemologists the specs for those specific gems on the off chance they might show up. Maurice kept that file on record. To make a long story short, because, if you must know, I'm starving, and your ex-husband is in possession of an extremely valuable gem. I don't even want to think about the other ones he put in his safe deposit box at the bank. How many did you say that was?"

"Um, there are four more. All about the same size. Holy cannoli! All this time Jordan was sleeping under half a million dollars and never knew it. You didn't notify the police yet, did you? Please tell me you didn't."

"Marcie, we went over this before. They have to be notified. We're in possession of stolen goods. Internationally stolen goods, I might add."

"Can't you hold off for one day? That's all I need. One day. I've been on the phone with Candace Pendleton and I have a good reason to believe she's in on this with Daisy Jamos. I kind of scared her into thinking some crime cartel in Brazil will be gunning for her so now she'll be in a hurry to unload those paintings she and Daisy had. You see, at first, I thought she was a buyer but now I'm convinced she's a sales rep. So to speak."

"I'm afraid to ask. What did you have in mind?"

"Nothing that would put me in jeopardy if that's what you're worried about. I plan to stakeout Daisy Jamos's place first thing in the morning. I guarantee those paintings will be unearthed from her residence and on their way to a buyer. All I plan to do is photograph the process. Or transaction for a better word. If nothing else, it will give the police all the evidence they need."

"Tell me, where does Tawn Hamlin fit in to any of this? Other than the fact she bought a painting."

"I'm not sure to be honest, but I don't believe she was part of the operation. I think she knew too much and that's what got her killed. Same with Josh Newburgh only I don't get the connection. Not yet anyway."

"Josh Newburgh? That project manager who had a heart attack?"

"A heart attack caused by potassium chloride. Your buddy at the Edina Police Department, Officer Conroy, called to let me know. You owe him a corned beef sandwich. Or was it pastrami? You owe Officer Demora a sandwich, too."

Max chuckled. "I'm in the wrong business. I should open up a deli."

"Officer Demora told me there were no viable prints on the nanny cams. Just hair styling gel. I'll explain when I see you. But right now I'm on to something."

"Look, I'm not too thrilled with the idea of you going it alone now that we know who we're dealing with. It's just as easy for the Minneapolis police to stakeout a residence."

"Come on, Max. It'll take forever and we'll miss the opportunity. First, someone will need to write a report. Then they'll need approval. By the time they step in, another half a million or more will be untraceable. Besides, I won't be alone. Hogan will be with me. He kind of insisted on it when I told him my idea."

"Huh. Doesn't surprise me. He caught the sleuthing bug from you with that Mystery Castle case and he hasn't gotten over it. Fine. Here's what we're going to do. Maurice will lock that tourmaline in the store's safe. It will eventually be turned over to the authorities and I don't want to chance anything by having it in my possession on the way home."

"But you had it in your possession on the way over."

"That's because I didn't know what I had. Truth be known, I thought it was an imitation. Some sort of kinky artwork thing. Now that I know, I'm a bit more circumspect."

"Max," I whispered, "can Maurice be trusted?"

"You don't need to whisper and the answer is yes. Believe me, the wrath of Doris and Camila is something no one would wish on an enemy. You don't have to worry about Maurice."

"When should I let Jordan in on the news?"

"I'd wait until you're certain of your next move."

"So you're okay with my stakeout?"

"I'll have to be. I'm stuck in Mankato and can't be two places at once. I don't have to tell you this but I will. If something doesn't feel right, get the hell out of there. Understood?"

"Naturally."

Angie was beside herself when I told her what Maurice had discovered, and like Max, she thought the police should've been called right away.

I shook my head and crinkled my nose. "No way. They'll muck it up with their paperwork and never-ending rubber stamping of who-has-got-permission-to-do-what-next. I've got an opportunity staring me in the face and if I don't take it, I don't know when the next one will come along. But you can relax. I'll still need a day or so to figure this out. "

"At least Hogan will be with you," she said. "Why are you giving me that look? I was standing inches from you when you told Max your plan. And if you want my two cents, wait until it's a done deal before you tell your ex-husband. He might muck things up, too."

We shut the lights, locked the door, and headed out. A little after five felt like mid-afternoon, one of things I liked best about daylight savings time. It was still warm a few hours later when Hogan and I grabbed a pizza at the Green Mill Restaurant and Bar. The sun had started to set and it was one of those quintessential summer evenings that are meant for long strolls, firefly watching, and hand holding. Unfortunately, we did none of those. We spent the evening strategizing our "game plan" for the following day.

Hogan looked at me from across the couch. "You sure you've got Candace Pendleton worked up enough to put the pressure on Daisy for a quick sale?"

I grinned. "Oh yeah. One mention of unidentifiable body parts and I knew I hit pay dirt."

The next morning we were up at an obscene hour and out the door by four. I left Byron enough kibble and treats to ensure he'd be fine until we got back. By five thirty we were parked across the street from Daisy's brownstone with a bird's eye view of her front steps. It was dumb luck really. The owner of a tan sedan pulled out of the parking space seconds before Hogan maneuvered the brewery van, a new addition to his business, into the spot. I hadn't thought of it at the time but Hogan did – Daisy might recognize my car and Candace would most certainly recognize his truck. Thankfully no one would notice a brewery van and Hogan removed the magnetic sign that said, "Ale Away at the Crooked Eye."

We finished the coffees we picked up on the way over and we were both wide awake and anxious. I stared at the distinctive brownstones with their large slate steps and wrought iron railings. Small garden areas dotted the front entrances and it appeared as if each house had a walkway to the back.

"Oh no," I mumbled.

"What? What's wrong?"

"What if Daisy and Candace's little operation takes place in the back of her house and not the front. Every house has a back door."

Hogan reached across the seat and gave my knee a squeeze. "True, but not every house has a back way out to another street. They'd still have to walk to the front. Look, if it's going to plague you, I'll slip out and have a quick look-see. It's early. No one's on the block."

Before I could protest, Hogan got out of the van and darted across the street. He ducked low behind the mulberry bushes in Daisy's front yard and disappeared from view. The last time he pulled a stunt like this was back in Biscay when a murderer broke into his brewery. Instinctively, I checked my ankle holster to make sure my Ruger was firmly in place. Not that I thought Daisy or Candace were murderesses but I've been fooled before.

I kept my eyes glued to Daisy's front entrance when I noticed someone else slipping behind the mulberry bushes and heading to the back of the house. The buyer? His back was to me but I could see it was the figure of a man in jeans and a dark shirt. The guy had come from nowhere. I hadn't seen any traffic on the street and that included bicycles. Whoever it was either lived nearby, parked on another street, or didn't mind taking a long walk.

The one thing I wasn't going to take was a chance he'd corner Hogan. I grabbed the keys from the ignition, put them in my pocket, locked the van, and raced across the street. The sudden slamming of a car door made me jump and I turned to see a blue Honda Accord pulling out of a parking spot a few yards ahead of our van. The car went straight down the block and turned left.

I told myself not to worry. It was someone heading off to work. Unlike the someone who headed behind Daisy's house. By now I had walked past the front yard and was halfway down a walkway to the backyard when I got a closer look at the man who followed Hogan. My footsteps must have alerted him because he turned and gave me a look.

I froze as if I'd seen a ghost. "Jordan?? What the hell! What the bloody hell are you doing here?"

"Shh! I could ask you the same thing."

"I'm investigating your wife's murder for crying out loud. I have no idea what you could possibly be doing."

"If you must know, I—"

At that second, Hogan came around from the back of house and motioned for us to get the heck out of there.

"Quick!" I said to Jordan. "We've got a van parked across the street. Hurry and get in!"

I clicked the open tab on the keyring, saw a flashing orange light and knew I had opened the doors. In a matter of seconds, the three of us were seated in Hogan's van.

"Hogan," I said, "meet Jordan Rayner, my ex-husband."

The two men grumbled some sort of a greeting or acknowledgment but before it could go any further, I broke in. "What's going on? Other than the fact I have no idea what Jordan is doing here or why we ran like mad to get back in the van."

Hogan took the keys from me and put them in the ignition. "We ran back because I heard a woman's voice at the back of the house and I was worried she might have seen us."

I looked across the street but no one had stepped outside. That didn't mean there wasn't someone eyeballing the parked cars. Jordan gave my shoulder a nudge from the backseat. "I don't know about the both of you but I was invited in a manner of speaking."

"What??? Daisy Jamos invited you to her house? At this hour? What on earth for?" I twisted my head around and glared at him.

"This is Daisy Jamos's house? That gallery owner who sold Tawn the painting?"

"Whose house did you think it was?" My voice had gotten sharp and whiny at the same time.

"Beats me. I got a text about an hour ago telling me that if I wanted to find out who killed my wife I needed to go to this address immediately. I thought whoever sent it was the guy in front of me so I followed him. How was I supposed to know it was your boyfriend?"

"Sounds like something straight out of a bad TV drama." Hogan said.

I reached my hand behind me and continued to glare at Jordan. "Let me see that text."

Sure enough, someone sent him an explicit text.

"How'd they get your number? You're using one of those cheap burner phones."

"Uh, let me think for a minute. Barry has the number and so does admin at the university. I had to update my information. Oh, and I also gave Classy Kitchens the new number in case they needed to reach me."

"Terrific. I'm surprised you didn't post it on Facebook." I took a closer look at the message and groaned. "Whoever sent it, they sent it anonymously."

Jordan took the phone back. "Isn't that something you could track down?"

"Not right away. Not now. And why didn't you call me instead of flying over here? You could've gotten yourself killed."

"If the caller wanted to kill me, he or she would've done it already. They tried twice before if you'd forgotten. Both times to look like accidents. I doubt they'd be texting me an invitation. Besides, what were you going to do? The address is over an hour from New Ulm."

Suddenly, Hogan slouched and motioned for us to do the same. "Try to stay out of view. Someone's pulling up to the house in a Lincoln Navigator and I doubt it's Matthew McConaughey or the woman who's into Sarah Vaughan's jazzy voice."

CHAPTER 22

The driver got out of the car, opened the rear passenger door and effectively blocked my ability to see who he was letting out of the vehicle. I held my breath and waited. Whoever it was, he or she would eventually walk past the front of the car and head toward the house, giving me a decent view to start snapping photos.

The small Canon Power Shot camera that I'd had for years still outshone the newer models, and while cell phone cameras were fine for everyday use, I needed the clarity that I knew my Canon would provide. Hogan and Jordan kept absolutely still as I started to take snapshots. From the person's rear, I ascertained it was a woman – pencil thin, loose fitting summer dress. It had to be Candace. I clenched my teeth and stayed focused on the image.

When she reached the front door she moved to the left giving me a crystal clear look at her face. There was no mistaking it – Candace Pendleton was paying an early morning visit to Daisy Jamos. I couldn't see who opened the door and ushered Candace inside but I imagined their visit would be brief since the driver was double parked in front of the residence.

"If Candace is about to unload those paintings, I seriously doubt she'll be the one to carry them to the car. They weigh a ton," I said.

Jordan leaned forward so his head was directly between Hogan and me. "I don't get it. What's going on?"

Hogan faced him for a second and then turned his attention to Daisy's house. "We think Candace Pendleton may be involved with that tourmaline theft. That's why we're here. Marcie sort of put the ball in motion by giving Candace a scare about Brazilian crime cartels. Plus Candace received a note from Daisy that was pretty explicit about a timeframe if Candace was going to buy the paintings. Or fence them. I think that's a better term in this case."

"I don't get it. What do you mean?"

I kept my eyes on the house but answered Jordan's question. "I led Candace to believe she would be murdered if those cartels caught up with her. I'm convinced she and Daisy are the masterminds behind those international thefts. Right about now Candace Pendleton is going to whisk those paintings out of the house and off to her buyers. She's not about to stall."

"Looney Candace Pendleton? That's what Tawn used to call her."

"Looney is probably the best act she's got going. Shh! She's turning around and motioning to the driver."

I heard the sound of the car door slamming and watched as the figure of a man walked up the front stairs and was ushered inside. Impossible to get a good look but from the rear I could tell he had a medium build and a medium height. Brownish hair. No uniform or hat. Dark trousers and a dark shirt.

I kept my eyes glued to the Lincoln Navigator. Candace and her driver were bound to return quickly. No one would risk getting a pricey ticket or worse yet, getting the vehicle towed. Especially that one. Nice color – deep blue. Sapphire blue. Way out of my league.

"Jordan," I asked, "Can you recognize the driver from the back? Is it someone from Classy Kitchens?"

"Sorry. Hard to tell."

"Never mind, I'll do what I can."

What I could do didn't amount to much. I was able to snap a few photos as the guy stepped inside the house but I couldn't tell who had opened the door. Jordan leaned his head forward again and I had to tell him to sit back in his seat. I desperately needed to get some good, clean shots with the camera.

"Okay, fine," he said. "I get what Candace's doing. What beats me is why did someone send *me* a text to be here? I'm not mixed up in this crap."

"No," I said, "but you might be the distraction they needed, if say, they were worried about getting caught while Candace moved the goods. If the police were to show up, the two women could point to you. You're already a suspect in your wife's murder as far as the authorities are concerned. Add a tourmaline theft and they'll figure you married Tawn because you knew about the stolen gems. The insurance policy was just icing on the cake."

"But I didn't know about the gems. Not until the painting fell!"

"It doesn't matter. Candace is a damn good actress and I wager Daisy isn't too far behind when it comes to that kind of talent."

Hogan rubbed the back of his neck and stretched. "Marcie's right. If anyone was to burst into their little scene, all they'd need to do was point to you and make up some lie. Whoa! Hold on! The driver is coming straight down the side walkway wheeling a suitcase. Are you getting the pictures, Marcie?"

"Fast and furious. But I can't tell who it is. He pulled a baseball cap over his eyes. He must have had it in his pocket. The only thing I can think of is that somehow Candace or Daisy was able to get Jordan's number from Renata or even John D'Angelo.

Maybe they gave one of them a line about wanting to call Jordan to offer condolences or even send flowers or something."

"Quick! Look at the front door." Hogan said. "Candace is on her way out."

"Yeah," I said, "And the driver's already stashed the suitcase in the car. Now he's opening the rear door for Candace. Damn it! I can't get a good look at the guy."

Hogan shook his head. "It probably doesn't matter. Most likely it's a paid employee of hers and for all he knows, Candace is picking up some designer shoes or clothing. I bet she tells him shoes. That would explain the weight in the suitcase."

I kept my eyes glued to the Lincoln. "Shoes. Rocks. Whatever… Uh-oh. The driver's pulling out. We've got two choices. We can follow the car but it'll probably go right back to Candace's place or Jordan can mosey up the front steps, announce himself and find out why he was summoned to Daisy's house. What do you think we should—"

"Oh what the heck! I might as well get this over with." Jordan slid the back door of the van open and jumped out.

"Not alone you won't." I opened my door and took a step.

"No one's expecting you, Marcie," he said. "How are you going to explain it?"

"I'll think of something."

"Be careful," Hogan shouted. "If you're not out of there in five minutes, I'll be joining you."

I stood behind Jordan as he rang the bell. No answer.

"Ring it again," I said. "Daisy's in there."

Jordan gave it another try. This time we heard the unmistakable sound of a door being unlocked and the knob turning. Daisy stood in front of us, a maroon caftan hanging gracefully over her tall, slender frame. She adjusted the scarf that was wrapped over her hair and I noticed her nails. Not polished or even manicured but stained with some sort of ink. The kind that gets into the small cracks and stays there forever. Funny that I never noticed it before when I was in her gallery.

"Miss Rayner?" she asked. "What brings you and your friend here?"

"I was invited," Jordan answered. "By you I presume. And I'm not her friend, I'm—"

I gave Jordan a not so subtle kick on the foot. "May we step aside? It's chilly out here so early in the morning."

Daisy took a step back and let us inside. I spoke as soon as I crossed the threshold. "What Jordan is trying to say, is, he received a not-so-subtle text message a few hours ago telling him that if he wanted to find out who killed his wife, he needed to go to this address. Oh, you've never met Jordan, have you? This is Tawn Hamlin's husband. He contacted me early this morning. *Very* early. My firm is consulting on the murder with the Edina Police Department and Jordan preferred to notify me in lieu of the local police. Fortunately for him, I was working another case a few blocks away."

My God! Lying is becoming second nature to me.

Jordan gave her a nod and she nodded back. I expected her face to register some sort of reaction but there was none. She'd make a great poker player.

"I'm sorry about your loss, Mr. Hamlin," Daisy said. "Your wife was a sheer genius when it came to design."

I gave Jordan a look that meant "don't you dare correct her as far as your name is concerned," and he got the point. Maybe our short-lived marriage wasn't all that lacking when it came to communication. He didn't say a word and neither did I. Instead, he handed his iPhone to Daisy with the text message prominently displayed on the screen. She stared at it for a few seconds and handed the phone back to him.

"That's my address all right but this must be someone's idea of a joke. I didn't send you that message and I certainly have no idea who could have murdered your wife. I didn't even have Tawn's private email address let alone yours. I had to reach her through Classy Kitchens."

I shifted my weight to my other foot. It was getting awkward standing in Daisy's foyer. "Do you have any idea who might have sent Jordan to your house? I couldn't help but notice a car pulling away from the front of the curb just as I was pulling up. It looked as if we're not the first morning visitors you've had. Maybe your earlier guest?"

"My earlier guest was a friend of mine. Helping out at the gallery. He offered to pick up some rather delicate artwork and take them there. Normally, that's something the artists arrange but in this case, there was a misunderstanding and the pieces were delivered to my residence. And the answer to your question is no. I have no idea who could have sent Mr. Hamlin to my house. None whatsoever."

"Okay then," I said. "Sorry to have inconvenienced you. We'd better get going." I turned to face the door, then turned back. "Um, would you mind terribly if I used your restroom? I'll only be a moment."

Jordan really must have picked up on my cue because he immediately blurted out, "And if it's all right with you, I'd really like to take a look at Tawn's kitchen project. I've never seen her work at an actual job site, only in photos."

Daisy's head darted in two directions almost as if she was on information overload. Then she looked at me. "There's a powder room to your left just past the living room. Kitchen's on the right. I'll show it to Mr. Hamlin in the meantime. It's in the final stages of its design renovation – detailing and contrast tiling. You can grasp the overall effect already and that's without its subtleties. "

"Thanks," I said and took off, but not before catching Jordan's eye and mouthing "Take your time."

Powder room my patootie. I had one chance to scope out Daisy's residence and I wasn't about to blow it. Like most brownstones, it was a three story building. I'd be lucky to navigate the first two given my time constraint. Still, I darted into the powder room and gave Hogan a quick call.

He must've been holding the phone. That's how quickly he took the call. "Is everything all right? I was about to charge on in there."

I kept my voice soft and low. "Everything's going smoothly but I need time to snoop around."

"What? That wasn't the plan."

"It is now. I think there's more to this gem trafficking. Listen carefully. Daisy's showing Jordan the kitchen and I'm in the powder room but I'm going to need more time and I don't think Jordan can keep her occupied with questions about design, style and function in a kitchen. Hell, he can barely tell the difference between the stove and the dishwasher."

"So what do you want me to do?"

"Daisy doesn't know who you are. In exactly five minutes, knock on the front door or ring the bell. Whatever. Then pretend to be taking a survey or something. Anything. Just keep her occupied. Tell her you're with a neighborhood alliance. They always have neighborhood alliances. Tell her a new zoning ordinance is about to be introduced. That should get her bristles up. Use your imagination. It doesn't matter. You've got that Crooked Eye inventory sheet in your middle console. Hold the clipboard close to your chest and ask questions."

"You have *got* to be kidding me."

"I'm not. Improvise. Now it's four minutes."

I ended the call before Hogan could say another word. Then, I meandered into what once was two smaller areas. A dining room perhaps and a sitting area? A prior renovation had turned it into a commanding family room/den complete with a large screen TV and equally large leather furniture. Colorful oil paintings of women and parrots filled the walls.

The staircase was in the front of the house. A long, narrow structure that was bound to get my heart pumping. Given the narrow space of the brownstone, a circular stairwell wouldn't have been feasible. I could hear Max laughing right now. I had once asked him if the firm had any sort of fitness amenities like gym membership and he broke up laughing. "You want exercise? Trust me, kid, you'll get it on the job." Today's escapade was proving him right.

I could hear Jordan's voice in the kitchen as I tip-toed up the stairs. *Please keep her talking. Ask to see the inside of the cabinets. Ask to see the plumbing under the sink. Anything!*

The top of the landing was a narrow sitting room. To my right, double doors opened into a grand bedroom complete with canopy bed and oversize furniture. Daisy must have a thing for grand and large furnishing. To my left was another bedroom, smaller but equally impressive. The window treatments allowed for plenty of light but there was nothing at all unusual about either of the rooms. I imagined they both had en suites but I didn't have the leisure to check.

Hogan hadn't made it to the door yet but I expected him to be there any second. I took a quick breath and continued up the stairs to the third floor. I swore the steps had gotten steeper. The top landing was a loft that Daisy was using as a studio. It was equally as messy as her desk at the gallery only this time with paint cans and brushes lying on white sheets instead of ashtrays filled with paperclips, stacks of books and piles of correspondence.

Like the artwork that hung in her living room, the pieces

in progress were all women and parrots. I was about to exit the room when I noticed a completed portrait of a Spanish dancer hanging on the wall. Her colorful costume caught my eye and I moseyed over for a fast look-see. At first I didn't notice anything unusual about it but when I glanced at the bottom right hand corner, I could all but feel the hairs standing up at the back of my neck. It was the signature – M. Jamos. And if I wasn't mistaken, I'd seen that M before.

At that precise second, I heard the doorbell ring. Hogan would keep Daisy occupied at the door but how was I going to explain my entrance from the stairwell instead of the powder room? I bit my lip and tried to think. These brownstone houses were built at a time when servants were common. And servants didn't use front staircases. I tip-toed down to the second floor and took a closer look at a small closed doorway off the rectangular sitting room but not before snapping a quick photo of the signature before I left the loft. I originally thought the door was a closet door, but now I was banking on the fact it would open into a back staircase.

I turned the knob slowly and held my breath. Absolute darkness coupled with a cloying, musty odor.

CHAPTER 23

Hogan's voice carried which meant Daisy must have let him inside. This wasn't good. If she thought she was about to sign a neighborhood petition she'd have a rude awakening with one look at a brewery inventory sheet.

Rather than poke a hand into a dark space in the hopes of finding a light switch, I used the flashlight on my phone to find out if indeed it was a stairwell and not a catch-all for Daisy's trash and treasurers. Whatever it was, given its stale odor, I doubted anyone had opened the door in a long, long time. Sure enough, it was a back staircase and under the illumination from my phone, I could see cobwebs on the walls and dust particles having a field day in the air. I also saw a light switch on my right and turned it on. At least the bulb hadn't blown and there was ample light for me to make my way to the first floor.

Unlike the main stairs, this version was totally closed in. Not even room for a handrail. I strained to hear the conversation from the floor below but it was impossible. The voices were jumbled. When I reached the bottom of the stairs, I shut the light and then opened the door praying I wouldn't be anywhere in Daisy's vicinity. As it turned out, I found myself standing in a small alcove staring at the most spectacular kitchen I'd ever seen in my life.

Hogan, Jordan and Daisy weren't in sight but that didn't mean I was in the clear. Last thing I needed to do was approach from a direction that was nowhere near the powder room. Rather than second guess myself, I went for a riskier move.

"Hey!" I shouted. "I turned the wrong way. I'm in the kitchen and it's truly spectacular!"

"Wait until the iridescent and textured tile is completed, then it will be spectacular. Exit from the archway by the double brick oven, then turn right." It was Daisy's voice and I did as she said. A moment later I saw her talking with Jordan in the foyer. Hogan was nowhere in sight.

"I thought I heard a third voice," I said.

Daisy adjusted her scarf, loosening a few curls on her forehead. "You did but he just left. It was someone from the next block over, looking for a missing dog. She got off her leash while he was walking her. I told him I'd keep an eye out."

Hogan's better at this than I thought.

"Thanks for letting me use your powder room. I need to get going and I'm sure the same applies for Mr. Hamlin."

Jordan glanced in the direction of the kitchen and then looked directly at Daisy. "I appreciate you showing me Tawn's work even though the circumstances were, well…a bit odd. It is disappointing, though. I really had hopes that text message would lead me to her killer."

Daisy rubbed her hands together, then grasped them so tight I thought she'd stop the circulation.

"I'm sure Tawn's killer will be brought to light," I said. "These things take time but eventually someone slips up and that's when our hard work pays off. Anyway, thanks again and have a good day."

"You as well."

When Jordan and I were on the sidewalk, I gave him a nudge. "Start walking down the block. We need to pass the van. I'm positive Hogan's watching us. When we're out of Daisy's sight, we'll wave to Hogan and he'll pull up to let us in."

"What an utter and complete waste of time," he bellyached. "Talk about being played."

"I wouldn't call it a complete waste of time. Not with what I found out."

"What's that?"

"There *is* no Margarida Tavares Branco. It's Daisy Jamos. She's the one who's been painting those oils and acrylics in Brazil and shipping them up here. This entire scheme is all hers."

Just then Hogan pulled up beside us. He didn't wait for a wave. Rolling down the window he asked, "Did your surveillance pay off?"

"Tell him," Jordan said.

"When my seatbelt is fastened and we're on our way. I'm too tempted to go back into Daisy's house guns a-blazing."

Hogan's voice got louder. "Uh-oh. I don't know if I should be relieved or worried. I'm going for worried. Get in the van before you do something we'll all regret."

I jumped into the front passenger seat and buckled up. Jordan did the same in the back. When we were two blocks down, I told Hogan exactly what I had discovered.

"That M on the bottom of her portraits is unique. Want to know what I think?" I continued before he or Jordan could say a word. "I think Daisy's got a studio somewhere near Barreiras. That's where she paints those God awful mixed media pieces and conceals the tourmalines in them. Very clever if you ask me. She then has the paintings shipped to Minneapolis. Customs probably doesn't even give them a second look."

"So how do you explain all the art world hype about Margarida Tavares Branco?" Hogan asked.

"Easy. It's hype and Daisy could do anything. No one's ever

really met Margarida. And if there are photos of her floating around the Internet, you can bet your bottom dollar, they're fake. Another really easy thing to pull off."

"You'll never find out who's behind the tourmaline theft in Brazil," Jordan said, again leaning his head between Hogan's and mine.

"I don't need to. That's Interpol's problem. All I need to do is expose the operation at this end. Once I do, I guarantee someone will come forward to point out Tawn's killer in order to save their own hide. Tawn *had* to know what was going on. What other motive for her death is there?"

Jordan slunk back in his seat. "Greed and insurance money according to the Edina Police."

"We'll see about that." I reached over and shook Hogan's shoulder. "Do you remember how to get to Candace's house? I'll wager she's unloading those paintings right now. We've got to hurry. Candace is really spooked and she's not wasting any time getting them into the hands of her buyers."

"No problem. It should take us about a half hour, forty minutes tops to get to Lake of the Isles."

"What about my car?" Jordan asked. "I parked it down the block."

"It'll only hold us up," I replied. "We'll come back for it later."

None of us said a word as Hogan drove out of the downtown area and west toward Candace's residence. Suddenly, I felt a pit in my stomach. "You don't suppose she had her driver go to her lake house, do you?"

"Doubtful," Hogan replied. "First of all, it's too far and she's in a hurry. Second, if her buyers are poised for a quick transaction they're not about to traipse all the way over to Lake Minnetonka. Trust your gut on this one."

Max always told me to trust my instincts but this was one of those times where I was really unsure. It didn't matter. It was a fifty percent chance either way. "I hope you're right."

Like clockwork, Jordan leaned forward. "Um, I don't want to sound pesky but, uh, do you have a plan once we get there?"

Yep. I have a plan all right and it's called "winging it."

"Actually, I do," I said, trying to put a little conviction into my voice. "You're going to do the exact same thing you did with that painting of yours."

"Break it? Break them?"

Hogan gave me a sideways glance as if to say, "This I've *got* to hear."

"Exactly. Right now I can't prove anything as far as possession of those tourmalines. But if one of Candace's paintings was to meet with a mishap and one of those stones just happened to come tumbling out, I'd be able to have all the evidence I needed to link her and Daisy with those international thefts."

"And how do you propose to pull this off?"

"Yeah, about that…I haven't gotten that far down in my thinking. My original plan was to get a good photo of the transaction but all I have is a picture of a guy who may or may not be Brom or Neil wheeling a suitcase up Daisy's walkway. I'd hoped for a photo of the painting or paintings, even if they were covered with butcher paper. At least the police would make the logical assumption the guy was carrying artwork. But a suitcase?"

Hogan patted my knee. "I see what you mean." Then he turned around to face Jordan for a split second before getting his eyes back on the road. "Hope you're good at improvising."

"I'd be better if we stopped for coffee and a breakfast roll or something. Ten or fifteen minutes more isn't going to make a difference."

A quick stop to the nearest Golden Arches and we were on our way to Candace's. The three of us batted around possible scenarios that would result in the terrible catastrophe of having Margarida Tavares Brancos's latest works end up trashed. Unfortunately, we weren't able to reach a consensus on anything by the time Hogan pulled into Candace's driveway.

No sign of the Lincoln Navigator but that didn't mean anything. As far as I was concerned, it could be parked in her garage. Probably alongside some equally pricey vehicles. What we did see, because it was impossible to miss, was a Black Dodge Charger. A Minnesota license plate but not the one from the Charger that tried to run me off the road. Unfortunately, with the Charger's tinted windows, it was impossible to tell if anyone was seated inside. It was too much of a coincidence even if the car had a different license plate. The driver could have easily switched them.

Hogan stopped a few feet into the driveway and shut the engine. "Now what?"

I grabbed my camera and took a good picture of the car. "Oh my gosh! Candace's driver, the guy with the baseball bat, is coming out of the house and he's carrying one of those paintings under his arm. He's headed to the Charger."

"The Charger's not going to get anywhere," Jordan said. "Hogan's van is blocking him."

In a flash, Hogan exited the van and ran like a quarterback straight at the driver.

Jordan poked my shoulder. "What's he doing?"

"What you should have been doing. Getting him to drop the painting."

I exited from my side of the van and hurried up the driveway with Jordan at my heels. Hogan had plowed into the man like nobody's business. It was as if he'd suddenly become Joe Greene of Pittsburgh Steeler's fame and both men were flat out on the asphalt. The painting was face down on the ground but still in one piece. I knew I had one chance to remedy that. I raced toward them, making sure I trounced on Daisy's precious artwork.

"Are you all right?" I asked.

Hogan stood up and brushed himself off. Meanwhile the guy with the baseball cap, who had his back to me, rushed to the painting and turned it over. I don't know who gasped more – the man when he realized Hogan's crash caused irreplaceable damage to the painting or me when I saw the small indents where the tourmalines had originally been affixed to the canvas.

"You just made me lose my summer job!" the driver exclaimed.

Like scavengers, Hogan, Jordan and I got on all fours to search for the tourmalines and in that instant, whoever was behind the wheel of the Dodge Charger, shot off past a line of trees turning Candace's perfectly manicured lawn into one huge mess.

"That was the buyer who bought the painting," the driver said. "You'd think he'd at least go in the house and get his money back from Mrs. Pendleton. And what the heck are you guys doing? Did someone drop something when the painting fell?"

The driver knelt to the ground at the same moment Hogan did but I didn't see the driver pick up anything. Hogan, on the other hand, made a sweeping gesture with his hand and dumped the contents in his pocket. "Just some loose change and my car keys. Both of them."

He furrowed his brow and mouthed the word "two." I wasn't sure if this was the painting with two tourmalines or the one with three. If it was the latter, then that meant the gem could still be lodged on the painting or somewhere on the ground. I looked down but didn't notice anything unusual.

"Do you know who that buyer was?" I asked the driver. I tried not to call attention to what might still be under our feet.

"No idea. Some art connoisseur according to Mrs. Pendleton. She had me arrive at an ungodly hour to drive her downtown in order to pick the painting up. Well, two of them actually. Now I'll lose my job for sure."

"So you knew you were picking up paintings and not, say, shoes or something?"

The driver looked at me as if I had two heads. "Yeah. Paintings. Strange thing dealing with the art world. Mrs. Pendleton always calls me at the last minute in a frantic rush to go downtown and get a painting or two. Once I had to carry four of them. Heavy suckers. But what the heck, the pay's good. Or *was* good I should say."

The sound of a screeching bobcat paled in comparison to what I heard next. It was Candace Pendleton flaying her arms and racing toward us. I was positive her scream could be heard all the way to Chicago.

CHAPTER 24

Candace stood over the shattered oil painting and clutched her chest. It was a move of hers I'd seen before at Classy Kitchens. "What have you done? My God! You've destroyed a priceless work of art!"

"I'm so terribly sorry," Hogan said, "I was running from a swarm of bees. They came out of nowhere. Crashing into your driver was entirely accidental. I'm surprised we didn't get stung. I'm sure your insurance company will cover the losses. We stopped by here because Marcie needed to ask you a few more questions regarding Tawn Hamlin but it can wait for another time. Right Marcie?"

"Um, yeah. Another time."

Jordan, Hogan, and I all shot each other looks and didn't say a word while Candace knelt to the ground to inspect the painting. Her fingers moved along the bumpy surface and given the expression of anguish on her face, I imagined she realized the tourmalines had come loose from the canvas and were scattered somewhere on the asphalt.

"Is something the matter? " I asked. "I mean, other than the painting's condition."

I wouldn't have wanted to be in Candace's position thinking there were priceless tourmalines scattered on the ground and unable to do a thing about it for fear her entire scheme would be exposed.

She scanned the immediate area and remained on the ground for what seemed like ages. "What on earth am I going to tell the buyer? This is a nightmare. A horrid, ghoulish nightmare..."

Jordan wasted no time cutting her off. "I think your buyer got the idea. He or she split when the painting hit the ground. It happened right in front of the car."

Candace crinkled her brow. "What do you mean? His car hasn't arrived yet."

"Hasn't arrived? Someone in the black Charger took off and made a mess of your lawn while they were at it."

"Lawn? Black Charger? My buyer doesn't own an American car. He only drives European models. I was expecting a white BMW if you must know. I sent my driver out to wait with the painting."

"Then who owns the black Charger?" I asked.

Candace shuttered as if I'd said, "Who owns the rusted out leaky jalopy?"

"How should I know?" she replied. "And what it was doing on my property is anyone's guess. Oh goodness. That BMW is going to be here any second. I need to make a call. Everyone step back from the painting and don't touch it! You'll only make things worse. In fact, you ought to leave. Now. This isn't a good time."

She ran into the house leaving the four of us to stare at the painting and at each other.

"I don't suppose you know who was behind the wheel of that Charger?" I asked the driver.

He shook his head. "Heck, I thought it was the buyer. Shows you how much I know. Look, I'd better go inside and have a word with Mrs. Pendleton when she gets off the phone."

When the driver was out of earshot, Hogan gave me a look. "How much do you want to bet she'll be on her hands and knees scouring this area for those tourmalines? You know, if what Max said was true, I've got the equivalent of two hundred thousand dollars in my pocket. I didn't spot another tourmaline so this must be the 'one with two.' We can call the police and tidy up this operation in a matter of minutes."

Jordan gave the painting a slight kick. "Not as far as I'm concerned. We're no closer to finding Tawn's killer and I doubt Candace will confess to anything. She'll be shocked, dismayed and distraught as soon as she's accused of trafficking Brazilian tourmalines."

"He's right," I said. "We need more evidence. *I* need more evidence. If the police arrive now she'll feign complete and utter surprise and she'll make Meryl Streep look like an amateur."

Hogan took a step toward me and widened his eyes. "What are you suggesting?"

"I need to get in that house and listen to every conversation that woman has. She'll be on the phone with Daisy, I all but guarantee it, and to her buyers to sort things out. There's still another painting in play. I might be able to record enough of the conversation to see if Tawn's name is mentioned and in what capacity."

"Incredible," Jordan said. "You actually carry a recording device with you?"

"Hey, I'm a licensed detective. You'd be surprised at what I carry with me."

Hogan and Jordan looked at each other. Then Hogan turned to me. "How do you plan to do this?"

"We'll make it look as if all of us are getting into the van but only you and Jordan will. I'll sneak around back and get inside from a window. Last time we were here she had all of her windows opened because she needed fresh air. Made a big deal about it, too. There are enough alcoves and hiding places for me to duck down and not get discovered."

"I'm not feeling good about this, Marcie," Hogan said. "Tell you what. I'll drive the van out of here but I'll park it on the road a few houses down in one of those lake view pull-offs. Then Jordan and I will hightail it back here and sneak around the rear of the house. If you let out a yell, we'll hear you. Or, use your cell phone. Text if you must. Got it?"

Jordan rubbed his chin and gave the painting another kick. "I hate to burst your sleuthing bubble, but what if the BMW buyer makes an appearance?"

"He won't," I said. "Candace is probably on the line with him, or her, this very second. She'll come up with some excuse to postpone the transaction. Relax."

"Okay, game on!" Hogan said and with that he darted to the van with Jordan only feet away. I took off to the left of the house where there were more bushes and trees.

I was happy with my SONY digital voice recorder and its four gigabytes of memory but Max insisted there'd be situations that called for a more discreet product so he bought us the latest in spyware – micro stick voice-activated recorders the size of large paperclips or flash drives. The sound quality was outstanding and they only made recordings when there was a voice, not empty airspace. I had taken it out of my bag and tucked it into my pocket along with my cell phone and wallet when I gave my bag to Hogan to stash in the van a few minutes earlier. Now I was a few yards away from an open window and moving at breakneck speed. Climbing in was the easy part.

Candace's voice was clearly audible as I peered into the room. Thank goodness I recognized my surroundings. I was in the Grand Foyer just shy of the small office where I had found her note. Given the intensity of her voice I knew that was where she was making her calls. I turned the recorder on and placed it behind a leafy fern on one of the accent tables in the Grand Foyer. Then, I listened to the one-sided conversation from behind a conveniently located four- panel bamboo room divider.

Thank goodness for decent acoustics. It felt as if Candace was standing right next to me. Her voice was that clear. "You must accept my apologies. Nothing like this has ever happened before. I can assure you. It was a mistake in inventory. And as I said before, I have another Margarida work with two exquisite adjuncts, both flawless. Naturally the price will be adjusted to reflect the change in numbers. I should have caught the error much sooner but since you're on your way over here, won't you consider the other piece?"

Oh my gosh! There's still a tourmaline missing. The driver dropped the painting with three of them encased it in. And adjuncts? For God sakes, Candace, use the word gemstone! Use the word tourmaline!

She didn't. "Fine. That would be fine. I'll refund the monies immediately to reflect the price difference. Yes, I have the routing number. My driver will bring the painting directly to your car. Park on the street. Don't use the driveway. Someone pulled in with a nasty oil spill and I wouldn't want it to get on your tires and splash onto the bottom of your car."

Nasty oil spill, hell. She's probably freaking out that a car could run over the tourmalines she thinks are still somewhere on the ground.

I held my breath waiting to hear if there was more to the conversation. There wasn't. I couldn't very well pull a second stint with Jordan knocking into the poor driver, not that it mattered. I had what I needed – two priceless tourmalines and three witnesses if I counted myself in the mix. What I didn't have and desperately needed was for Candace to open up about

Tawn. Either Jordan's late wife would be exonerated as far as the tourmaline thefts were concerned or she would be implicated posthumously.

My heart was racing as I waited to see if Candace would place another call. Sure enough, her voice was crystal clear.

"Daisy? Are you alone? Good. The most awful thing happened minutes ago. That snoopy detective showed up unannounced with two associates from her office. I met one of them a few days ago. Have no clue about the other. It doesn't matter. What matters is that one of the associates smashed into my driver while he had the painting with three under his arm. What?... No, not with a car. The associate said he was running from bees…You heard me. Bees! He crashed right into my driver and…. What? I *am* getting to the point. The point being, the painting fell and broke and the…"

Say it! Just say it! Tourmalines!

"My God Daisy! Those lovely embellishments to the painting are missing. They must have become dislodged when the painting fell. What? Of course I looked and I intend to look again!"

Great! Now they're embellishments.

"My buyer's agreed to continue with the transaction. I told him I'd substitute the piece with the other one and refund the difference…What? Of course I know what a half a million dollars looks like. I'm not an idiot…Yes, I'll call you back."

I expected Candace to be done with her calls but I was mistaken and my body paid the price. It was uncomfortable crouching under that screen but the darn thing was at least a foot shorter than I was. Candace's next conversation carried into the Grand Foyer and I knew I could count on my spyware micro stick to pick up every nuance of that call.

"I told you not to come to my place of residence unannounced. If it's about our little business deal, it could have been handled over the phone. I don't have time right now. We can deal with it later this week. I'll call you or leave a message with Renata."

The sound of the receiver being put back in its cradle all but reverberated in my ears. Nothing is quite as satisfying as slamming a phone. Too bad the millennials would never know the pleasure. Obviously Candace was angry with whoever was at the other end and I was frantically running through the possibilities. The moment she said *Renata,* I knew Candace's caller had to be associated with Classy Kitchens. Renata's not exactly a common name. That left me with a narrow playing field – John D'Angelo, Brom, Alexis or Neil. Unfortunately, it wasn't narrow enough and no mention of Tawn.

I crept slowly to the accent table to retrieve my micro stick when I heard footsteps. Without wasting a second, I hurried back to my hiding spot and tried to catch my breath. The bamboo screen was porous and I had a decent, if not shaded, view of Candace in the hallway. That meant she probably could see me as well if she decided to enter the room and look around. I didn't take a chance. I got down on all fours and held my breath while she continued down the hall. At that instant, I heard the driver call out.

"That BMW 4 Series is a beauty. Must be another buyer parked on the street in front of the driveway. I can see the shine on that baby all the way up the drive. I wonder why they didn't pull in."

"Be careful this time. That painting's worth a fortune, like the other one. The one you dropped. I'd deduct the cost from your pay but you'd have to work the next century to compensate me. Never mind, we'll work something out. Oh, use the walkway adjacent to the driveway even if you have to skirt around the little bushes. I wouldn't want to risk another mishap should a car pull in. Understood?"

"Absolutely."

Candace was covering her bases all right. She had to keep up the ruse of an oil spill and make sure the driver didn't accidently discover the fallen tourmalines that she thought were still on the ground.

"When you're done," she said to the driver, "please go around back and wash the Navigator. Trips into downtown always result in dust and grime. Oh, and be sure to give it a good polish while you're at it."

The poor driver. I figured he'd be enslaved to Candace Pendleton for the rest of his young life. Her voice drifted back toward the kitchen and it was time for me to get out of there. Not a red banner day as far as sleuthing was concerned but not a washout either. I still had to decide whether or not to call in the Minneapolis Police or let it ride a tad longer. As it turned out, the decision was made for me. The moment I heard the front door open and close, I heard Candace's footsteps going up the stairs. It was now or never if I had any chance at all to snoop around in that office of hers to see if I could find anything whatsoever that would link Tawn Hamlin to the international world of gem smuggling. A memo perhaps or a receipt? No one's that good at covering their tracks.

CHAPTER 25

I pocketed the micro stick and walked directly to the office, thankful that for once in my life I had decided to wear soft soled sandals instead of my usual wedge heels or espadrilles. Suddenly my phone vibrated in my pocket. Hogan had sent a text.

"R U OK?"

"Yes. Need more time."

No sooner did I push the Send button when I heard footsteps again.

Damn it! Candace is on her way back down.

With no viable options other than to duck under the desk, I moved as if I was following a nineteen fifties air raid drill, the ones I'd seen on those old black and white movies. My elbow was jammed into the underside of the desk fighting for the same space as her trash basket. That was the moment that changed everything. The basket got tipped over and as I frantically tossed the crumbled papers, torn slips of paper, post-its and notepad pages back into the bin, one word caught my eye – Tawn.

It was part of an email that had been printed out, crumpled up, and tossed in the trash along with lots of other emails. Apparently Candace must be as old school as my mother and prints them out. Too bad the sender's address was missing. While the email wasn't incriminating, it gave me the chills. Someone had written "The little bitch is going to cost us an arm and a leg. I found another alternative. Time to kiss Tawn goodbye. I'll talk with you later. Delete this email."

My first hunch was Daisy. She and Candace were already embroiled in their tourmaline scheme so having the same kitchen designer would make sense. But murder? I had to catch a breath and think it out.

Whoever sent the email didn't exactly come right out and say they planned on murdering Tawn, but what did the sender mean by another alternative? Surely people don't go around knocking off their designers or contractors if the price gets too out of hand. They simply hire someone else. Then again, if there were ironclad contracts specifying the designer, aka Tawn, then Daisy and Candace would be stuck. With Tawn out of the picture, the contract would be null and void. Why then, was Josh Newburgh murdered? Unless his name was specified on the contract as well. It would make sense except for one thing - the timing. If Daisy and Candace wanted to drop Classy Kitchens and go with another designer, why wait until their projects were near completion?

Suddenly something dawned on me. Something Candace had said about Ernie Star. She was adamant that Ernie couldn't possibly have been involved in Tawn's death because only a fool would cut her off before their project was completed. With Daisy and Candace's kitchens fast on the way for finalization, another company could easily step in making Tawn expendable. But that didn't make sense either. After all, the bulk of the job had been completed, so there would be no real monetary savings.

A new theory crystalized in my mind as I squirmed to alleviate the pain I felt in my legs from being cramped under the desk. Tawn must have found out about Daisy and Candace's operation and since Tawn worked so closely with Josh Newburgh, she shared that information with him. They must have let it slip and that's what got them killed. Not their kitchen design work. Too bad I couldn't prove it.

Candace's footsteps got closer but they moved in the direction of the kitchen. If I hurried, I could make it back to the Grand Foyer and out the window. I was about to make a mad dash when my cell phoned vibrated. Hogan again with a new message.

"Blk Charger back. B careful."

The Black Charger must have passed the van on its way back to Candace's. Maybe the phone call with Candace pissed off the driver. At any rate, I needed to get a good look at who was behind the wheel, even if it meant taking a hell of a chance. I didn't hear any footsteps but that didn't mean the lady of the house wasn't within screaming distance.

With no other option, I moved as furiously as I could to get to the Great Foyer and the great outdoors. In fact, I moved so fast I practically threw my body out the window, scraping both elbows on one of Candace's carefully manicured bushes. Granted, there was a window in the little office but it was one of those narrow decorative ones that don't open.

I remained crouched down behind the bushes waiting for the Black Charger to pull in to the driveway. With my right hand, I pulled out my cell phone and sent Hogan a quick text. "B hind bush, must C who driver is."

He returned my message immediately. "Don't do anything stupid."

Seconds later the Charger pulled in but the driver drove to the rear of the house by the garage making it impossible to identify him or her. So much for the front door.

Damn it! I hadn't climbed in and out a window so much since ninth grade when I was grounded for two weeks and snuck out of the house. Back in the Great Foyer again, I put the micro stick on the accent table and took my familiar place behind the bamboo screen. Maybe that would be enough. Maybe I'd be able to recognize the driver by the sound of his or her voice. I was breathing really hard and forced myself to take long, slow breaths.

Just then I heard Candace's voice. "I told you not to come here without calling first. I don't have time to talk. Whatever it is, it can wait. Oh dear God! You drove that car of yours up my driveway. It better not be too late. Stay here in the kitchen and don't move until I get back. I mean it if you ever expect to do business with me."

I had a darned good hunch Candace was going to go back to that spot in the driveway to hunt for the missing tourmalines but I was wrong. Instead, I heard her yell to the driver, "Get me a flashlight from the Navigator and bring it to the Charger."

Then, I heard a door slam. No reason for me to stay put. Once again, I exited the Great Foyer. This time with skill and finesse. No scrapes or scratches. Using the line of bushes to conceal my whereabouts, I snuck behind the house to see what she was up to. The frantic woman shone the flashlight on the front driver's side tire and moved in to inspect it. I watched as she ran her hand around the tire tread. She did the same with the other three tires. Then, I heard her call out. "I need some help. And bring me something to wipe my hands."

Next thing I knew, Candace got behind the wheel and her driver gave the car a push. That business with the tires meant one thing only to me. Clearly, she was smarter than I thought to check the underside of the tires for any tourmalines caught in the treads. And double check in case a stone was lodged in the tread that faced the pavement.

The driver walked back to the Navigator and Candace hurried past the side of the house to the spot on the driveway where the painting had fallen. She was huffing and gasping to the point I thought she might have a stroke. Meanwhile, I had managed to skirt around to the front entrance and ducked behind some taller but thinner bushes. Candace was way too preoccupied to notice my presence.

I watched as she got on all fours reaching her hands in every which direction to see if she could find the stones. She shone the flashlight on the asphalt but it was no good. She moved farther up the driveway, then farther down. If I didn't think I was watching a possible gem smuggler/murderer in action, it would have been quite comical. Finally, she stood up and yelled to the driver, "I need something to wipe my hands. Hurry up!" Then, she stormed back to the house.

Too late for me to make a move. All I could do was hold still, keep low and pray she didn't notice the change in color scheme behind her bushes. Like it or not, I still had to retrieve my micro stick from the Great Foyer and I absolutely had to identify who the heck was behind the wheel of that Charger.

I held my breath as Candace opened the front door and slammed it behind her. I remembered it being locked when Hogan and I paid her a formal visit so I was surprised it had been left open. Then I recalled the door having one of those keypad entry systems and made a mental note that if I ever owned a home to get one of those. Takes the worry out of losing keys.

Her voice was so loud I could hear every word she said. "Where's a towel or damp cloth? What took you so long? I thought you'd bring it to me while I was outside."

Then I heard another voice but it wasn't the driver's. It was a woman's voice and it sounded familiar. "What the heck were you doing to my tires? So help me if you slashed them I'll have you arrested for vandalism. I looked out a window and watched you."

"I wasn't vandalizing your car. Although it might be an improvement."

"Then what?"

"I thought you might have run over something in the driveway."

"Seriously? You were concerned I'd get a flat? Please, don't even answer that because I know what you were looking for – tourmalines. Precious and rare tourmalines. The minute that hideous painting hit the pavement and broke, I knew they'd come tumbling out. That's why I left in such a hurry. I didn't want to be around when your buyer showed up. For all I knew he or she could've been a loosely hinged psychopath who would've taken it out on anyone in the vicinity when he or she found out the prize tourmalines went bye-bye."

Candace and the woman from the Charger must have moved away from the entrance and farther into the house. Their conversation got muffled but I was positive the micro stick would pick it up. Still, I wanted to hear every word that went on between them. Every single utterance. I made my way back to the window that I now treated as my own personal back door to the house. It was a good move because I picked up Candace's response as I hoisted my right leg on the sill.

Her voice was shrill to the point of causing serious damage to my ears. "What? How do you know about the tourmalines? This is outrageous. I demand to know how you, of all people, found out."

"Don't look so surprised. I ought to be the one with the private investigator license and not Marcie Rayner. The woman's as clueless as they get."

Clueless? Clueless? It's a good thing I'm not face-to-face with you. Whoever you are.

Just then, the woman laughed. It was a breezy laugh and in that instant I knew exactly who it was – Alexis, Tawn's assistant designer. So that's who planted the GPS tracker and tried to run me off the road. I figured she was either trying to scare me or she wanted me out of the way. But why? And for the life of me, I couldn't figure out how she was involved with Candace if it didn't have to do with kitchen design.

I reached for my cell phone and was about to shoot off a text to Hogan when someone grabbed me from behind and yanked me off the window sill. A large moist hand covered my mouth and I was thrown backward.

It happened so fast I could barely catch my breath let alone reach for my gun. At least my legs were working and I gave my assailant a good, sharp kick on whatever part of his or her body they came in contact with. I was about to let loose with another kick when my attacker spoke.

"Hell! Quit it, Marcie. It's me. Jordan. I had to get you out of there. With the black and blue marks all over me to prove it. Hogan's sneaking around on the other side. When he didn't hear back from you he insisted we run over here. He thinks the person in the black Charger could be dangerous. Geez, I can't believe how fast we ran here. My muscles have been worked to the point of no return."

I got up and looked Jordan in the eye. "Oh brother. Listen, you've got to edge your way around the house and catch up with Hogan. I'm on to something and it can't wait. There's a row of rocket junipers on the left. Wait behind them. Tell Hogan I'll text or call if things get dicey."

With that, I lifted my leg onto the sill and hoisted myself inside. At least Jordan didn't argue with me. Candace was still talking but I had to strain to hear her. I wasn't sure if her voice was coming from the office area or farther down in the kitchen. It didn't matter. I could still make out what she was saying. "How did you find out? Damn it. Do you have any inkling of what's going on?"

Alexis's voice was louder. "I'm learning fast but you're the one who'll need to take notes. Listen, I want in on that little tourmaline deal of yours. Whoever's working with you and Daisy, tell them you've just added a partner."

I swore Candace's voice hit a new decibel level. "Are you insane?"

"Insane enough to let the Minneapolis Police Department in on your secret. Or maybe I should cut to the chase and call the FBI."

"Don't be ridiculous. They'd never believe you. You don't have any evidence."

"Really? How do you think I found out about your *extended* business, shall we say, if I didn't have substantial evidence in the first place? It sort of fell off a bedroom wall and into my lap. Although at the time, I thought the painting on the wall was a one-shot deal and not a major enterprise. Hell, I thought I was procuring those client lists from Classy Kitchens so you could talk those millionaires into buying high priced art from Daisy's gallery. Now, come to find out, it's all about rare gems, not fine art. So, yes or no?"

Alexis paused and it felt like minutes, not seconds. Then, she continued. "It should be an easy choice. Funny, but I originally came here with a few more names I dug up from our archives, which, by the way isn't that easy to pull off with Brom snooping all around."

Okay, I can cross Brom off the list.

Candace voice was more of a growl. "You insufferable little wench!"

"Humph. I've been called worse. Much worse. Anyway, when I saw your driver... that *is* your driver, isn't it? Well, when I witnessed that catastrophic collision in front of my car and the resulting aftermath, I realized it was time for me to negotiate another deal with you. Pity such a lovely painting got destroyed. Tsk-tsk. I take it you haven't located the tourmalines that spilled out of it."

"I'll find them."

"Last chance. Am I going to partner up with you or make a teeny weeny little phone call? Take your time. I'm not in a hurry."

I couldn't believe what I heard. Alexis was brazen enough to blackmail Candace. Maybe Hogan was right about the danger part of this deal. For all I knew, Alexis could be carrying a gun with every intention of using it. I tried to put the immediacy of the situation in the back of my mind as I struggled to piece together what I knew and what I needed to do about it.

From what Alexis said, she had to be the person who ransacked Jordan's apartment and placed the nanny cams there. How else would she know about the tourmalines that Jordan discovered? It was beginning to make sense except for one thing – the reason she was in his apartment to begin with. If I believed what she told Candace, then Alexis learned about the tourmalines when she saw the video and pieced together the larger operation when she witnessed the second Margarida Tavares Bronco painting hit the dust on Candace's driveway. Maybe she was a better investigator than I gave her credit for.

If I followed that line of reasoning, then Alexis was telling Candace the truth about her impromptu visit. It had nothing to do with the tourmalines because at the time, Alexis hadn't made the connection.

What I couldn't wrap myself around was why on earth did Alexis break in to Jordan's and place spyware around the place if she wasn't looking for those gems in the first place? None of this came close to explaining a motive for Tawn's murder nor did it link Alexis to it. I figured everything would unravel once I retrieved my micro stick and contacted the police. Hogan was right. I *did* have what I needed.

CHAPTER 26

The room was empty and I was about to make a quick dash to the accent table, retrieve the micro stick, and exit the room the same way I got in. That was before I heard footsteps approaching and Candace saying, "No sense standing in the hall. We might as well talk this over like civilized people. Follow me into the Grand Foyer."

The bamboo screen, although sufficient cover when Candace was at a distance, would never suffice. I had to get the hell out of there and do it quickly. Like Tom Sawyer running from his Aunt Polly, I all but threw myself out of the window. I landed unceremoniously with my butt on the ground and a few new scratches. Without wasting a second, I texted Hogan. "Need more time."

I kept low to the ground and thanks to the open window, continued to listen to the conversation between Candace and Alexis. Candace's voice was at a level pitch. Maybe she was resigned to being found out or maybe she thought it would be best not to show Alexis how nervous she really was. Whatever the case, at least the micro stick would get a clear reading.

"A bedroom wall, you said? Well aren't you the little Mata Hari getting your information from under the sheets."

The breezy tone in Alexis's voice was gone. "How dare you. If this stupid fern wasn't in the way, I'd be tempted to do something unladylike."

Oh no. The fern. That means they're sitting inches away from the recorder.

"You don't consider blackmail unladylike?"

"I consider it a necessity. By the way, Candace, it looks like you left a flash drive behind this fern."

"A what? Good grief. It must belong to my husband. Honestly. I hope there's nothing important on it. He's always bringing work home from the office but it's not like him to leave things lying around. Oh well, I'll stick it in my pocket and when I go upstairs, I'll put it on his dresser. Right now we have some other matters to discuss."

The micro stick! My God! It's in Candace's pocket on its way to a dresser upstairs.

My hands began to tremble and my pulse quickened. I felt lightheaded and queasy as if I was about to lose my lunch. Only I wasn't sick to my stomach, I was sick, period. Without that micro stick, there was no way I could implicate Candace Pendleton in the tourmaline theft or a possible motive for murder. I had to think fast but the more I tried to focus, the more I began to shake.

I took a deep breath and let it out slowly. Then I did it again. I read somewhere that taking a series of deep breaths allows the mind to focus. That, and chewing gum. Only I didn't have any gum. In the three or four seconds it took me to calm down, I envisioned a number of scenarios. None of them were great.

My initial thought was to have Hogan retrieve the van and pull into the driveway so I could ring the bell and concoct some reason for Candace to let me in the house. Then, I would inadvertently spill the coffee I was holding on her slacks so she'd be compelled to change out of them. Then, I'd find a way to sneak upstairs and get the micro stick. Unfortunately, it was way too complicated. Besides, I didn't have any coffee to spill.

Nope. I had to get up close and personal with her. So up close and personal that I'd be able to lift that micro stick from her pocket like the Artful Dodger on a busy London street. It would take a diversion but with Hogan and Jordan yards away behind those juniper bushes, I wasn't so sure I could pull it off. I needed their help desperately.

I pulled out my cell phone and fired off a text to Hogan. "Pull van up drive. C U & J at door. Hurry."

While I waited for Hogan and Jordan to make a mad run from the juniper bushes to the street where the van was parked, I leaned in to listen to the on-going conversation between Candace and Alexis.

What I heard instead was the driver's voice. "The Navigator is cleaned and buffed dry. I'll give it a good waxing next time. So, if you don't need me for anything else today, I've got to get going. I'll get my motorbike from the garage. Okay?"

"Fine. Fine." Candace sounded dismissive. "I'll call you if I need you sooner than what's on your schedule."

Talk about serendipitous. At least that meant there was one less player to contend with if I had any hopes of getting my hands on that micro stick. I kept my body low to ground, thankful the bushes provided ample cover.

Candace's voice was steady, almost as if she had rehearsed what she was about to say. "You know very well I can't simply partner you up. I have to discuss the matter with—"

Just then, the only sound I heard was the engine from the driver's motorcycle. Apparently the guy enjoyed revving it up. The sound blared in my ears as he took off down the driveway and onto the street. The next noise I heard was a car pulling in the driveway. Hogan! I heard the door slam shut. He must have had his foot glued to the gas pedal.

I stood up and edged my way around the house until I had reached the front corner where the bushes were closely spaced. Expecting to see the familiar Crooked Eye Brewery van, I stood up and waved without looking down the driveway and when I did, I saw Daisy Jamos waving back.

She got out of her red Audi and thundered to the front entrance, turning her head slightly to address my presence. "Marcie. What are you doing here?"

At that instant, Hogan's van pulled up behind her and he and Jordan shot out of it like nobody's business and positioned themselves next to me. I brushed some loose strands of hair from my face and gave Daisy a smile. "I, um, came here earlier with colleagues to discuss something with Candace but she was preoccupied. We left but then I remembered I dropped my cell phone near the front entrance so I did a quick jaunt up the drive with the van parked on the street."

Then I turned to Hogan and Jordan. "It's okay. You didn't have to get out of the van to help me, I found it. So clumsy of me, huh?"

Daisy gave me a funny look as if to say, 'What a feeble explanation," but at least she didn't question it. In fact, she turned away and pushed the doorbell before any of us could say anything. Just as well. I worried we'd dig ourselves in deeper. Seconds later, Candace swung the front door open. I'd seen photos of birds whose pouches under their bills weren't as wide as her mouth. She glared at us, turned around to where Alexis was standing a few yards away and yelled right at her, "You monstrous little weasel! You called Daisy, didn't you?"

Alexis's voice was loud and brash. "What? I've been here with you all along. What are you saying? That I conjured her up?"

By now, Alexis had made it to the front door just as Daisy brushed Candace aside and walked in. The three of us, Hogan,

Jordan and I, followed her as if we had a royal invitation. I whispered, "Candace pocketed my recorder" and bit my lip.

"Which pocket?" Hogan mouthed when no one was looking at us. "Don't know," I mouthed back.

"Um," I said to Candace, "I suppose you're wondering why we came back so—"

Before Candace could acknowledge me, Daisy grabbed her by the wrist and yanked her off to the side, nearly colliding with an occasional table that held a large cream colored vase with fresh flowers. "You know why I'm here, don't you? You didn't think I was going to sit around and wait for you to call me back, did you? Well? Did you find them?"

Candace's face looked ashen. "I, er, well, that is..."

Out of nowhere, Jordan blurted out, "Uh, pardon me but whatever it is, look in your pockets. People stash stuff in their pockets all the time and forget they put it there until they go to do the laundry."

With that, Daisy shook Candace by the shoulders and screamed in her face. "You've had them all along in your pockets?"

"No! I don't. Of course not. Here, see for yourself!"

With that, she turned her pockets inside out and tossed the micro stick on the occasional table. "There's nothing in my pockets except for a stupid flash drive. Now are you satisfied?"

I lunged for the table while Candace and Daisy locked eyes and glared at each other. If they were giving out Olympic metals for dash-and-grab, I would've taken the gold. I snatched the micro stick and shoved it in my pocket while pretending to have a coughing fit.

"I'm okay, everyone," I said but no one paid any attention to me. Daisy was still giving Candace the evil eye while Hogan and Jordan watched silently.

Daisy ran her fingers through her hair and shook her head as if she were ridding herself of lice. "Where's the painting? Where's the damn painting you twit?"

"I had my driver put it in the garage."

"Did you inspect it? Did you get a flashlight and inspect it?"

"No, like I told you over the phone, I felt the surface and there weren't any distinguishable texturized features. And I saw all that clay dust on the ground where it had fallen."

"Show me that painting right now!"

"We can wait here," I said. "It's not a problem."

"My God!" Candace shrieked. "Are you still here? Didn't I tell you before that this was not a good time to ask me questions. Can't you see I'm otherwise engaged? If you hadn't arrived, those bees wouldn't have had anyone to attack and my painting would still be in one piece. It's a very valuable Margarida Tavares Branco, but I wouldn't expect you to know anything about art."

"I know Tawn Hamlin bought one of those. And I know Daisy's gallery sponsored the artist. Is there something else I should know?"

Just then I heard the faint sound of sirens. At first I thought it might be an ambulance somewhere in the vicinity but as I listened closely I realized it was more than one siren. A fire maybe? No, those sirens have a different wail. Suddenly everyone heard the sirens and Candace went ballistic.

She shoved Daisy into the occasional table and when Daisy tried to steady herself, Candace gave her another shove. "You called the police, didn't you? What did you tell them? You're not going to pin all of this on me. The painting! I've got to hide it. *We've* got to hide it."

Daisy stood up and pointed a finger directly at Candace's face. "Why on earth would I call the police? Don't be a moron. For all I know that buyer of yours might've been an undercover cop. Did you vet him like we discussed?"

"Of course I did. He's a hospital administrator for goodness sakes. They make more money than any of us."

"Are you ladies dealing in stolen art?" I asked. I tried to sound as naïve as possible. No sense letting on that I knew about the tourmalines.

At that moment, the sirens got louder. It sounded as if there were at least two, possibly three vehicles and if I wasn't mistaken, they were headed down Lake of the Isles Parkway. I was positive Hogan had made the call. To say he was uncomfortable with the equivalent of a million dollars in his pocket would be an understatement. Max would've made the call as well. It was the prudent and logical thing to do, but why now? Why, when we were so close to finding out Tawn's involvement with the Paraiba tourmalines, did he jump the gun and call in the big guns?

I crinkled my nose and gave him a look to which he brushed off by shrugging his shoulders. Terrific. I was about to whisper something to him when Candace clapped her hands and spoke. "Everyone remain calm. There's no evidence of any wrongdoing should the police descend on my household like seventeen-year locusts. Besides, those sirens could be responding to a situation at one of the neighbor's houses."

"Uh, I don't think so," Jordan said. "Unless they got the address wrong. Look out the window. They're pulling in your driveway. Cripes. They've got one marked car and another unmarked one."

"Quick!" Candace said. "Everyone take a seat here in the Grand Foyer and act nonchalant. Everything is under control." Then she turned to me, "I don't have to let them in, do I? I mean, they would need a search warrant, wouldn't they?"

"Unless they think someone's in danger. Then they could enter the premises."

"Let me in on the deal," Alexis said, "or I'll start screaming bloody murder."

CHAPTER 27

The flashing lights from the police vehicles created a strange strobe-like feature in the hallway. Apparently Candace's large living room windows in the front of the house literally brought the outdoors in.

"I mean it," Alexis said. "My voice will carry all the way to St. Paul. You don't think I came unprepared, do you? I must admit, it's one of those templates I pulled off from the Internet when I thought we'd be discussing something entirely different but that's the beauty of fill-in-the-blank, don't you think?" She took out a folded piece of paper from her bag and along with a pen, handed it to Candace. "It's a partnership agreement. Plain and simple. I become your third partner in that little concealed prize within the painting scheme or I scream my lungs out. What will it be?"

"Oh for God sakes!" Daisy exclaimed. "Sign the damn thing and give it to me. Our lawyers can deal with it later."

Candace acquiesced, scrawled her name on the sheet of paper and handed it to Daisy who did the same. Alexis then re-folded the paper and put it back in her bag just as the doorbell rang.

"Remember," Candace said. "Act calm."

The doorbell rang again followed by a loud, male voice. "Darryl Flemming, this is the Minneapolis Police Department and we have a warrant for your arrest! Open the door now."

Candace bounced out of her seat as if she was a debutant about to take a first dance. "Darryl Flemming? The Flemmings live next door. He holds the wildest high stakes poker games in his basement. I'll bet someone wised up. Oh joy of joys! The police aren't here for me."

With that, she flew to the front door and I bounded out of my chair to get a glimpse of the action. She flung the door open wide and announced, "Officers, you have the wrong house. The Flemmings, Darryl and Portia, are my next door neighbors. Dear me! This isn't one of those domestic violence things, is it? The Flemmings are such quiet, unassuming people. Should I be worried? Are either of them brandishing a weapon?"

Clearly, the woman missed her golden opportunity to appear in footlights. I continued to listen to her spout off. "Do you need to see my identification? I'm Candace Pendleton and—"

"Sorry to disturb you, Ma'am," was the response and the door was promptly closed.

So much for Hogan calling the police. In retrospect, I should've given that assumption more thought. If anyone was going to rat me out, it would've been Jordan. I surveyed the group and took a breath. I was perhaps the only one in the room who knew exactly what was going on, having overheard Candace's earlier conversation with Alexis. My best bet was to play dumb and let the micro stick continue to take notes.

Daisy stood and walked toward Candace. "I want to see that painting now."

"Not so fast," I said. "Are you involved with stolen artwork? Is that what this is about?"

"Certainly not," Daisy said. "I run a legitimate business. Unfortunately, I took in a partner who obviously did not understand how precious art pieces should be handled."

Then, Candace pointed her finger at me. "They were handled fine until those bees showed up. First thing tomorrow I intend to call an exterminator. For all I know the hive could be close by."

Hogan rolled his eyes when she wasn't looking and I had all I could do to hold myself back from laughing. I stood and walked toward Daisy and Candace. "It must be quite the business for Alexis to threaten you into making her a partner as well. What I'd like to know is how Tawn Hamlin figured into it. Was she on your payroll, too?"

Daisy shot back at me like a dagger. "Don't be absurd. She bought a painting, that's all. I give the woman some credit for recognizing artistic talent."

Then, I did the unthinkable in an attempt to get to the truth. "I'm not so sure it was the artwork itself that captured her attention. More like the overall illusion it provided. I mean, after all, I've seen kindergarteners who could put Margarida Tavares Branco to shame."

Candace grabbed Daisy by the wrist. "She doesn't mean that. She's trying to pry information out of us and it's not going to work because Tawn had nothing to do with Visual Fields of Vision's art inventory."

Daisy shook off Candace's hand and strode to the archway that separated the Grand Foyer from the corridor. "I don't care what she thinks. I want to see that painting now! It's in the garage you said?"

"I, um, er..." Candace babbled.

Meanwhile, I tried a new tact. This time with Alexis. "When did you become an art connoisseur? Seems to me you mentioned some sort of concealed prize in the package. Care to expound on that?"

Alexis bit her lower lip and grimaced. "What I meant was the style Margarida used. The visual style. You know, like those puzzles that show one picture when there's really another one that requires a closer eye. The term is trompe l'oeil and those paintings are worth a fortune."

Good Grief! You're a better liar than I am.

Candace and Daisy were now standing in the archway and having words. I wasted no time joining them. "I suppose not, but I can always learn. I wouldn't mind taking a closer look at that painting myself. Mind if I join you in the garage? In fact, I think it would be a terrific learning experience for all of us."

"No one's going to the garage without me," Alexis said, all but elbowing me away from Daisy and Candace. Meanwhile, Hogan and Jordan, who were still seated, got up and sauntered toward us.

Everyone began talking at once and it was only when a loud knock on the front door caused us to stand still. Another knock followed, this time with the ringing of the bell.

"Now what?" Candace huffed. "This is an untenable afternoon and I haven't even had time to enjoy a leisurely lunch."

"None of us have," Jordan said under his breath but I don't think she heard him. She walked to the front of the house but instead of opening the door or asking who was there, she peered out of one of the large picture windows and exclaimed, "Dear God, it's the police again. I imagine they want to question me about the Flemmings. Good Lord! We can't have all of us standing around like some sort of sideshow. Find a seat somewhere in the living room. Act casual."

Hogan and I plopped ourselves on one of her fancy couches while everyone else scrambled for a chair, an ottoman or a bench. Hogan leaned into my ear and kept his voice low. "Now are you ready to give this up?"

"Maybe they're collecting money for the Police Benevolent

Society. I mean, no one tipped them off about the tourmalines, right?"

"None of us," Hogan whispered but who the hell knows what Candace's got going on."

At that moment, the door opened and two uniformed police officers stepped inside. Clean shaven, middle aged and not shy around a food table. The taller of the two, with short brown hair spoke. "I'm Officer Gelaney with the Minnesota Police Department and I have a search warrant to check the premises of one Candace Pendleton."

"What??" Candace shrieked, all but rendering everyone in the room deaf. "What for? This has got to be a mistake. A horrible, wretched mistake. I'm Candace Pendleton and I am certainly not a terrorist. I'm an American citizen with rights!"

"Mrs. Pendleton," Officer Gelaney said, "No one is accusing you of being a terrorist, nor are we about to violate your constitutional rights."

He showed her the search warrant and for a few seconds she was quiet. Then, not so much.

"I demand to know what this is all about. The warrant says stolen jewels. I can assure you, my jewels were purchased from reliable sources. Do you know who my husband is? He's an executive with Cargill Salt. Do you think he'd buy me jewelry that wasn't from a certified jeweler?"

Candace shoved the search warrant at the officer and shouted, "I cannot have you traipse through my house. This is an outrage. I have wool carpeting upstairs. You'll destroy it."

The officer kept his gaze on Candace. "Then perhaps we can spare your carpets if you'll kindly direct my men to the painting with the hidden gems." With that, the officer went to the door and motioned for two plain clothed officers to enter.

Daisy looked as if she had aged overnight. Her face no longer reflected the casual Bohemian lightheartedness it did when I first met her and the dark Kohl make-up that accentuated her eyes was now dull and smudged. She appeared as if she could try out for one of Macbeth's witches without much effort. She gave Candace a frosty stare and shook her head.

"I don't know what you're talking about," Candace said. "I can assure you none of my paintings have hidden gems in them."

Just then, Candace's driver, who was standing behind the second set of police officers, peered into the living room and spoke. "I'm really sorry, Mrs. Pendleton. Honestly. But I can't afford to get caught up in any of this. I'd be expelled from college. I have enough problems with finances. I couldn't afford a lawyer if I tried. I'm really, really sorry. Things were a little fishy when you called me at weird hours to pick up artwork from Ms. Jamos but I figured you were both kind of eccentric. Then, when I put that painting in the garage, I saw something round tumble out of it and I picked it up. I had no choice. I had to go to the police and tell them."

That clinches it. It's the one with three and Hogan's got the other two.

"You imbecile!" Candace screamed. "Tell them what? What did you tell them?"

Before the driver could answer, Alexis took out the signed partnership agreement from her purse and tore it up in little pieces making sure all the pieces went back into her purse. "I've decided not to do business with either of you ladies," she said, "especially under the circumstances."

Jordan muttered "Oh brother" and Hogan had all he could do to keep a straight face.

"We're wasting time, Mrs. Pendleton," the officer said. "Please direct us to that painting."

The driver stepped back from the front door and announced, "It's in the garage. I can show it to you."

Behind him Candace's voice bellowed like a medieval fishwife but I don't think he heard her. He and the two plain clothed officers had already left the front entrance and had turned right toward the rear of the house. They were followed by the uniformed officers. Meanwhile, Candace continued to shout as she raced through the house followed by Daisy at her heels.

"Hurry!' she said. "We can get there first, move the painting into the kitchen and hide it in one of the concealed cabinets."

For a brief moment I considered the irony of the situation. Tawn Hamlin may have been killed because she found out about Daisy and Candace's enterprise and now her kitchen design with its concealed cabinetry and deep visual illusion would serve to protect the two women who might have been responsible for her death.

"There won't be enough time," Daisy replied. "Besides, all they'll find is a painting. You said yourself the tourmalines were gone. It's your driver's word against ours. For all anyone knows maybe he's trying to set you up."

Hogan, Jordan and I followed Daisy and Candace into the garage. Unfortunately for them, her driver and the police officers were faster and had opened the garage door, letting in sufficient light for us to see the freshly washed and buffed Lincoln Navigator as well as the tattered painting. It leaned against the wall and practically screamed for someone to put it out of its misery.

"That's it," the driver said. "That's where the gemstone I gave you came from. Like I said, it tumbled out when I put the painting against the wall. If you look carefully you'll see some indents."

"What's that painting supposed to be?" one of the officers asked.

"Beats me," was the response. "Looks like a set of teeth wedged between two mountains. Damned if I know."

I heard a gasp but I wasn't sure where it came from. At first glance it appeared as if everyone from Candace's living room had converged into her tandem garage so it could have been any one in that crowd. I started to scan their faces when I heard the unmistakable sound of a car starting. Five seconds later I figured it out. Alexis had left the premises.

CHAPTER 28

Daisy crossed her arms and looked directly at Candace's driver. "Gemstone? You're most likely holding a clump of acrylic paint or at the very least a glass fragment. Artists are known to infuse those elements to texturize their pieces."

"Um, I don't think so. You see I'm majoring in seismic geology and one of the requirements for graduation is to be able to identify certain gemstones, minerals and rocks. What came out of that painting was a tourmaline encased in some sort of clay. The clay fell out and when I saw the color of the gem I knew I was holding something rare. Then I remembered a post I saw a few weeks ago on Facebook. Something about stolen Brazilian tourmalines and how the police in Minnesota were following a lead."

"Some lead," Jordan muttered under his breath.

"That's ridiculous," Daisy said. She turned to the two police officers who brought the warrant. "Are you going to take the word of some college student? He's no gemologist."

The taller officer took a quick breath and glanced at the driver. "He may not be a gemologist but the one we have on staff working the stolen tourmaline case most certainly is. One look at that gem and our guy was positive it was a…." Then he looked at his partner. "What did the gemologist call that thing? A pariah?"

The other officer shrugged. "Something like that. Anyway, our department received a tip-off a while back about rare gems being routed into the U.S. Interpol believed Minneapolis was the destination but our lead went cold. Until today."

"This is circumstantial evidence," Candace said. "Nothing will hold up in court."

"You may be right," the taller officer replied, "but it's enough evidence to book you on suspicion of theft and gem smuggling."

"Me?" Candace shouted. "You're arresting *me*? I'm the innocent victim here. If anyone needs to be arrested, it's that lady in that shapeless maroon caftan. She's the one who sold that painting to me. How was I supposed to know she was a gem smuggler?"

Suddenly Daisy lunged for Candace, all but knocking over Jordan who was a few inches away. "You lousy little turncoat! How dare you implicate me! I ought to—"

I never got to find out what Daisy thought she ought to do because at that very second Candace pounced on her like a wildcat. The two of them tore at each other with flailing arms, misdirected punches and kicks to the shins. Only the shins that got kicked weren't Daisy's or Candace's. They belonged to the two police officers who tried to separate them.

Next thing I knew, the plain clothes officers tried to intervene but they got embroiled in the melee as well. If it was one thing I learned in junior high, it was to get the heck out of the way when things like that happened. Oddly enough, it was drummed into my head by my mother in reference to my uncle Phil's early days teaching seventh grade social studies.

My uncle had the unfortunate assignment of lunch duty during his first year of teaching. Needless to say a food fight broke out and kids were hurling milk, mashed potatoes and anything they could get their hands on. In an effort to quell the fracas, my uncle stepped into the middle of the cafeteria and demanded that the students cease and desist immediately. Four minutes later, when he found himself covered in cling peaches with no relief in sight, an older, more experienced teacher yanked him from the middle of the room and said, "Don't you know you can't stop these things? Do what the rest of us do – stand against the wall and write down names."

Granted, the officers weren't going to wind up covered in canned fruit, but their shins and their ankles would be bruised for days. I plastered myself against the driver side of the Lincoln Navigator along with Hogan, Jordan, and the driver. Hogan was on my right and Jordan and the driver on the left.

"I give it ten more seconds," Jordan said, "and they'll trump up the charges to include assaulting an officer."

Hogan shifted his weight and gave me a nudge. "Give it another ten seconds and when they cart those two off, we'll be next."

"Relax," I said. "If that happens, I'll show them my identification and explain."

"Good luck with that once Candace concocts some story about your involvement. We've got no choice or we'll be named accessories. You've got to tell them about the tape recording and I've got to hand over the other two tourmalines. That should give them all the evidence they need for a solid arrest."

"The tape won't play out in court because it was obtained illegally. I was hoping to use it as leverage to get Candace to tell me the truth about Tawn's involvement but I think I pieced it together. It was something Candace mentioned."

"I can't hear you," Hogan said. "Not with that frenzy going on in front of us."

Daisy and Candace refused to give up and no matter how hard the officers tried to separate them; it was impossible. At one point, one of the plain clothed officers reached in to tear them apart but Daisy bit his wrist.

Yep, Jordan's right. Assault will be the next charge.

I leaned into Hogan's ear and said, "The concealed cabinets. Tawn must have designed cabinets that aren't easily spotted. Cabinets are large. Especially if they don't have shelves. I'll wager Candace's kitchen was built to hide Daisy's artwork. I mean, after all, most businesses keep an inventory."

"I thought Tawn was working on Candace's lake house. You know, the one in Minnetonka."

"True, but who's to say she didn't design this one first?"

Next thing I knew, Jordan elbowed me. "What are you two talking about? I can't hear a damn thing with that circus in front of us."

"Jordan, do you know if Tawn did a renovation on this house?"

"Not sure. Although I do know it wasn't the first project she did for Candace. Why?"

"I'm pretty positive your wife might have inadvertently paved the way for Candace to conceal certain art pieces in the kitchen cabinetry. Tawn was all about design and illusion for artistic purposes but Candace had more nefarious motives in mind."

"Huh?"

"Candace needed a secure spot to hide those Margarida paintings but something must have spooked her so she silenced Tawn for good."

"What???"

Then, like something out of one of those horror movies where a creature goes totally berserk, Jordan charged toward Candace. He paid no attention to the officers who tried to subdue her and with one lightning fast gesture, he yanked her to her feet and screamed at the top of his lungs, "You murderous witch! You killed my wife."

At that point Daisy grabbed Candace by the shoulders and shook her. "You killed his wife? You're the one who did it?"

"I didn't kill anyone, you conniving baboon! I don't even know who he is. I thought he was Marcie Rayner's boss."

My boss? Please tell me I'm not hearing things.

"It's the husband," Daisy said. "Tawn's husband. He showed up at my place because someone sent him a text."

"Well don't look at me," Candace huffed.

And then, silence. An actual lull. It gave the police officers enough time to get firm grasps on Daisy and Candace and cuff them. Jordan was still shouting at Candace and I thought he'd never stop.

"If you don't quit it," Hogan said as he yanked Jordan away from her, "You'll be next. Hope you have lots of bail money."

Jordan struggled to get back in Candace's face but Hogan made sure that didn't happen. "Take it easy," he told him. "They've got it under control."

The police may have had it under control but Jordan didn't. It was as if all the tension and anger resulting from his wife's murder finally found the outlet he needed – Candace Pendleton. He took out a car key and waved it in front of her as the police tried to remove her from the garage.

"So help me I'll etch this sucker right into the finish of your car if you don't tell the police the truth! I mean it." Then, to prove his point, he held the key on top of the car's hood and waited.

"Do something," Candace wailed "before that lunatic destroys a classic car."

"No one is going to destroy anything," one of the plain clothed officers said. He stepped toward Jordan and gave him one of those "don't make it harder on yourself than it has to be" looks. "If this woman committed a murder, we'll know soon enough."

With that, Jordan moved away from the car and the

uniformed officers escorted Candace and Daisy out of the garage and around the front of the house where their cars were parked. Candace kept screaming two things – "I didn't kill anyone" and "Don't you dare ruin my Belgium wool carpeting."

Daisy wasn't without words either. "Don't trust anything that woman says. She's a pathological liar!"

I turned toward one of the plain clothed officers and showed him my identification. "I came here to question Mrs. Pendleton about the murder of her kitchen designer, Tawn Hamlin. Then, pointing to Hogan and Jordan, I added, "These two gentlemen came with me. We've got information that needs to be shared with your department. If you give me your precinct address, we can be there in an hour. Um, make that an hour and a half. We haven't eaten since breakfast and I also need to take care of some other business."

The officer turned to his partner and said, "Secure the house. We'll be back later." Then he gave me a nod and took out a business card. "See you in an hour or so. My shift doesn't end until eight. Ask for Mikey Abrams."

"Guess I might as well split," said the driver as he gave the Lincoln a quick pat on its roof.

"Hold on a sec, will you?" Mikey motioned for the driver to approach. "I'll need your name and contact information in case we need to ask you some questions."

The driver complied and stood dutifully in front of him. I waved and followed Hogan and Jordan, who were already part way out of Candace's garage.

The three of us wasted no time getting into Hogan's van.

"Hey, I'm really sorry about losing it back there," Jordan said, "but all of a sudden it was like something went off in my head."

I turned in my seat and glared. "Yeah, your brain backfiring. You could've really messed things up."

"I said I was sorry, didn't I?"

"Forget it."

Hogan patted me on the knee and I began to relax.

"What did you mean by "other business?" he asked. "You mentioned eating, which is number one on my list, but what else did you have in mind?"

"You don't think I'm going to hand over this micro stick without making a copy first? Best bet is for me to make a copy on Jordan's laptop and email it to myself. If we hurry, we can get to his friend's apartment, take care of the copy and go grab a bite to eat. We'll make it to the precinct in plenty of time." Then I swiveled my head around and faced Jordan. "That's okay with you, isn't it?"

"Absolutely. Anything to nail that witch. Oh, and by the way, I'm not staying at Barry's any longer. A couple of nights were enough for me. The guy's idea of music is listening to Yanni. The laptop's back at my place."

"Swell."

CHAPTER 29

I didn't realize how uncomfortable Hogan was with the two precious tourmalines in his pocket until we finally handed them over to Mikey Abrams along with the micro stick. It felt like hours since the time I originally told the officer I'd be at the precinct. First, we had to drop Jordan off at his car, which was parked on Daisy Jamos's street. Then, over to his place so I could make a copy of the micro stick and email to myself. I also emailed one to Max as well.

There was a Wendy's only a few yards from Jordan's so I wound up devouring my second fast food meal of the day. My junk food threshold had reached its limit and I swore the only thing I'd let into my mouth in the next twenty –four hours would be leafy and green. Okay, leafy and green with ample salad dressing but positively no more greasy food.

I tried to call Max to keep him posted but wound up leaving him a voice mail. Jordan was adamant I let him know if Candace confessed to anything at the police station but I was doubtful I'd be privy to that information. Not right away anyhow.

"Look," I said as Hogan and I headed out of Jordan's apartment, "I promise I'll call if I find out anything else. Whatever you do, don't be lax with the security measures. For all any of us knows, there's still a murderer at large if Candace wasn't acting alone."

"Terrific."

Jordan double locked the door and Hogan and I drove to twenty seventh and Lake of Isles where the Fifth Precinct was located. Mikey Abrams was expecting us because we were ushered right into his office by the duty clerk when we arrived. I had made the assumption he was a plain-clothed officer but as it turned out, he was a detective-sergeant who stepped in at the last minute for an officer who had taken ill.

Without pausing to catch a breath, I handed him the micro stick, took a seat near his desk along with Hogan, and smiled. "You'll have enough evidence on this tape to make an arrest. It won't hold up in court because it was obtained without Mrs. Pendleton's permission, or Ms. Jamos's for that matter, but it will be enough to get them talking."

I then proceeded to tell Mikey Abrams everything I had uncovered about the clandestine tourmaline operation including my take on how Daisy Jamos managed to pull it off. I must have been more excited than I realized because Hogan had to bump my elbow a few times to get me to stop tapping my foot on the floor.

"You see," I said, "she used her art gallery downtown to introduce the artwork of one Brazilian artist by the name of Margarida Tavares Branco, only there is no such person. It's Daisy. She's the artist. I used Google to do a little translating and guess what I found out? Margarida is Portuguese for daisy. Portuguese is what they speak in Brazil. But it was the signature, the M, that sealed the deal."

"Fascinating," he said.

"Oh, there's more. Speculation on my part, but with researched-based evidence to support it. Daisy would go off to Brazil for weeks at a time. Candace as well. Daisy has an art studio not far from Barreiras. That's where she paints her

Margarida's and encases the tourmalines in them. Very clever. No one scrutinizes imported artwork the way they do for illegal drugs. Heck, dogs are trained to sniff out drugs or food products, not gems. Anyway, I've got half the puzzle down pat. I have no idea where the tourmalines are getting mined or how Daisy is getting ahold of them. I only know what happens once they land in her hot little hand."

"We've reached the same conclusion you have. Mrs. Pendleton was fencing the gems for Ms. Jamos. Whether or not she's a partner in a greater operation, we have yet to learn."

"She didn't tell you?"

"Not as of yet. But she was insistent about something – the murder of her kitchen designer. She said that's why you were at her house. To question her again. She demanded to take a polygraph test for that explicit reason and only that reason. It took some finagling but we managed to have one administered a short while ago."

"And?"

"She was telling the truth about the murder. At least according to the polygraph. She had nothing to do with it and has no knowledge of who Tawn Hamlin's killer is. Given her relationship with Ms. Jamos, Candace Pendleton would have more than an inkling if Daisy Jamos was the killer."

I was stunned. Totally and completely stunned. My theory evaporated in a nanosecond and I was left with what? An international gem smuggling ring? Granted, it was a high profile case but it wasn't the one I was paid to investigate. It took me a few seconds to grapple with a new reality. If Candace and Daisy were out of the picture regarding Tawn's death, then there had to be another player. Certainly not Alexis. True, she was up to something but it wasn't tourmalines. She'd only recently come on to that scene.

"If you ask me," I said, "Tawn's demise was the result of her unwittingly designing kitchen cabinets that on the surface appeared to look normal but were actually secret compartments built to store stolen gems fused into canvases. Poor Tawn. She had no idea whatsoever that it wasn't the *design* her clients were interested in as much as the *purpose.* I still believe she knew too much and someone killed her. That would explain Josh Newburgh's suspicious death as well."

"Who?"

"Josh Newburgh. He was the project manager for Leo McCellan, the contractor whose company built the kitchens. Josh suffered a massive heart attack which was thought to be from natural causes but it was later discovered someone had given him a high dose of potassium chloride. Someone on your police force has to be working on it. Josh died in Minneapolis but the Edina Police are in the loop as well since Classy Kitchens is the catalyst, so to speak."

"Let me get this straight. You believe Tawn and this Newburgh guy somehow found out about the gem smuggling operation and someone other than the two ladies we have in custody was responsible for killing them."

"I do."

"It's a viable theory, I'll give you that, but as far as we can tell, only Ms. Jamos and Mrs. Pendleton were the only ones involved with the storage and transfer of the artwork. Look, I can really understand how you'd want to wrap this up in a neat little package but most times it doesn't work that way. Don't take this the wrong way but you're still a neophyte investigator. I'll bet you haven't even turned thirty yet."

Whoa. I don't know whether to be insulted or tickled pink.

Mikey Abrams rubbed his salt and pepper goatee and continued. "I'm five years off from retiring so I've seen a whole lot more. It could very well be that whoever murdered Ms. Hamlin had nothing to do with the tourmaline theft. Same deal with the Newburgh guy. For all we know it could be two separate killers. Two separate motives. And apparently two separate police jurisdictions. Always a whole lot of fun."

"What did Daisy say?"

"Not much. She's waiting on her lawyer."

"That figures. Whoever it is must be on retainer."

With that I gave Hogan a poke and he reached into his pocket and handed Mikey Abrams two of the most beautiful gems I'd ever seen in my life. They were mesmerizing blue with a hue that seemed to glow.

"These are two of the three tourmalines that were hidden in that painting. The driver found the other one," he said.

Mikey Abrams stood up, walked to his file cabinet and came back with a small plastic evidence bag. "Three, huh?" he asked and I nodded.

"Three, and I can substantiate that with a little note written to Mrs. Pendleton that I acquired under some questionable circumstances. As I explained earlier, there are more tourmalines. They spilled out of the painting that hung over Tawn and her husband's bed. When she died, he started to take the painting down. Had he not lost his grip on it, we would never have known it housed rare tourmalines. Tawn herself didn't even know. It was a fluke. That painting was probably destined for a high-price sale but wound up in auction. She bought it because she liked it. God knows why. The thing gave me the creeps and it didn't do much for her husband."

"Where are those tourmalines now?"

"With the exception of one that my boss, Max Blake, took for authentication with a certified gemologist, the others are in her husband's bank vault. Max will contact you and make arrangements to get the tourmaline to your department. I'll make sure Tawn's husband phones you so that those gems can be turned over as well."

Mikey smiled. "They won't be with us for long. Interpol's investigators have all but been camping on our doorsteps. Do you have any idea how massive this operation is? It spanned over a decade. If it hadn't been for your involvement and your persistence in trying to solve Ms. Hamlin's murder, none of this would have come to light."

I clasped my hands and shrugged.

"Hey," he said, "don't beat yourself up over not getting the result you wanted. You eliminated two players from the game, now go after the rest."

Hogan told me the same thing on the drive home but I couldn't help but feel as if everything had been a wasted effort.

"I was positive it was Candace," I moaned. "And when we had her dead to rights, I was even more positive she'd break down and confess to the murder. Now I'm back to square one."

"Yep. Been there. Done that."

"Huh? What are you talking about?"

"The brewery. What else? When something goes kerflooey, I tend to fixate on one reason for the mess-up. When it turns out I'm wrong, there's no consoling me until I get it right."

"So how do you do it?"

"Same way you will. Same thing Mikey Abrams said. Start over. And by the way, I liked the guy. Real down to earth and not full of himself. Look, what do you say we give this a break for tonight and chill out at your place? Geez, it's past six already. We'll get take-out, hang out on the couch and I'll even rub the soles of your feet."

I gave his arm a squeeze. "What girl can resist that?"

Hogan and I staggered to bed at a little before midnight. A

combination of nerves and exhaustion had claimed me and I imagined it did a number on him as well. I conked out as soon as my head hit the pillow but at three in the morning, a small detail that I had neglected to pursue surfaced in the recesses of my brain and made sure I wouldn't be able to get back to sleep. A small detail by the name of Alexis.

By all accounts, she was a gold-digging opportunist who would stop at nothing to get what she wanted. And she almost did, had it not been for the Minneapolis Police Department sending over a few of their finest to search Candace's Pendleton's place for stolen Brazilian tourmalines.

But she didn't happen on that tourmaline information serendipitously. She found out from the spyware she planted at Jordan's. She said so herself when she was alone with Candace. So what was that scheming little minx up to?

I got up from the bed and tiptoed into the kitchen where I made myself a cup of tea. As I lifted the teabag up and down in the hot water, bits and pieces of the information I had gleaned began to crystalize. That note I found at Candace's said something about someone, most likely Daisy, finding another alternative that would result in her and Candace "kissing Tawn good-bye." At first I thought it might be a reference to murder but now, given my firsthand experience witnessing Alexis in action, I had a completely different take.

If I was right, then Alexis was more Machiavellian than anyone gave her credit for. The trouble was, until I could find out what the hell she was doing in Jordan's apartment, I had no way of proving anything.

My first instinct was to call Mikey Abrams and have him bring her in for questioning but unless Classy Kitchens was going to press charges regarding Alexis's unauthorized use of the client files, there was nothing to hold her on. Same deal with the little blackmail scheme she offered up to Candace. Candace would only dig herself in deeper. Nope. I had to find another way to get to the truth regarding Tawn's murder.

I finished my tea, made a quick restroom stop and crept back in bed. Hogan's body was warm and within minutes I dozed off snuggled next to him. It was a light sleep that incorporated the extraneous noises in my apartment that I had gotten accustomed to hearing. The hum of the ceiling fan, the sound of the icemaker in the refrigerator, and the traffic noises outside that the windows couldn't totally block.

When I awoke the next morning, I had a renewed sense of direction. I leaned on Hogan's chest and whispered one word – Alexis.

"Think you've got it figured out?" he asked.

"Not yet. But I will."

CHAPTER 30

Hogan had to leave early the next morning to get back to the brewery but insisted he'd be able to slip away for an evening with me later on in the week. Once again, I told him I'd make the drive to Biscay the following weekend but he chuckled. "Let's play it by ear until you wrap up this case. Relax, I don't mind driving to New Ulm to see my favorite detective. Even if it means dealing with her ex-husband."

"Yeah, that was kind of weird, wasn't it?"

"Not as awkward as I expected. He seemed like a nice enough guy."

"Oh, he's nice enough. That was the problem. Too nice to too many women."

Hogan gave me a giant bear hug followed by a super long kiss. "I've got the only woman I want so you'll have to get used to it."

"With pleasure."

After he left, I rinsed our breakfast dishes off in the sink and decided to spend the day reviewing my notes and double checking the timeline for Tawn's murder. Max had always told me whenever in doubt, scrutinize the timeline. And that's exactly what I planned to do in-between loads of laundry and some much needed housework. So much for a lazy Sunday at home.

By noon, the dust bunnies that had accumulated under the furniture were gone and fresh linens were on my bed. The kitchen and bathroom didn't look too shabby either. As far as the timeline went, everyone's story matched up. I was at a standstill and uncertain of my next move but thanks to a phone call from my mother, everything changed.

"Marcie! When were you going to call me to tell me you were involved in that Brazilian tourmaline case? It was on the Sunday morning news. Dee Dee called to tell me. She said they mentioned Blake Investigations out of New Ulm. The Minneapolis Police Department made some arrests following an intensified confrontation at the smuggler's residence. Were you there? Dee Dee said the news anchors weren't all that specific but more details will emerge as they get deeper into the case. Don't tell me Blake Investigations is going to be sending you to Brazil or I'll wring Max's neck."

It took me a full twenty minutes to explain to my mother that I was never in any real danger and Max and I were certainly not going to Brazil. "That's why Interpol exists," I said. "To deal with those international crimes in cooperation with law enforcement agencies around the world."

"What about Jordan's second wife? Did she figure into any of this?"

"As far as everyone knows, she didn't. It's an open case and I'm working on it."

"Work on it from your desk."

Having reassured my mother I had no plans to leave the country, she went on to tell me about a new Publix they were opening near her house and some musical show she and her friends got tickets to attend. From there she went on to let me know about a potluck dinner the women in her complex planned to have. I muttered "uh-huh" sporadically and didn't realize she had asked me a question.

"So, do you have any idea where it could be?"

"Um, uh, what could be?"

"The handwritten cookbook with Nonnie's recipes. Marcie, aren't you paying attention?"

"Um, sure. I must not have heard."

"Your grandmother Nonnie had a handwritten book with all of her special recipes and for the life of me I can't find it."

The last time I had seen my grandmother's recipe book was eons ago when my mother still lived in New Ulm. The thing was tattered and full of grease stains. I think the grease was the only thing keeping the paper from disintegrating.

"Sorry, Mom, but I have no idea. Can't you use another recipe for whatever it is you're making?"

"Absolutely not. It's those secret spices of hers that make the dish. Without knowing what they are and how she used them, I'll wind up with something ordinary, not extraordinary."

Ordinary. Not extraordinary.

In that split second, the fog surrounding Alexis's motive for breaking into Jordan's house lifted and I was ecstatic. "I'm sure it will turn up. Don't worry. Have no fear. Keep looking. Well, I've got to go. I'll talk to you this week."

"Are you all right, Marcie? You're running off at the mouth."

"Am I? Oh well. It's been great talking to you. Love you!"

The second the call ended, I placed one to Jordan. It was as if he'd been waiting all morning for his cell phone to ring. "Marcie. Did you find out something? That was fast."

"I might have. Listen carefully. I know you went through the apartment looking for any flash drives that Tawn might have stashed and I know you downloaded her laptop files and sent them to me, but did you find any notebooks of hers? Notebooks that would be frayed from overuse?"

"No, and I looked all through her things."

My mother's reference to grandma Nonnie hit a nerve. "What about the cookbooks in your kitchen? Did you go through them?"

"Cookbooks. Tawn hardly cooked."

"But I'll bet she had cookbooks. Go check. I'm staying on the line."

Jordan let out a really audible sigh. "Give me a sec and hang on."

I had a hunch and kept my fingers crossed. Jordan got back on the line with a monotonous list of cookbooks. "Betty Crocker, South Beach Diet, Atkins Diet, The Lutheran Women's Cookbook, The New Keto Diet, The Shakeology Diet, and Weight Watchers Famous Recipes."

"That's it?"

"What did you expect? You asked for cookbooks."

I tried not to sound too annoyed. "Pull the largest ones out and see if there's anything crammed inside."

"Oh brother. There's lots of stuff crammed into Betty Crocker. Newspaper clippings of recipes, handwritten recipes, and lots of stapled pages that are folded together. It's so old the cover sheet says Mary Ann Locaste. Geez, Tawn's probably kept favorite recipes from her childhood."

"Un-do the Mary Ann Locaste pages. Tell me what you see."

"Holy Crap! These aren't recipes at all. They're designs with crazy math formulas. She's got a boatload of them and they're really weird. Hard to explain."

"Don't. Don't explain. When we get off the phone, take as many photos as you can and email them to me right away. I mean it. Right away!"

"What do you think they are?"

"The reason your apartment was ransacked. I'll explain later. Meanwhile, start snapping photos and get them to me. Talk to you later."

Granted, it was a Sunday but this couldn't wait. I phoned Max the instant I was done speaking with Jordan. "Hey, it's me. Sorry to interrupt your weekend but I really need to speak with your brother-in-law. Can you give me his phone number? Wallis should be back from that architectural symposium by now. It's really important or I wouldn't have bothered you."

"Hold your horses. I can't do two things at once – look up his number and talk to you."

Just then, I heard someone in the background. It sounded like Doris, his wife. I couldn't make out what she was saying but Max clarified. "Make it three things at once. Doris needs me to deal with a spider in the bathroom. Give me two minutes and I'll call back."

An hour and a half later, I got the answers I needed. I spoke with Wallis and emailed him the photos Jordan had sent me. Wallis, in turn, took a full forty five minutes to review them before calling me back and when he did, he sounded as if he was holding a lottery ticket with the winning Powerball numbers on it."

"I've never seen anything like this. It's unbelievable. Mind-boggling. I keep staring at the designs and pinching myself. Of course it would take me days, weeks even, to figure out how she made those formulas work but OH MY GOD! It's like I'm looking at something Leonardo Da Vinci and M.C. Escher would've come up with if they were working together. And her use of mirrors is pure genius."

"So, um, these designs of Tawn's aren't the usual architectural renderings?"

"That would be the understatement of the year. These aren't designs that can be easily replicated. Without the blueprints I'm looking at, it would be impossible to come up with something that even remotely approached what she created."

"Even if the project was already completed and someone wanted to duplicate it?"

"They'd never be able to figure out how she used geometry, angles, color and glass to pull it off. It's not like conducting an autopsy although that does make for an interesting analogy."

And an even more interesting motive for murder.

I was pretty sure I had it figured out and needed to act on it first thing in the morning. I thanked Wallis and promised to fill him in once I was done with the case. He assured me he wouldn't breathe a word of it to anyone even though his findings were astounding.

Granted, Alexis was present at Candace's house during that dreadful debacle yesterday but she was more of a pawn in that smuggling operation than an actual party to it. At this juncture in time, I imagined the police were going after the big guns and putting Alexis on a back burner. Still, she didn't need to know that and I had to use every bit of leverage I could to get that manipulative little snake to fess up. Too bad it would have to wait until the next day when Classy Kitchens opened for business.

"I'm in and I'm out, Angie," I said the following morning. "I checked my emails, gulped down a double expresso I bought on my way in, and now I'm off to Classy Kitchens to nail a killer."

Angie had just poured herself a cup of coffee and booted up her computer. "Aren't you going to wait until Max gets here so you can let him know what's going on?"

"No time to waste. Tell him I'm on to something and I'll call him from the road. Or wherever."

I needed to catch Alexis off-guard. The same way I did with Leo. I crossed my fingers she'd be at Classy Kitchens and not at some job site. It was a chance I was willing to take.

Traffic from New Ulm to Edina was steady. No slowdowns in spite of the usual summer road construction. When I arrived at the Classy Kitchens showroom there were only two cars parked in front – a silver Maserati Quattroporte and a white Audi Sportback. I made sure to park my blue secondhand Honda equidistant from both of those.

Neil was at his usual place at the door and greeted me. "Marcie, right? I guess you saw the news, huh? Everyone's flipping out about the fact two of our clients were involved in an international gem smuggling ring. Oops. I shouldn't have opened my big mouth. I overheard Mr. D'Angelo and Renata this morning. Something about it being bad for business but I don't know how. I mean, it's not as if Classy Kitchens or any of its employees was smuggling anything."

"It's okay. I won't say anything. Do you know if Brom and Alexis are in? I was hoping to catch them."

"Their cars were parked around back when I pulled in so they must be here. You remember where the concierge area is, right by the Asian fusion kitchen."

"I'll find it. Thanks, Neil."

Renata was on the phone with someone when I reached her desk and from the sound of her voice, the conversation wasn't going very well. Then again, I knew from experience how fussy and demanding the Classy Kitchens' clients were.

"Yes, yes, I already told you. I expect it later today. You'll have it first thing in the morning. Please hold off."

I mouthed the words "Brom and Alexis" when I approached her and she motioned for me to proceed into their area, just beyond the glass doors. I wasn't sure but it looked as if she hadn't slept well the night before. Her hair was hastily combed and her make-up wasn't as finely done. Maybe this Daisy-Candace thing really got to her.

I could see that both of the assistant designers were in their own offices. Brom was working at his computer and Alexis seemed to be shuffling papers on her desk. I went straight toward Alexis and rapped on the doorjamb.

"Quite the vanishing act you pulled on Saturday," I said, "when you were at Candace Pendleton's house."

"Miss Rayner. Marcie. This isn't a good time. You'll have to come back later."

"Fine with me, but when I do, I won't be alone. I'll be accompanied by a police officer."

Alexis moved her chair back from the desk. "Close the door. Please."

I did as she said and pulled a chair close to the edge of her desk. Then I sat without waiting for an invitation. The desk made an easy prop for my elbow and I took the liberty of leaning in so that we were eye-to-eye. "I won't waste your time about the incident at Mrs. Pendleton's. I'll be brief. That natural flip of your hair isn't all that natural. My guess would be ultra-firm control gel."

"My hair? Why are you interested in my hair?"

"You might have been careful about not leaving any fingerprints on those nanny cams you planted at Jordan Rayner's apartment but you weren't so fastidious when it came to the residue of your styling gel."

"Nanny cams? How did you— I mean, I didn't—"

"Save it. We both know you did. What do you think I did with those recording devices once we found them? They're in a Minneapolis forensic lab and I can assure you the police will have no problem issuing a search warrant for your home and office. Once that brand of gel matches up, well…who's to say what they'll arrest you for but I know where I'd start."

"My God. This isn't what you think."

"Really? Maybe I should tell you exactly what I think and what I know. Then you can tell me how close to being right I am."

And how close I am to pulling this off.

Alexis squirmed in her chair and bit her lip. Her hands were on the desk and I could detect a slight tremor. I didn't give her a chance to say a word. My eyes never left hers as I spoke. "You had a deal with Daisy Jamos and Candace Pendleton to provide them with client names for their art business in return for monetary compensation. How am I doing so far?"

"I, um, er…"

"I'll take that as a yes. Working in a place like this, I'm sure you're privy to lots of information regarding client wealth. I suppose when the opportunity came up to augment your income, it was hard to resist. And after all, no real harm was done. I mean, it wasn't as if you were giving away trade secrets, although I do believe certain privacy laws apply."

Alexis voice cracked. "What are you getting at?"

"You left the Pendleton residence in a sure-fire hurry because you didn't want to be named in the real business those two women ran. You really didn't know about their gem smuggling operation until you observed some interesting video from Jordan's apartment. I'm talking about the discovery of rare tourmalines that were ensconced in Tawn's painting. A painting that came from none other than Daisy Jamos's gallery at one time or another."

"I had nothing to do with those tourmalines."

"Oh, I believe you, don't get me wrong. But what you did was far worse. You broke into Jordan's place, *Tawn's* place and ransacked it. When you couldn't find what you were looking for, you planted nanny cams to observe Jordan's moves in the hope of finding what you were really after – Tawn's geometric formulas, color intensity combinations and one-of-a-kind designs that created the deep illusion she was known for. You knew how secretive Tawn was when it came to guarding her projects, that's why her office was so sterile. The real information had to be at her place of residence."

"You wouldn't understand. I—"

"I understand this much. You also put a damn GPS tracker on my car. And don't bother denying it. Those things do have prints and I have lots of friends at the crime lab."

Lots of friends in the crime lab my you-know-what but what does she know?

"Okay, so maybe I was trying to scare you away. I knew it was just a matter of time when a private investigator would show up at Classy Kitchens and get under our noses. I didn't need anyone to find out about my intentions and interfere. Unlike the police, you guys have no boundaries. That GPS tracker is top of the line for your information – ninety six hours' worth of video and I still had to swap it out a few times when you were in the area. Good thing Ernie Star had a big mouth."

"All of this is child's play and we both know it. The real motive for Tawn's murder was your relentless desire to take her place. To be the next deep illusion designer but you couldn't do that if she was in the picture so you murdered her."

At that point, all color left Alexis's face and her hands shook so badly she had to sit on them. "My God! What are you saying? My God! I didn't kill Tawn."

I'm not sure where I learned it, probably from Max, but sometimes silence can be the best interrogator. I sat as still as I could and looked at her. It felt as if hours had passed but it couldn't have been more than a minute or so. Finally, Alexis broke into sobs. Complete and total sobs.

"I won't deny it. I wanted to be as brilliant and famous as Tawn but I didn't kill her for it. If you're going to have me arrested, it's for being an opportunist, not a murderer. I could've taken over for Tawn as far as Daisy and Candace were concerned, so yes, I ransacked Tawn's apartment. I never figured the husband would find out it was me. Yes, I was looking for her design book. And yes, yes, I was the one who sent Jordan a text so I could try one more time. And it might have worked if it wasn't for the police officers patrolling the block. Since when did they start that? I gave up and paid a visit to Candace but you already know about that."

"Seems you've had quite the busy schedule and quite the motive for murder."

"I admit it. I was unstoppable. I wanted to be the one who got to hobnob with the Property Brothers and Joanna Gaines. But not so driven that I'd kill someone. Especially someone I knew. I'm not a cold-blooded murderer."

I stared at her and didn't say a word.

"I know this doesn't look good for me but I did all those things *after* Tawn was murdered. *After.* I took advantage of her death to further my own position but I wasn't the one who grabbed that meat mallet. Heck, I don't even know what's in half of the kitchen drawers around here. I didn't stock them."

In that split second, I knew she had told me the truth. I also knew my entire theory had blown up in my face. Alexis may have been the vulture picking apart the carrion on the road but she wasn't the one who put it there. I started to say something but the words wouldn't come out of my mouth.

CHAPTER 31

"Now what?" she asked. "If you must know, I told John D'Angelo everything this morning. About the client list, that is. I violated a trust and I handed him my resignation. He accepted it and didn't say a word. That was the worst part. It would've been better if he tore into me but he didn't. I was cleaning out my office when you walked in. Later today I plan to go to the Minneapolis police about Jordan's apartment. If you talk to him, tell him I'll pay for any damages. Looks like my career is in the toilet. Brom's been secretly gloating all morning."

I sat there stunned. Alexis had managed to take the wind out of me for a second time.

"I guess there's not much more for me to say. I'll let you get back to what you were doing."

"Even with all this mess, I'm probably having a better morning than Renata. At least I wasn't left with a crap load of bills, a house in foreclosure, an army of creditors, and a husband who walked out on me. There's only so much overtime a person can handle, and even with it, they find the money's still not enough."

"What did you just say?"

"I said, 'there's only so much overtime—'

"No, no. Before that. Something about creditors."

Alexis put a hand over her mouth and widened her eyes. "I shouldn't have told you that. I'm flying on nerves and not thinking. Look, I've got to get this office cleaned out. So are we good?"

"Yeah, we're good. Oh, do you mind if I use the employee restroom in here? I'll only be a minute."

"Sure. No problem."

My mind flashed back to the first time I met Renata. She had a paper on her desk about collections. At the time, I assumed it was from some high-priced company that specialized in kitchen utensils or the like. I closed my eyes and tried to recall what it said. Something that began with the letter B... "Bountiful Collections?" "Beautiful Collections?" No. It was a name. A last name. "Beauregard Collections?" I took a chance and googled it on my phone. The answer came back as "Do you mean Beaumont Collections?"

I immediately clicked yes and it took me to the website. So much for a fancy-dancy retailer. Beaumont Collections was one of the ten best rated debt collection agencies. That meant Alexis was right – Renata was struggling. But that didn't make her a killer. Unless there was more to it.

I raced out of the restroom and went straight to Alexis. "You said you didn't stock the kitchen drawers. Who did?"

"Um, well, they were already stocked when Brom and I were hired. I imagine Renata ordered the stuff because that's the kind of thing she does, but I haven't a clue as to who actually stocked them. Neil wasn't working for us yet so it couldn't have been him. Lots of times when businesses like this are set up, temps are used but I think Mr. D'Angelo would've been too fussy to hire a temp agency."

But maybe not too fussy to pay Renata overtime.

If I overheard Renata correctly on the phone, she expected something to come through later today. Whoever was on the other end of the call would have it by morning. It had to be money. What else could it possibly be?

"One more question, Alexis, and I won't bug you anymore. Can you tell by looking at your computer if Ernie Star has an appointment today? He's the last of Tawn's remaining clients and I'm curious."

"Mr. Star doesn't have one with me but I can check Brom's schedule and Mr. D'Angelo's as far as client appointments are concerned. Their other appointments are for their eyes only."

I felt like a racehorse chomping at the bit. "I really need you to see if Ernie Star will be in."

Alexis sat back in her seat and gave me a funny look. "Does it mean enough to you to talk to Jordan and maybe convince him not to press charges against me? I'll still pay for damages but a police record will destroy me."

"Okay, I'll see what I can do. Now please, pull the schedules up."

Alexis tapped a few letters on her keyboard and pointed to the monitor. "Mr. Sunshine himself has an appointment at four thirty. Gee, that's cutting it close. We close at five tonight. Hmm, and there's another thing."

"What?"

"The appointment doesn't specify with whom. If it's for me, there's an A coded in, for Brom, a B. Maybe he's just coming in to go over his contract with Renata."

"Thanks, Alexis."

"You won't forget to talk with Jordan, will you?"

"I won't."

I let myself out of the inner office and walked past Renata again. She was on the phone and this time her tone was different. "All of it by four thirty. An agreement is an agreement, so don't think about reneging. It wouldn't be in your best interests."

I forced a smile and kept walking. I had plenty of time. Ernie Star wasn't going to make an appearance at Classy Kitchens until the end of the day. And, if things went right, he wouldn't be making an appearance at all. He'd be behind bars.

With nothing in my stomach but a double expresso, I headed out for the nearest breakfast place – a Denny's not too far from Classy Kitchens. One Grand Slam later and I was on my way to the future Star residence on Lowery Hill in Mt. Curve. To ensure it wouldn't be a wasted trip, I had Angie do a little playacting for me.

Angie all but shrieked. "You want me to what? Pretend I'm from the City of Minneapolis Water Department?"

"Yes. Tell him you're going to send an inspector to his location within the hour. Look, I'd do it myself but he'd recognize my voice. Tell him they've had some issues with sewage seepage. That should get his attention. Insist he be at his residence on Lowry Hill or they won't be able to address the sewage issue until later in the week."

"You owe me, you know," she said.

"Mocha cappuccinos for the next two days?"

"Fine. Let me write down the number."

"Numbers. I'll need you to make another call as well."

"Aargh. Mocha cappuccinos for the next three days."

It wasn't simply the process of elimination I used to reach my decision, although that was always one of Max's favorites. Ernie Star had told me he wanted a one-of-a-kind masterpiece whose elements could never be duplicated. By ensuring Tawn was out of the picture, he'd get his wish. The only other obstacle was Josh Newburgh. Josh knew how to convert Tawn's blueprints into viable structures. That meant he had to be eliminated as well.

Driving east on the 394, I couldn't help but think about something I'd read years ago. I wasn't sure if it was from the Middle Ages or the Byzantine Empire but whatever it was, it gave me the chills. It wasn't uncommon for kings to kill off their architects once the projects were completed. That way, the secrets would die with them and the structures could never be replicated. I thought of Ernie Star and shuddered. His visions of grandeur coupled with his self-absorption and arrogance certainly put him in that category.

I wasn't sure if Angie's call would work but the minute Ernie Star appeared at the front door of his Lowry Hill mansion-in-progress, I let out a sigh of relief.

"Miss Rayner? I'm not sure what you're doing here but I don't have time to chit-chat with you. Damn water utility company is having an issue with the waste water. I expect a crew to be here any minute."

"Um, I won't take up much of your time. Can I come in? By the way, where is everyone? Last time I was here there were enough trucks to open a used car lot."

"Oh, *that.* First of all, it's lunchtime and the two men who were on the job this morning decided to go out to eat. Leo McCellan sent the others to another job site for today. That's how it is with contractors. They get started and then they leave to go off on another job. A royal pain in the ass."

"So, uh, can I have a few words with you?"

"Make it fast. We can talk in the kitchen."

I leaned over and touched the side of my leg where my gun was holstered. It was a habit I'd gotten used to ever since Max insisted I carry a concealed weapon on me. I also made sure my wallet and cell phone were safely tucked in my pant pockets.

Ernie was a few feet ahead of me and waved me into the kitchen. One look and the term jaw-dropping wouldn't have come close to describing it. Since my last visit, the contractors had made tremendous progress.

I could have sworn the room looked larger than I remembered but that was before all of the design nuances were in place. I wasn't sure if it was the dimensionality of the tiles or the color hues but it gave the room the effect of something live, something moving. Then I remembered the carousel component. Ernie said it could be programmed to move so subtly that no one would notice, much like those restaurants on the top of skyscrapers.

With my back to the cabinets, I got a panoramic view of the expansive lawn and lake in the distance. Ernie was a few feet away by the center island. He leaned against a bistro chair and lifted his brows. "So, what's this about?"

"I know you were the one responsible for the murders of Tawn Hamlin and Josh Newburgh."

"Now why the hell would I go and do something like that?"

"So you could be assured you'd be the only person in the world whose kitchen was an architectural treasure that could never be replicated."

"I don't suppose you've got any evidence to back-up your ludicrous claim?"

"I've got better. I've got Renata Florio's word."

Ernie steadied himself with the bistro chair. "You're lying. You've got nothing."

"Really? How about I start with the night Tawn's body was discovered? Funny how Renata locked the showroom when she, Alexis and Brom exited the place. The designers insisted they watched her double check the lock and try the door. Only Renata didn't lock it, did she? She made it look as if she did but she was really leaving it open for you to access."

"Why would she do that?"

"For money, what else? Your money to be precise. Renata was drowning in debt and about to lose her house. Somehow you got wind of it and made her a proposition – leave the showroom door open so you could have some alone time with Tawn. In exchange, Renata would receive a substantial amount of money from you. Enough money to make her creditors disappear."

"She told you all of that?"

I nodded. I had to keep my ruse going so he'd admit to everything. "You'd be surprised what I found out, including how you slipped the potassium chloride into Josh Newburgh's coffee. Leo McCellan must have let it slip that Josh had a family history of ventricular arrhythmia. I bet you still have that half-empty shaker of Lo-Salt in one of your cabinets unless of course you decided to dump it. No one ever suspected tainted coffee when Josh succumbed to a heart attack. By the time the lab report came in, his coffee cup was long gone."

Ernie bent his head down, his hand pressed against the underside of the kitchen island. "You think you've got this figured out, don't you?"

"I know I do."

Just then, I felt a sudden jerk and I was thrown backwards into the cabinets. Damn it. He must have pushed a button to set that carousel moving and God knows what else. Next thing I knew I was trying to stop myself from tumbling sideways down a dark flight of stairs. My only thought was that sideways was better than backwards as the cabinet door closed behind me.

My hands instinctively reached for the walls and I was relieved to find a handrail in the dark. Four or five steps of fumbling but I managed to remain vertical. I grabbed for my cell phone and tapped the flashlight feature. Ahead of me were fancy shelves that I assumed were for a future wine cellar but when I got closer, I realized it was an illusion. Some sort of painting. Then, the room began to get smaller. At least that's how it appeared to me. The walls were getting closer and I could hear my heart thumping.

I held out my hands expecting to be able to feel both sides of the wall but nothing happened. It was another illusion and a darned good one. Suddenly Wallis's commentary about mirrors hit me. I reasoned if Tawn could use mirrors to create the illusion, maybe I could do the same to get the hell out.

The only mirror I had was on the back of a small compact I kept in my wallet. *Small* being the pivotal word. Nevertheless it was a mirror. The combined juggling act of balancing my iPhone's flashlight in conjunction with the mirror was mindboggling yet somehow I was able to pull it off. I continued down a corridor in the vast expanse of Ernie's basement. Horrific visions of funhouses and mad scientist labs kept appearing in my mind. I expected some diabolical creature to pop out at me at any given second but I knew the only madman around here was Ernie. Not very consoling.

The corridor seemed endless but I figured there had to be more than one entrance into a basement this expansive. I hate it when I'm right if it means the circumstances go against me. In this case, the circumstance being Ernie. I could see his face clearly in the tiny handheld mirror. He came out of a hidden doorway and flicked the lights on. In his hand was a large wrench. Too late for me to reach for my gun but not too late to duck down, tighten my fist and land a punch in his groin.

He let out a yowl and dropped the wrench. The same time I dropped my phone and my compact. That meant I had two free hands to reach for the wrench. "What's the matter?" I asked. "Couldn't find a meat mallet in your high-priced kitchen?"

The pain that Ernie was feeling from my well-aimed punch must have subsided because he lunged at me, both hands straight out. I wasted no time putting one of his wrists out of commission with the wrench before bending down to grab my phone. As for my compact, it wasn't worth taking my eyes off of him.

"Hear that noise upstairs? Those are footsteps. The police are in there looking for me."

"I don't hear anything."

"You will."

I prayed I wasn't mistaken and that Angie had done what I asked – Called Detective-Sergeant Mikey Abrams an hour after I left for Lowry Hill and told him to get over to Ernie Star's residence ASAP. There wouldn't be enough mocha cappuccinos to thank her.

CHAPTER 32

"Miss Rayner! Are you in here? Miss Rayner?"

"I'm down here!" I yelled. So loud, in fact, my throat hurt. "In the basement. With the killer. Hurry!"

Ernie made his way back to the entrance he had used and flicked off the lights.

"The killer's at large," I screamed. Then, I turned on my flashlight and tried to locate the doorway he had used. It was no use. It was as if the man had vanished in thin air, leaving me in a maze of long corridors and dead ends.

I could hear footsteps upstairs and lots of them. Maybe Mikey had brought the cavalry. No sense going crazy in the dark. I did the only sensible thing under the circumstances. I called Wallis.

"No time to talk, Wallis. I'm trapped in the basement of Ernie Star's house on Lowry Hill. You've got the blueprint from that email Jordan sent. Quick! It's still on your phone. Look at it and tell me how the hell I can get out."

Fifteen minutes later, I found myself standing yards away from the house. I had exited from a passageway that went directly to the lake. Without wasting another second, I raced to the house, only this time my gun was in my hand and not my holster.

I circled to the front entrance and caught site of two police vehicles. Ernie Star was being escorted to one of them by a uniformed police officer. As soon as Ernie spotted me, he yelled, "It's your word against mine, you witch!"

"No, I yelled back. It's your word, period." Then, I took out the only other device I had on me, another micro stick. I handed it to Mikey Abrams who was out of breath from running toward me.

"It's always cheaper when you buy these in bulk," I said.

"You took an awful chance, you know, by going it alone. You should've called us first."

"What? And spoiled all the fun?"

"Your office secretary explained everything. We had the Edina Police bring Renata Florio in for questioning and she confessed to letting Ernie into Classy Kitchens in exchange for payment. She swears she had no idea he was going to kill Tawn but that will be up to a jury to decide."

"She might not have known at the time but she withheld evidence once the deed was done."

"Yep," Mikey said. "Glad I don't have to sit on that jury. You going to be okay? You didn't get hurt, did you?"

"No, I'm fine. I'm going to stop at the nearest coffee shop, catch my breath and make a few calls. If you don't mind, I'd like to call Jordan Rayner first, before you guys do. He was the one who hired me to find out who killed his wife."

"I know."

"How? I never said anything."

"You didn't have to. It was pretty obvious when we first met. Like I said, I've been in this business for a long time. And from the looks of things, you will be, too. You're one heck of an investigator, Marcie Rayner."

I was on my second Starbucks Blonde Vanilla Latte when I called Max. I had already spoken to Jordan and he was relieved the entire ordeal was over.

"Tawn poured out her soul to accomplish those designs," Jordan said. "And look what it got her."

"Listen, her killer will get what he deserves. I'm certain of it. And as for your late wife, her work will be acknowledged in the architectural world if you'll agree to have Max's brother-in-law, Wallis, address it at the next international symposium in Sydney, Australia."

"Absolutely. Um, er, I don't how to say it so I'll just come out with it. You didn't have to help me but you did. You didn't have to believe me but you did. And I can't possibly thank you enough. Hogan's one heck of a lucky guy. But he already knows it."

I wished Jordan well and ended the call.

Max's response when I told him what happened wasn't nearly as calm and reflective as Jordan's. "You could've gotten yourself killed!"

"Relax, I had a pretty good backup plan in place thanks to Angie. But the real hero was Wallis. If it wasn't for him I'd still be wandering around Ernie Star's basement. Maybe you and I could take him out to lunch or something."

"He'd like that. He has to live with Camila's cooking every day. I only get to suffer with it when Doris makes us visit. Look, go straight home and take it easy. The office can wait for another day. Understood?"

"Understood. And thanks, Max."

"For what?"

"For believing I could do this. You were right, you know. About this job being more gratifying than my prior work as a crime statistician."

"I've known you since you were a little girl, Marcie. You had Nancy Drew written all over you."

"Yeesh."

My next call was to Hogan and it was a brief one. "Any chance

I could convince you to drive to my place tonight? I caught Tawn's killer! It was Ernie Star. Mikey Abrams apprehended him. I'm dying to tell you ever single detail."

"I'm already on my way."

"What? How?"

"Jordan called the brewery to thank me. You can fill me in over dinner. Take-out or dine out, whatever you want."

"I just want to see you. You know, if I hadn't watched you fiddle around with that deadbolt on the brewery's front door a zillion times, it wouldn't have occurred to me that Renata never locked up. She only made it look that way. She was the one who left the door unlocked for the killer."

"Hmm, does that mean I'm the one who really solved this?"

"I'll give you all the credit you deserve when I see you."

There was another phone call I had to make whether I was in the mood or not. I took a last sip of my latte and dialed my mother.

"The Minneapolis police arrested Tawn Hamlin's killer. It was one of her clients. I thought you'd want to know."

"I thought she was murdered in Edina."

"She was, but the killer lives in Minneapolis."

"Good. I'm glad you listened to me and stayed at your desk."

I didn't have the heart to tell her my desk was the last place I'd be. I tossed my empty coffee cup in the trash and headed for my car. I never wanted to see another designer kitchen again. As far as I was concerned, a decent microwave and a long list of take-out places were all I needed in this business.

EPILOGUE

About a month later, Angie received the full payment from Jordan for our services. He included a note thanking all of us and had enclosed a recent article from the university newsletter with the following headline, "Campus Police Catch Tire Slasher." Apparently Jordan's car fell victim to a disgruntled student who randomly targeted faculty cars and slashed their tires or put nails in them. The article went on to say it would be difficult for those staff members whose vehicles were vandalized to prove it was indeed that perpetrator. At the bottom of the article Jordan had penciled in, "That's because they don't have Marcie working for them."

I smiled when I read the note. Jordan Rayner had learned to appreciate me, and with that, we could both move on.

THE END

About the Authors

Ann I. Goldfarb

A former teacher and middle school principal from upstate New York, Ann always had a passion for writing. As a sideline to her career in education, Ann wrote for a number of trade journals before turning her attention to mysteries. She got her feet wet writing YA time travel novels and then joined forces with her husband, James Clapp, to write cozy mysteries under the pen name of J.C. Eaton. To date, they are penning three mystery series – The Sophie Kimball Mysteries, The Wine Trail Mysteries, and the Marcie Rayner Mysteries. The couple resides with their four-legged friends in Sun City West, Arizona, where sunshine doesn't need to be shoveled. Visit the websites at: *www.jceatonmysteries.com* and *www.timetravelmysteries.com*

James E. Clapp

With a background in construction, a degree in business and a successful tour of duty with the U.S. Navy, James never envisioned himself writing cozy mysteries along with his wife, Ann I. Goldfarb. In fact, the only writing he did was for informational brochures and workshop material for the winery industry where he worked as a tasting room manager in his home state of New York. When he and his wife left the Snow Belt for the Arizona desert, he was hit with the writing bug. Under the pen name of J.C. Eaton, he began the journey into cozy mysteries, complete with quirky characters and determined sleuths. Visit the website at: *www.jceatonmysteries.com*